Normal Miguel

Normal Miguel

Erik Orrantia

Cheyenne Publishing
Camas, Washington
www.cheyennepublishing.com

ISBN: 978-0-9797773-9-4

Edited by Tracey Pennington
Cover art by Alex Beecroft

Published by Cheyenne Publishing
Camas, Washington
Mailing Address:
    P. O. Box 872412 Vancouver, WA 98687-2412
Website: www.cheyennepublishing.com

Other Young Adult Books from Cheyenne Publishing

The Glass Minstrel by Hayden Thorne
Hidden Conflict: Tales from Lost Voices in Battle
The Filly by Mark R. Probst

Acknowledgements

I would like to thank the following people whose commitment, patience, insight, and many hours of work helped to bring this work to fruition:

Jerry McCullough

Millard Billings

Heide Harrier

Michael Solari

Richard McBreen

Jesus Francisco Orrantia Peralta

Tracey Pennington

Mark Probst

One

A RANDOM BOLT with a nut attached about half way up kept Miguel transfixed for the hours-long bus ride from Puebla to Comalticán. With every bump and turn of the bus up the semi-paved road, the bolt jumped and bobbed like a drop of hot water on a frying pan. The road was semi-paved because the election-year pavement had not been maintained past the election year and the common freezes and thaws and downpours and floods had begun to wear potholes in it before the yellow stripe down the middle was ever painted.

The bus and passengers slowly made their way through the winding hills, leaning to and fro at every curve. Miguel had never heard a bus screech and rattle so much; it seemed that every piece of it made noise. A broken window sealed with tape banged in its aluminum frame. The accordion exit door slammed into the metal of the doorway. The naked springs of the driver's chair squealed incessantly as the driver's body read the road like a blind man's finger reading Braille. The engine roared at upturns and the brakes ground at every curve. The few other passengers had stopped talking to each other hours before, their monotonous faces revealed their local origins—this wasn't their first time on this bus. It was the bolt that caught Miguel's attention the most, though, sliding up and back down the aisle, knocking around the people feet and the chair feet, always reappearing. It probably belonged in some other place but it seemed to have found a new home among the travelers and their many belongings. Whatever it was supposed to hold together would have to make do without it.

The ride from Mexico City to Puebla had been far smoother. But Miguel was no longer thinking of the past; it was

9

August now, and muggy. His foot tapped his backpack from force of habit. He couldn't bear to lose it, for it held his only Normal uniform, the tell-tale maroon pants and white shirt of a neophyte teacher, and his other few possessions: some articles of casual clothing, a hair brush, razor blade, tooth brush, and a couple of condoms that were passed out by the AIDS prevention guy at a bar a few weeks before. His hands began to sweat at the idea of fifty pairs of brown eyes in a cramped room that would ultimately decide if he were a success or a failure. People back home had already decided, thought they already knew, thought leaving the city was a bad idea. *But that's what they think about any idea. No more thinking of the past; I'm on my own now.*

In the canyon between the green hills, a creek flowed. Its rippling could occasionally be heard over the scandalous noise of the bus, usually just before the bus passed over a rickety bridge or a shallow bridgeless crossing. The clear water looked fresh but cold in the gray afternoon fog between the foliage. The bus must have crossed it a dozen times before it finally reached the fringes of Comalticán. Miguel guessed this was Comalticán because the coordinator at the Normal School had told him that the town would be at the first cemetery, not that she'd ever been here, either. He felt a spasm in his stomach, yet as he looked at the outcropping of homes, perhaps no more than fifty or a hundred, chickens pecking in the road and the faint rhythm of Mexican banda in the background, he felt less afraid, less threatened. It was nothing like the busy streets and honking of cars back home. The brakes ground a final time, the bus gasped, and a few of the people gathered their bags and made their way to the exit. The rest would move on to destinations farther down the windy road.

The bus stopped in front of a slightly crooked wooden post that suspended a single black electric line. Miguel took one last look at his reflection in the bus window. His dark skin contrasted with his white shirt, and he looked more like a skinny, smooth-faced teenager than the twenty-five-year-old that he was. He took a final breath before stepping off the bus. About halfway up the post hung a round ceramic platter, a *comal*, with the word "Comaltícan" written across the diameter in childlike writing. Beneath that was the word "Population" followed by either the number 110 or, given the angle between the ones, the word "Yo." Miguel couldn't tell.

To the left of the post was the cemetery, where crosses and gaudy statues of the Virgin Mary abounded. It looked untended, typical for cemeteries of the less-privileged. Tall grasses protruded from the sides of boxy shrines where artificial flowers faded and real ones had long ago wilted. Familiar battles between life and death, occurring in the very place that memorialized them.

He asked for directions to the Internado, the boarding school, and a friendly lady with a wrinkled face steered him up a rocky road toward his destination. "Do you see the cross?" she asked, pointing to the top of the hill above the town. He nodded. Her pointing finger moved down to a set of peach-colored buildings about a hundred meters from the tilted electric post. "That's the Internado."

He followed the dirt road toward the gate. Gray rocks were exposed beneath the coarse brown dirt at his feet. When he entered, the campus seemed deserted. There was a padlock on the office door. There were three rows of rooms that were obviously classrooms and two two-story buildings, apparently dormitories, in close proximity, but they, too, were quiet and abandoned. He wondered if he had made a mistake.

From a small hut a couple hundred meters from the campus, on the other side of a brown soccer field, rose puffs of smoke from a tiny chimney.

Miguel walked over and knocked on the wooden door. After a moment of no response, he creaked the door open. He felt the heat from the stone oven built in to the corner of the small shack. A stone chimney reached to the roof. He saw the back of a man working at a table, swiftly kneading dough with his strong arms. A tattoo on his arm extended below the sleeve of his worn-out white t-shirt.

"Good afternoon," Miguel said.

The man turned around. "Good day." He was tall and rugged, his face not shaven for a few days. His sweaty white t-shirt revealed a broad chest from years of hard work, and a round belly from years of hard play. "Can I help you?"

"I just got here," replied Miguel. "I'm Miguel, the new teacher from the Normal School."

"You're the new teacher from the Normal School, huh?" he responded. Miguel couldn't tell if his response was mocking or clarifying. "I'm Captain, the baker." He held out his right arm, his floury hand turned in so that Miguel might shake his forearm. "You're kind of early, Miguel. The Directora won't be back for another hour or so." He belched loudly and Miguel smelled beer. "Why don't you stay here, *cabrón,* till they get back? You want a beer?"

Miguel shook his head. "No thanks, I just got off the bus."

"Well, you want some bread?" Captain held two round rolls up to his chest and squeezed them provocatively. He smiled at Miguel and laughed out loud, looking him in the eyes. "I'll bet you do." An awkward second passed. Captain burst out in laughter again. "I'm just fucking with you, Miguel." He handed one piece of bread over to Miguel and bit into the other. "Put your things down and help me out with the dough, if you want. We'll be seeing a lot of each other, so just take it easy."

Not long after, the voices of children could be heard. Miguel peered through the door and saw several children enter the campus with a stout woman. "That's the Directora," said Captain. "Wash up your hands and go down to her office so she can show you where your room is." As Miguel picked up his things, Captain said, "You'll have to come to town with me and check out the cantina or the pool hall. We always watch the soccer games down there, too, *cabrón.*"

"Sure," replied Miguel as he began walking down to the office. "Thanks for the invitation."

The padlock was now removed, so Miguel walked directly in. The stout woman was there, shuffling through papers. "Good afternoon, Señora. I'm Miguel Hernández, the new Normal student."

She looked up from her business. Her face was brown and the vertical lines between her eyebrows gave her a serious expression; she was the kind of woman that could not be deceived. Her lips were closed tight and her black hair was graying. She looked as if she had worked her way up in the school system and took her job with utmost gravity. Miguel awaited a response from her and swallowed nervously. She reminded him of his mother.

But then her head tilted and her lips parted to reveal the most welcoming of smiles. "Of course," she said. "I am glad you made it safely. The bus didn't shake your brain loose, did it?" She shook his hand firmly and directed him to a seat. "I am Sandra Zaragoza but everyone calls me Directora. You must be hungry, too?"

"A bit, uh, Directora. But Captain gave me some bread already."

"Ah, so you met the Captain? Don't pay him any attention. That old soldier's just a baker now. He's probably invited you down to the bars already, right? But I'm sure you have other things on your mind. We have lots of children to attend to. I'll get one of the children to show you your room and then we'll see you in the dining house for dinner. Work starts tomorrow, so you'll want to get rested.

"You'll be working under Viviana, who will help you with your lesson plans and oversee your teaching. She is one of the mayor's nieces and lives in town, in Arbolito, so won't be in till early tomorrow. Most of the children were picked up by their families this weekend but will be here first thing in the morning, too.

"If there is anything you need, you be sure to let me know."

"Yes, Directora."

"Any questions?"

"Um, what room will I go to in the morning?"

"You will be in room eight, sixth grade," she said, nodding her head. "Miguel." She waited for him to look at her. "These children need you. They need *us*. We're the only chance they have."

Two

THE ROAD UP THE CANYON along the creek bed was the same route that missionaries had followed two hundred years before in search of gold, silver, and unsaved souls. A small tributary that fed the creek came from up yet a narrower canyon among the thick flora. It was barely a trickle this time of year, but had seen raging waters the likes of which in a rainy season some time ago had burst open hard rock in the mountainside from which it sprang. Abimael had been no more than a toddler at the time. The women in his family made a paltry living stitching sandals of leather and used tires for sale to the local folk, while the men of the family found day labor jobs hauling rubble at construction sites, sorting rocks for the cobblestone roads, or beating back the jungle that was encroaching on someone's hillside farm. One way or another, corn had to find its way to the table, and some cut of meat might even grace the pot beside the lardy beans above the fire.

But water…never in short supply. Although its stream was only a trickle at times, the mountainside was a benevolent giver. So Abi's house, not twenty meters from the fissure, was never without a fresh drink or a soup base or an automatic rinse cycle. So grateful was his family to the water gods that one particularly rainy season, the rock split open and gave birth to a new beginning.

Not one of them had been inside a cave before, nor had any of the family ever imagined that such unusual formations comprised the innards of the sierra on whose belly they and their ancestors had clung like ticks for generations. Stalactites and stalagmites stretched down from the high ceiling and up from the dank floor, nearly touching each other in some places while

14

barely grown in others. Tiny limestone straws hung from the ceiling in quirky places, releasing clear water at their leisure. In some places, rock kernels formed like popcorn on the ceiling above and thick colored veins ran through the mountain as if her heart were in proximity. Gigantic columns of white rock poured down majestically in one chamber. It was like liquid rock frozen in time, the fluid motion halted in one blink of the eye.

Over four kilometers of mountain guts had been explored since the cave's discovery. There were so many things to see, only limited by the cost of D-cell batteries.

The stream that carved the cave was unbearably cold on their sandaled feet at first exploration, but after years of their journeying within, it became as familiar and automatic as descending into your basement. Once the footholds were learned and a few cinderblocks strategically lodged in place, the water was but a joist in the basement to be dodged.

It wasn't long before the mayor in the no-longer-distant town found out and, predictably, took steps to snuff out the family's dream. Anything so awe-inspiring and mysterious must be lucrative, must be regulated. People would want to see. It cost the third born daughter to live in the mayor's house for the federal government to approve a permit for Mexico's newest natural resource. The Patiño Juarez family, who never legally owned the hilly plot on which they lived, became the honorary custodians of the "Open-Rock Cave."

There never was any road that went to the Patiño residence, of course, so locals began offering to guide travelers up to the cave site or to take them up on horseback. When a national newspaper caught wind of it, visitors from faraway places came to see. And when the hysteria finally died down a bit, the Patiños were left with a couple dozen plastic flashlights and a tall stack of brown pamphlets.

The sudden influx of cash helped the family to pay off some long-standing debts, but the stream of visitors became more like the creek in summertime. Occasionally, groups of foreign spelunkers came with fancy harnesses and strap-on flashlights. But the most common visitor was one who rented his flashlight and disappeared for an hour or two beneath the earth and that was the end of that.

Abimael wasn't even a meter tall. The youngest born, he was always lost in someone's skirt. *Get away from the fire. Don't stand by the river. Don't tease the pig. Get away from the ant nest.* Someone always had to watch out for him. They passed him into the cave like a sandbag just to squelch his complaining. They knew he was too little to handle the current of the stream by himself, especially a few minutes into the narrow straightaway where the cave wall formed a tight tunnel.

One night, at bedtime, they noticed he wasn't on his mat. The dim light of the kerosene lamp didn't illuminate his corner much. They began to furiously look around the home, calling out his name, "Abi!" They checked the outhouse, they looked down the trail, they looked up his favorite climbing tree until they all converged at the stream where they filled their drinking gourds and washed their clothes, not ten meters away from the black hole of the cave entrance, which was even darker in the nighttime. It was what they all feared most, what they all knew was going to be true, and what they all secretly felt guilty about, not even having noticed his absence. They went for the flashlights without saying another word, knowing that the cave mouth had swallowed him down and hoping that it hadn't chewed very much.

Everyone had been lost in the cave from time to time. It was a twisting labyrinth of solid rock. If your lights went out, the darkness and silence were like a kiss of death that would instantly cease your breathing and make your hair stand on end. A mouse in the bowels of an eagle. When the rich spelunkers came with their high-powered lights, the caverns were yet again a different world as formations could be seen in their entirety. But with twenty-five-peso flashlights, only pieces could be seen at a time. Every move of the light changed the shadows; the still air kept its secrets. One never knew which way to go, except if one followed the stream. But the stream had long dried up in many chambers, save for an occasional tapping of drops from the ceiling above.

They had gotten used to it. After a couple years of finding

tourists and visitors who had lost their way, all of the Patiños knew their general way around. They recognized the shapes and colors, the slippery parts, the steps and protrusions. Tourists were easy to find, though, because they wouldn't stray far from the main paths. Perhaps directional signs would serve, suggested some folks, but who would put the signs in? The mayor was gone as soon as their sister left with his family, so the government was no longer of assistance. Besides, the spelunkers liked it unspoiled; they said that many caves had been ruined by over-regulation. And someone was always around to haul out a lost soul. It made for good tips.

They weren't sure about Abi, though. He was small, liable to crawl up in one of an infinite number of crevices. He was quiet, too, less likely to scream out, though perhaps he would quietly cry. They weren't even sure if he had a light, as the flashlights were never counted, their batteries only tested by a rapid light-in-the-face check. But the current in the stream was the principal concern, for surely they could find him in the cave if he hadn't drowned.

They searched for hours through the darkness. The women and girls concentrated on the stream, feeling their way through the streambed with their feet, hoping to not feel a soft thump. Their extremities grew numb and the yellow light of the flashlights died down in the toiling. The men and boys squeezed up in the fissures, searching high and low, stopping now and then to listen for whimpering or crying from their son and brother. More often than anything, they found unknown passages that might have led on to other unknown passages, places that a little corpse could be digested by the earth, a corpse whose bones might someday be discovered after Abi was forgotten.

They returned from the dark hole as dawn broke. Tired and saddened, they trod back to their wooden hut to find Abi lying on his mat, curled up like a fetus. He was as wet as the girls and as muddy as the boys, shivering in his sleep. He had found his way into the cave and had found his way out again without the assistance of his astonished kin. They looked at each other, surprised, but more appalled at the hours they had spent in anguish, guilt, and mud. They gathered around his mat quietly, no one inspired to so much as pick him up. He must have felt their presence for he awoke and looked around at them, the black hair on his tiny head awry. They waited for some moment and then he unapologetically said, "I hate that cave," before he turned his back to them and fell back asleep.

Breakfast was the usual tortillas and beans, but unusually late. There was little talk amongst the family. Abimael's mother and father had spoken privately as the others went about their business. They had left Abi asleep. As the family gathered around the morning fire, the father decided: "He is too little to stay with us here. It is not good for him to be so close to this cave where he can get lost or killed. He does not understand the blessing we have received. He will go to the Internado at Co-maltican where we will visit him and make sure he is content. Anyway, he will receive a better education there than he will get with us here." And with that, and with no voiced opinion to the contrary, five-year-old Abimael was taken on the three hour trip to the Internado, not to see his family again for a long, long time.

Three

CLASSROOM NUMBER EIGHT was made of red bricks. The many double desks were so close together that the forty-two students were like a sea of black heads that bobbed on waves of white shirts, and their blue uniform pants were like the ocean depths. Their sneakered and sandaled feet inevitably kicked at each other and pushed backpacks to and fro. Viviana, Miguel's master teacher, hadn't shown up until ten o'clock or so to check and make sure he was all right. The students greeted her with a choral "Good morning, Maestra." She warned them to behave for the new student teacher, and then she left as quickly as she had appeared.

The students didn't seem much different from those in Mexico City. Their uniforms were the same, there was the same number of them, and they were equally likely to tease each other, disobey directions, and resist learning in one form or another. Of course, many were quiet and interested in learning, but what new teacher paid attention to them? When loud boys made fun of him or each other, when they twisted his words to interrupt the class: "How can I answer when you said to be quiet, Doce?" "You said to write on a piece of paper with pencil but I only have a pen."

How could a person teach under these conditions? Miguel wondered if his family was right. Had he made another mistake?

He remembered his favorite song, *"A Quien Le Importa?"*—to whom does it matter?—by Alaska y Dinarama that he sang so often in his head. It reminded him that it didn't matter what people thought of what he said or did, he just had to be himself. Something had to keep him going, for there was always so much to endure and so seemingly little for which to endure it.

The nighttime chores didn't make it much easier. He was assigned to cook in the kitchen, stirring great pots of pork chops for nearly three hundred hungry children. The huge wooden spoon was like a witch's tool and the meat, he imagined, like body parts dispensed to the young people who mindlessly gnawed flesh from the bone. Only nine months and twenty-eight days left. He could manage.

That night, Miguel was sent across the field to return the bread trays to the Captain, for children were not allowed in the bakery at night. The Captain sat in his soiled white shirt, his powdery apron hung on a hook near the oven. The smoldering fire could be heard as it died down for the night.

"Ay, *cabrón*, how'd it go?" he asked Miguel.

Miguel just shook his head.

"Ha, ha! It always seems rough at first, but you'll get used to it. Look at me."

Miguel turned up and saw him as he sucked in his breath and flexed his biceps. He hadn't really noticed that the Captain was actually quite strong. It was the smell of alcohol that he had noticed.

"Still as buffed as in the old days, *cabrón*," he said, and then leaned back in a wooden chair to touch his hand to the wall above him. "The ladies still want some of this." His hand came down to squeeze his crotch and Miguel, embarrassed, turned his head toward the door.

"Don't go, Doce," Captain said to him. "Have a seat, have a drink, relax for a while. What else is there to do?"

It was true, Miguel thought. What else was there to do? A drink sounded like just the right medicine and, although he hated to admit it, the vulgarity and machismo of the Captain were intriguing.

"Here, suck on this," the Captain said, as he passed him a bottle of cane alcohol. "I got no glasses."

It went down like jalapeño juice and made Miguel cough abruptly.

"Yeah, I knew you'd like to suck some, right? All you

Mexico City boys like that, don't you?" He looked down at his hand as he squeezed his crotch again. This time Miguel's eyes fixed on the Captain's crotch. He hated himself for wanting it, but he knew he did.

Captain's face turned more serious and his tone more quiet. "Come on, suck on it for me."

Miguel thought about the sea of children, the stern brown face of the Directora, and the greasy cauldron with the thick cooking bones. He didn't want Captain to think he was queer, let alone an easy queer. He didn't want Captain to feel like he could treat him that way. But he *was* like that and some part of him liked to be treated that way. Another swig of the alcohol pushed him to his knees. And, as Miguel opened the Captain's pants where he sat and serviced the baker, he liked to hear the Captain's moans.

Captain put his hands up behind his head. "Ah, just like the old days," he whispered, "You boys always do it better than women."

Miguel felt Captain's hands pull at his backside so that he'd slide his butt over to within Captain's reach. Miguel was disgusted with himself; he felt like he was a cheap trinket. But he was excited. At least somebody valued him today.

Captain came in his mouth without warning and then closed his pants back up. "I told you you'll have to come to town with me one night." Miguel took another gulp of alcohol before trudging down to his quarters in the dark night air.

He realized he hadn't said a single word to the Captain through the entire encounter. But that seemed somehow typical for him. He thought about the next day of work and the children, and he hoped they'd never find out.

It was the tiniest of moments, really a non-event. Yet the utter sincerity of it began Miguel's journey in a whole new direction. It was the kind of moment that people who've never had them could not even understand. Perhaps only those sorts of people, like teachers or parents, who work with those whose gratitude is almost always implicit, recognize it. A good waiter receives a tip, a good salesman a bonus, a good artist sells work for high prices and hears about the brilliance of her work. What does a teacher get? Poor students have no money to give and, even if they did, they couldn't give it. And any overt praising of a teacher is always suspect. But Abimael had no idea that the teacher was listening.

Abimael was still pretty short for his age. A few years back, he had developed some warts on his face, just to the left of his lower lip. They grew nearly one on top of the other to form something of a ridiculous larva that would have stuck out straight if it wasn't for their own weight bending it downward. He had a couple of others on his nose and cheeks, and on his hands and fingertips, and it was hard to talk to him without looking at them. He had a bit of a raspy voice and an abundance of baby fat, but was a cheerful kid with lots of friends despite his visible defects.

Abi had developed into an eager student, probably more interested in the teacher's attention than whatever material he was supposed to learn. He made it hard for Miguel to focus, at times, with his constant questions. "Where are you from, Doce? Why did you come here? Are you leaving soon like all the other student teachers? Do you like goat milk? What type of dance will you do for Christmas, Doce? Do you have a girl-friend?" But for Miguel, an abundance of questions was prefer-able to the outright defiance of some of the students. Also, Abi's warts were sometimes a distraction for Miguel, if a repul-sive one. What if he caught them from him?

Abi was sitting against a wall beside his best friend, Johana, in such a way that Miguel could spot their feet from a distance without seeing their faces. He had been approaching to send them off to dinner but stopped before turning the corner when he heard their conversation.

"He's the best teacher I ever had," Miguel heard him say. It made Miguel attentive and silent as he pushed his back against the adjacent wall. "He tries really hard to teach us stuff and does it in funny ways. He doesn't let the other kids walk all over him like Maestra Viviana does. And you can tell that he likes us. He makes me want to learn."

"I like him, too," Johana said. "He doesn't just make us sit there and write dictations until the school day ends. And we never have to watch the bad boys hold up books in their outstretched arms!"

Miguel couldn't believe his ears. He couldn't believe that anyone, much less his students, noticed his efforts. It became worth it all of a sudden, as in his head the sweet voice of Christina Aguilera sang that song about being beautiful regardless of the things that people say, and he applied it to Abimael and Johana and then himself and then Abimael again. And those ugly warts on his face had all but vanished in Miguel's mind.

Four

HIGH, HIGH, HIGH UP THE TWISTY HIGHWAY, horses, mules and, rarely, cars meandered along pockmarked asphalt. The temperature dropped off markedly, tall trees gave way to shorter shrubs, and mist flowed down the mountainside like soda foam down the side of a cup. The land was solitary and spacious and seemed to be almost completely without a human soul. But it was ideal for the coffee plants that spread their branches amongst the endless acres of mountain tops, and it was here that Johana's family had the fortune of settling generations ago to harvest the reddened berries of an addictive drink. Johana missed the smell of coffee roasting on the patio.

It was just this year that her family had decided that the Internado would be best. As much as she would be missed, education was the only way for her to be successful in life. Maybe she would even go to the university and come back to tell great tales of faraway adventures. It was for love that she had to leave and for love that her parents came to see her so often. They would bring the Directora sacks of freshly roasted coffee and invite her to dinner in town at the best restaurant with real wooden tables. The Internado was still a closer option for their daughter than the faraway private schools that would keep her out of reach. It would allow her to grow up in the heartland of Puebla culture and know the Poblanos from the very root.

But it was hard for her not to feel punished at times, as if the Internado were a prison and all the students merely inmates. There was no freedom, such as when she would climb papaya trees and haul in the fresh booty for her family. The dogs at the Internado were scruffy and unkempt, not like the dachshunds at home. The diet of meat and bread was dreary. And the great chamber of beds was nothing like the tranquil bedroom where her mother used to tuck her in.

Why did she have to grow up? Why couldn't Don Manuel just take care of her for the rest of her life, as her father worked the plantation and her mother supervised the house? The mature side of her knew and understood, but she'd loved the indulgences of childhood.

Her father explained to her how the green coffee beans grew up, too. *They take in the Sun and enjoy the falling rains, just like a child. But then the times change and they begin to change color, first yellow like a young lady and then red like an adult.* And then it was time for them to move on, as their time for watching the mist roll by and counting lightning bolts in the gray clouds was over. They'd lie out and dry in the afternoon heat until they were ready to be converted, and able to release the perfect flavor. Finally, those dark beans would be toasted to a rich brown like the dark brown hair on her father's head, the head that she would look down upon when she sat upon his shoulders as he explained to her the ways of the world. Father would always make time to stroll the mountain trails with his favorite second daughter. "You never know *when* your colors will change," he would tell her, "but you know that they will." It reminded her of her older sister, Julieta.

Julieta's colors had changed, too. And then Julieta, like Johana, had to leave. In fact, Julieta's quinceañera and Julieta's wedding were two of her fondest memories. She couldn't decide which one she loved the best. The two events were about a year apart and were both about a year in the making.

The first was the quinceañera. Every girl dreamed about her quinceañera—the boys in black tuxedos waltzing in her honor, the decorated cake like an edible painting, the food and drink served to a hundred guests who came to witness her transition into a señorita, and, of course, the dress. Johana hadn't felt at all left out or jealous of Julieta, for she had played an important part in the procession—after Julieta walked up the aisle of the church filled with spectators, and the priest spoke about the duties of a woman, Johana got to place the sparkly crown on her head. Besides, she knew her time would come—she would turn fifteen, too. She saw this as practice.

Baby blue was the color scheme. There were baby blue ribbons on the white chair covers, roses dyed baby blue at every table, baby blue frosting on the cake, and baby blue chiffon in the dresses. She loved her dress. It made her feel like a princess. And the high-heeled shoes, the ones that her mother made her practice walking in on the cobblestone terrace, made her look like a grown woman. She put her dress on first thing in the morning that day so that she could pretend all day that she was royalty. She didn't tell anyone, but her feet were killing her by early afternoon. She stuffed the shoes in a box after the procession. But the dress she slept in that night. Julieta's had been even better, fluffier than hers at the bottom, like a huge ball of cotton candy from the fair.

The second great memory was Julieta's wedding. Her parents had met frequently with Julieta's boyfriend and his parents behind closed doors. It was shortly after the quinceañera and Johana was unsure what they were talking about. They seemed so stern and serious. They must have been discussing which colors it was going to be this time or where it would be held or who was going to pay for it. Well, she didn't really think that his parents could pay, since they worked for her father. He told Johana not to play with any of the workers' children, that she was not to have her wedding so early. She didn't understand. She thought weddings were wonderful events and wanted to start talking about her dress. She knew the colors would be changing.

It was a smaller celebration this time, and dark green was the color scheme. There were fewer tables and far fewer people. Even the dresses were simpler. She had a green satin sash around her waist that was exactly the color of the leaves on the coffee trees. This time she felt more like a fairy born in the mystical mountains who came down between the trees on the backs of slithering iguanas whose scales were made of diamonds and whose collars were made of gold. She also remembered the wrought-iron centerpieces on the tables, filled with long green leaves of freshly cut plants and crooked branches arranged in unique ways that would call attention to themselves yet allow you to see the person across the table, too.

After the wedding, Julieta left with her husband to Monterrey where he would work and she would study. Father thought it would be best where few people knew them, and they could get a fresh start. They would come to visit with their baby and tell of tall buildings covered with glass, and coffee shops, not like home where they roasted the coffee, but where people sat with their computers and bought cups of steaming lattes or mochas and sat for hours to watch four lanes of traffic whiz by. It wasn't long after that Johana left to the Internado.

She befriended Abimael but never pitied him. She knew that they were different. And since she looked forward to her parents coming and visiting her for the weekend or taking her home for the holidays, she sometimes felt bad that Abi's parents rarely came. Johana and her family took him with them sometimes, but it would never be the same for him as it was for her. Nor was it her duty to make it all better for him; that was something he'd have to do for himself. Knowing that didn't stop her frustration when Abi would clam up and then she'd hear from the boys that he'd crawl beneath his bed and curl up in the fetal position. Trouble was to be confronted standing up.

Five

INDEPENDENCE DAY, September Fifteenth, was the first major event of the school year. Miguel was still getting his bearings—clarifying the daily classroom schedule, nailing down such things as pencil-sharpening procedures and bathroom-visiting rules, and figuring out who should sit where. He had not a single thought about contributing to the Independence Day celebration and, despite a few children's suggestions, he had no idea how. He would be a passive observer.

Independence Day in Mexico City was a huge affair, perhaps the biggest of the year. The country actually had fewer than a hundred years under its current political system; Mexico would never forget the years of pillage, starting with the Spaniards in the 1600's, ending with the Americans in the mid-1800's, and including just about everyone else in between. Now Mexico was a proud independent country.

In Mexico City, Miguel knew, hundreds of thousands would gather in the town center, the Zócalo, just outside the grand government palace downtown where the enormous Mexican flag—perhaps thirty meters in length—would wave in the wind. The perfectly-disciplined guard would come to play the national anthem and then would lower the flag at sunset as the cheers of the crowd rivaled those at the World Soccer Championship. Then the party would begin and the lines would grow in front of the beer vendors and the public restrooms. The Aztec dancers, hoping to earn some tips, would come out of the crowd with their lofty feathered headdresses and obsidian spears, and the President of Mexico himself would emerge onto the balcony of the palace to scream: "Viva Mexico! Viva Mexico!" to the roars and the hollers of the populace. As the moment came to a climax, a great series of fireworks would explode in the sky directly above the throngs of people, most of them drunk by now, who would marvel at the dizzying array of light and color…forgetting, for the moment, that the fireworks were paid for by their tax money.

In Comalticán, however, Miguel and his class sat on the sidelines of the soccer field watching a mediocre performance. The third grade teacher had trained half a dozen chubby and uncoordinated children at the so-called art of Aztec dancing. Their headdresses consisted of a few unimpressive feathers each, and they donned what appeared more like clown make-up than war paint. An eighth grade boy then stood upon the shoulders of two classmates as he screamed "Viva Mexico!" in a high-pitched voice, his fake moustache clinging on by a thread. Then the anti-climactic sparklers were lit in the twilight, spun in overhead circles by some fourth graders. Miguel was unimpressed, feeling little connection to the Internado. But he vowed that their next performance would be better than this embarrassment, and he regretted having not contributed.

Orfil and Jesse were the tallest students in the class. This made sense, since they were also the oldest students, having repeated two grades each. They were also the loud, difficult ones. And they constantly made requests to go swim at the river or to do a class barbecue or to hike up to the cross. Miguel didn't dare take forty-two students anyplace by himself. What if the students went crazy? What if they got lost or somebody got hurt? In the few weeks he had been there, he learned that news traveled fast in a small town and that gossip was everywhere.

Nevertheless, he gave in. Since none of the punishments of Maestra Viviana or any of the other teachers had worked, he decided to resort to bribery. "If you behave well for the entire week and complete your assignments and homework," he announced, "we'll go on your hiking trip up to the cross." The class burst out in cheers. "But you have to pass Thursday's test," he went on. Their faces became more serious.

Of course, Miguel never imagined they'd actually do it. But when he witnessed the entire class quietly reading and doing their exercises for the first time, he knew that he had better get a plan ready for the trip.

The students weren't perfect. Nor were their past test scores. But instead of wanting to keep the prize from them, he wanted more than anything to give it to them. He hadn't felt too popular with these students, and he thought it would be a constant struggle, but when Orfil and Jesse began to rouse the younger ones, yelling at them to get their books out, telling them to sit down and follow directions, he knew he couldn't waste their energy.

Thursday afternoon, the class was quiet with anticipation, watching Maestro Miguel at the little teacher's desk, poring over the completed tests. "Well, Maestro?" the students asked anxiously.

"Not done yet." He looked intently at the papers, trying hard not to crack a smile. Then, when the tension had peaked, he put his red marker down and frowned. The students' shoulders slumped.

"Not everybody passed like I had hoped for…"

They looked down quietly.

"But I have to say that everyone improved." He put his arms up triumphantly. "Put your sweatpants on tomorrow, because we're headed up the hill!"

The students screamed out and smacked each others' hands. They were shining with joy.

When they all left the classroom, Miguel went back to the teacher's seat, where he saw a tiny wooden shrimp with fourteen carved legs in sixteen little leg holes. The word "Acapulco" was written on the side. There was a little note attached. "Maestro, you're the coolest teacher I know." He didn't know who gave it to him. But it didn't matter. It was the most beautiful broken shrimp he had ever seen.

The Directora gave Miguel the night off from kitchen duty so that he could go into town. He wanted to surprise the students with an extra treat. Although his pay from the Internado was next to nothing, so were his living expenses. He had no rent nor bills to pay whatsoever, so he could spend his money freely.

At a candy store in Arbolito, Miguel browsed through the mounds of gummy bears and gummy worms and gummy frogs, dodged the dozens of piñatas hanging from the ceiling, and looked through the pistachios, almonds, and walnuts before he decided on the *moheganos*, sticky corn balls in plastic wrap, for all forty-two of his students. "You're the new teacher at the Internado, no?" asked a young man tending the store.

"Yes. Miguel." He shook hands with him.

"Ruben." He handed Miguel the plastic bag and thanked him for the business. "Tell the Captain I sent my greetings." And he went about his chores in the candy shop, swatting away the bees on the guava pastes. "Come back again."

The students all showed up early and they awaited no instructions before they began the march up toward the cross on the mountain peak. As they marched past neighboring classrooms, children from the other classes gathered at the windows to watch them go by. Miguel's students gleefully waved at them. In all honesty, Miguel didn't understand the thrill of sweating up the mountain, but would never mention it to them. If earning these children's affection and, hence, obedience cost some sore muscles and eighty pesos at the candy store, so be it. Teaching oftentimes thrusts one into the most unexpected situations.

Jesse was unusually determined. The normal "idiot" or "faggot" or "asshole" only came out of his mouth when he was provoked. He had taken his shirt off and tied it around his waist, and constantly looked up toward the lone white cross that stood steadfastly before the passing clouds. His mother might be up there looking down upon him, he thought, coaxing him closer.

She had been both hoping and giving up hope on the family trek, years prior, to see the Virgin of Guadalupe. Every year at the end of October, they used to make a shrine for the Day of the Dead to her mother, Jesse's grandmother, who had died at an early age from cancer. His mother wasn't sure in her last year of life why God had given her the same affliction, nor why

He made her battle with the social security medical care just like He did her mother. But she supposed He had His reasons and it was up to her to accept His judgment and know that He would take care of her children in one way or another. After all, He had put the words in the doctors' mouths—"There is really no hope for treatment. Be prepared and say goodbye." She wasn't the only one that thought of that last shrine for her mother as her own shrine.

She would make it to the Basilica, she decided, if it was the last thing she did. So she and her family walked amongst the pilgrims from their small town toward the Basilica of Guadalupe north of Mexico City, nearly two hundred miles away. They camped in small outcroppings arranged by supporters in towns along the way, were served meatballs with nopal cactus strips and pork skin tacos by kind hands, and were encouraged by warm eyes. She was one of many in a wheelchair. Jesse had been too young to grasp it all, but he could feel the gravity of the situation and feared for his mother's plight and his own. "Have faith, son," were the words she repeated over and over.

They reached the Basilica by December twelfth. Jesse remembered, more than anything, the crowds and crowds of people, the colorfully garbed dancers, the white-faced mimes, and having to go to the bathroom very badly. His father led him to some public park where he peed on a tree like the other children, and he returned to find his mother waiting in line at the Chapel of the Spring. It seemed like he stood forever. But the image of his mother's closed eyes and clenched fists rising above the chrome of the wheelchair, her knitted sweater, and then the saddest of wails would never escape him. They doused her with the water from the spring on that afternoon that, for her, was like the last sprig of hope. Then she died two days after Christmas.

When he looked up at the cross on the hill, he could imagine her smiling face as she sat in the same wheelchair with the same knitted sweater. She didn't mean for him to ever be sent to the Internado. His father had no choice since he worked on the highways in distant states. She had promised to never leave him alone. And he imagined her there with him. But then why did he feel so lonely at times?

He felt the sweat on his back and the dry dust in his throat as his own penitence, his sacrifice, for having not been the perfect son that he promised to be. He didn't have faith at times. He couldn't always accept this life as it was given to him. And he wasn't sure where else in this whole world he might belong. The cross was solace.

Orfil was never the leader that Jesse was. He looked up to Jesse as Jesse looked up to the cross. And he, like Jesse, also had a flame of anger which, of course, he didn't understand. But it burned within him like a pilot light nonetheless.

When Orfil was a toddler, his young father had no patience for the slow life and minute incomes of a rural town. He was far more ambitious and carried illusions of fast cars with bright decals and endless banda music from waist-high patio speakers. He wanted the good life. He left Orfil's young mother, his common-law wife, with promises to return from the north with money the likes of which that town had never seen. He went to smuggle drugs with a friend of a friend from secondary school through the desert mountains on the Chihuahua-New Mexico border and then further north all the way up to Canada. The drug traffickers were always looking for new deliverers, cheap ones, for their ever-blossoming markets in "the other side."

Orfil waited for Papi to come home. He'd set aside a slice of flan or a portion of bananas with cream and explain to his mother that that was Papi's piece. "You eat it," she would tell him stoically, "Papi's not coming home for a long time."

What do four-year-olds know of time? The next day he'd pour an extra glass of milk for Papi since he knew he'd be thirsty when he arrived. *Stupid child*, his family thought. They hadn't planned on his being there, but then they hadn't planned anything, really. His mother hadn't planned to stop going to school or get kicked out of her mother's house. She hadn't planned to develop a drinking problem like her aunts and her grandmother. Orfil's father hadn't planned to get caught or serve two years in an American prison. They hadn't planned Orfil's bedroom, either; they just put another bed in their room.

Papi came back home after four years, about three years

and nine months after crusty servings of rice pudding stopped being thrown in the garbage. "Papi's back! Papi's back!" Orfil's screams of joy could have penetrated even the most bitter soul. He rejoiced that he'd been right to keep alive that flicker of hope of seeing Papi walk in every time the door opened. He had never let himself believe all the bad things they said about him. Life was about to be set on track again.

It didn't take anyone, even Orfil, too long to see that Papi wasn't the same person anymore. He wasn't really Papi. He had done too much product sampling; he had become cold like his prison cell. He didn't even stay a year before he left again, unable to meet even the most minimal expectations. He had lost his soul.

The second time that his father left, Orfil had some growing up to do, or at least he had to thicken his skin. That flame, his little pilot light that had once flickered in hope, had changed. It burned hot and uncaring, then and forevermore. He lost. He learned to say "fuck it." Two years after that, his father was dead. Fuck it.

His mother's alcoholism made it necessary to send him to the Internado. His ailing grandfather couldn't care for such a troubled child.

Although Orfil no longer remembered most of his own story, that angry flame had never been extinguished. Though Jesse took the lead in disrupting the class and acting immaturely and foolishly, Orfil's constant scowl expressed a different story for anyone who was willing to read it.

As the students hiked up the hill, their shiny blue polyester sweatpants made a rubbing noise as the pant legs slid past each other. Most of the students traveled in groups of two or three, the boys usually with boys and the girls usually with girls. The bigger ones like Orfil and Jesse were up in the front while the smaller or fatter ones were further behind, as were Abi and Johana. As they passed their teacher or he passed them, they exchanged salutations or a question or two. Miguel realized that each tidbit from a child inevitably revealed some tiny puzzle piece that began to explain how and why their personalities and ways of being were so perfect for each of them. It amazed him how even one piece of information about someone's past could entirely change one's perception of that person, and the judgments which were based upon that perception. How might truly knowing another create a relationship based upon acceptance of who he or she truly is? He thought of his students once again, from whom he now began to hear screams and yells as they arrived at the cross. He doubted that type of acceptance could ever erase some of those things that most irritated him about others, but he supposed that knowing someone through and through was preferable to not.

By the time he reached the cross, Miguel had picked up the littlest of his students, Rebeca, who clung to him happily from her perch on his back. The cross was not as tall as he had imagined, perhaps two meters in height, and he wasn't convinced that the children's climbing on it was very respectful, either. But he was too tired to get them off of it and he figured that other adults should have scolded them enough on previous trips to extinguish such behavior on this one.

The taller trees had been cleared away from in front of the cross. From this view, the Internado could be seen below along with the dozens of homes in its vicinity. The settlement actually was rather circular as the valley formed a sort of broad and flat bowl like the earthenware *comals* on which tortillas were heated over the fire; hence the name, Comalticán. The small cemetery could be seen near the entrance to the *comal* as well as the river that ran from left to right just beyond. This country village was quite a contrast to the graffitied buildings, squeezed wall to wall and block to block, in Mexico City. The light breeze might have actually been relaxing if it hadn't been for the forty-two children under his charge who, now that he noticed, were all sipping on ice-cold soft drinks.

At his right side was a middle-aged lady with one foot propped up on a blue ice chest. She was looking out at Comalticán as if mocking Miguel, who was looking at her quizzically. She seemed to be wearing several multi-colored layers of clothing haphazardly strewn upon her solid, lard-fed body. She wore a faded purple gypsy hat from which her straggly hair protruded

in all directions. Her soiled white tennis shoes were accented by
striped knee-high socks into which her pants were tucked.
When she looked left, their gaze met and she shuddered as if
startled. And then a semi-toothed grin opened in her face and
she confirmed in a raspy voice, "It's beautiful, isn't it?"

Miguel only nodded as she continued, "The air is thin but
it's refreshing…Coke?" Her hand pointed to the ice chest.

"Uh, who are you?" he asked.

"Oh, Teresa. Nice to meet you. You're the new teacher,
right? The students like it up here. My children do too, when
they come up here. They're not here right now, of course." She
spoke quickly, as if trying to fit in all the words before her
breath ran out. After each sentence, she nodded, reaffirming to
herself what she just said.

"Yes, I'm the new teacher. Are you always up here?"

"No, of course not. I'm just working. I heard you guys were
coming up here so I brought some sodas. I thought you might
need a cool drink, no? It's a tough climb but got to work,
right?" she nodded again, still smiling.

"Right. Got to work."

"Well, when you got five kids, you got to feed them, right?
I mean, there are things you just have to do, right?"

"Right." He looked down at the ice chest again. "How
much are they?"

"Ten pesos. That's pretty fair, right? I mean, they are pretty
heavy to get up this hill, you know? But, whatever, got to work,
right?"

"Yeah," he agreed feeling rather disarmed. It was true, you
got to work, right? He couldn't believe this lady was for real,
but took an instant liking to her. He saw his students pulling
together coins from their sweatpants' pockets as her ice chest
continued emptying itself. He recalled the *moheganos* and
passed little Rebeca the bag to disperse amongst the students.

"Let's get these out, Rebeca," he told her. "We got lots of
things to do, right?"

Six

MIGUEL HAD NEVER SEEN A CANTINA with urinals on the wall.
They weren't on the bathroom wall, for there was no bathroom;
they were on the wall directly to the right of the front door. He
wasn't sure if the smell of pee was really there or only in his
head, but the gobs of flies circling around were real enough. He
had finally agreed to "come down to Arbolito for a cold one"
with the Captain, but hardly fancied this as a place to relax. He
seemed to be the only one in the place who felt that way.

There were fifteen or so men in the joint, most with the
typical garb of the mountain dwellers—white linen pants that
were strapped around at the waist and rolled up at the ankles, a
white linen long-sleeved shirt, a colored bandana around the
neck, and a sombrero. They mostly sat a few to a table, every
man with a brown beer bottle in his hand or in front of him on
the plastic table. There were no women allowed in the bar except for the two waitresses, who not-so-quietly talked to each
other at the corner of the bar much more than they waited on
their patrons. One had to call out one of their names before they
sprang to duty.

"Maestro!" called the Captain from the far corner table. "Sit
down!" He waved his hand beckoningly. Then he shouted at the
waitress, "Ilse! Get the Doce a beer!" Ilse plopped one leg off
the bar stool and then the other, as the story from Mariana
would have to wait. "That's it, old lady," he shouted again,
laughing wide to reveal silver fillings beside his tongue. She
held up her fist to him in feigned defiance.

Miguel watched the interaction until his eyes fixed on one
of the men in dirty white linen passed out at the adjacent table.
His cheek was flat on the plastic and it looked as if his head had

37

long since slipped off of his forearm, since the puddle of spit beneath his open mouth implied he'd been this way for a while. He was breathing, though, which was a relief.

Captain looked over at Miguel and shook his head. "Fuckin' Pablo," he offered. "Get the fuck up, Pablo!" he shouted. But the drunkard didn't flinch.

They passed the next hour between banda music from the jukebox and the only brand of beer that the cantina sold. The place was actually pretty quiet, as the patrons mostly focused on self-medicating with their drinks. There was a single bottle of tequila on a shelf at the bar, untouched.

"See that waitress?" said the Captain in Miguel's ear. His breath by this time smelled like an old beer and an ashtray. Miguel was getting drunk, too. He wasn't used to drinking on school nights. "She has a nipple ring in her left titty. She likes it when you tug on it with your teeth." He laughed diabolically and put his arm on Miguel's back. "But she screams too much, goes kind of crazy on you. I quit messing with her a long time ago." He nodded to Miguel as he raised his eyebrows. Miguel nodded and smiled politely in return. Captain continued, "She still wants me, though. Don't you see her looking over here all the time?"

Miguel hadn't seen her look over toward their table at all. On the contrary, he noticed how dirty the tables were and how little the two waitresses paid attention to them. He had been resisting the urge to relieve his bladder at the public urinals but could no longer endure. He got up slowly from his chair and as he did so one of the Captain's hands descended from his shoulder to his butt. The man grabbed strongly and pulled at Miguel's shoulders with his other hand. "Hey," he said, "those chicks had nice tight pussies but I'll bet nothing beats this sweet ass, Maestro." He squeezed his butt cheek again. Miguel smiled politely again, both repulsed and slightly aroused. He walked over to the urinals trying to conceal his stagger.

After a couple more beers and Captain's unending commentary, he suggested they get going. "You should see my place, Maestro. It's just around the corner from the school." No more politeness from Miguel; it was all he could do to stand up straight.

One of the town's three taxis gave them a lift back to Comaltícan. The air was crisp and the night black like charcoal. When they arrived at the Captain's house, Miguel went directly to the bathroom for another piss. Even with the absence of a toilet seat, he could barely hit the toilet water without wetting the rim. When he walked out to the living room, he found the Captain on the tattered sofa, one hand holding a beer and the other hand holding his crotch. "I know what you're hoping for, Doce." It was the diabolical laugh again.

Miguel's eyes alternated between Captain's crotch and face, preferring the crotch. He hated for the Captain to think he was right, to think he could treat him like some perverted sex toy. But he *did* want it.

"You are a little butterfly boy, aren't you?" the Captain asked, looking him straight in the face. Miguel's eyes went back to Captain's crotch where his hand hadn't stopped rubbing it. Miguel couldn't deny how big it was nor how fit the Captain must have once been.

Miguel's tongue betrayed his dignity. It slipped out and wet his lips. Then he heard himself say, "Yeah, I guess so."

"Then come and suck this" was the last comment that Miguel could remember when he woke up the next morning. He couldn't even remember how he got back to the school. If it hadn't been for the crowing of some infernal roosters, Miguel doubted that he would have ever awakened in time. His head pounded. His butt was sore and his underwear slightly soiled. In a daze, he searched for the white shirt and maroon pants of a Normal student.

He wasn't too out of it to chuckle at the irony. He had to look "normal" for his students. Who ever came up with that word for teachers? He thought of his students and then his mother. He shuddered at the notion of their discovering his "abnormality." He brushed his black hair back, determined to avoid a run to the bakery that day.

Seven

"THREE TIMES SEVEN?" Miguel pointed at Orfil, whose eyes looked about the room before he shrugged his shoulders.

Miguel couldn't tell which was worse, their math or their spelling. Little Rebeca always seemed to know the answers, but most of them had a long ways to go. He wouldn't forget the spelling contest that he had designed. He would pick words out of a hat. Each time they misspelled a word, they'd get eliminated, he had planned, until the final round where the champion would have to correctly spell the word his or her opponent had misspelled. But everyone had been eliminated by the second round. "Stupid faggots," screamed Juan, "F-A-G-O-T-S!" Miguel sent him the look.

The championship round consisted of the last two students who spelled fourteen words in a row incorrectly. Neither could eliminate the other. Miguel called it a tie to save face and decided to go with easier words the next time.

The sea of black heads was now *his* sea of black heads, despite the occasional meddling of Maestra Viviana, who explained that her being in charge of the Christmas festival would keep her from helping him much. "You're doing fine, anyhow, although the monsters seem out of control, at times," she said.

He mentally scoffed at her complaints about her paychecks and the burdens of her duties. He was on a meager allowance yet won his students over with his dedication and creativity, he thought. He tired of her belittling them. *And the Christmas festival?* he wondered. They were still in September.

Having taken his students up to the cross, he wasn't sure what he could bribe them with next. "The swimming hole!" they cried in unison.

"Swimming hole? What swimming hole?"

"Down at the river!" they cried again.

Miguel shook his head. "It's getting too cold to go swimming."

"We don't care!" they shouted.

"You don't even have bathing clothes…"

"We don't care!" again.

"I don't even know where it is."

"We'll show you!"

The deal was set. Times tables, spelling lists, and state capitals. One swimming hole for the girls, one for the boys. He wondered if he was too permissive. The other teachers didn't take the students on outings, they didn't buy them candies or play games with them. But his students seemed to be learning and they loved him, he told himself. He was too far in now anyway; there was no turning back.

It was the Directora's insistence that the boys and girls be separated. She knew the kids would swim naked and that they wouldn't care if they were all in the same swimming hole. But word gets around, she knew, and it would be better to prevent any gossip. So she agreed to chaperone them and watch the girls' swimming hole, but only if they kept their part of the bargain—and she was going to judge their academic results.

It was the first week that Miguel ever saw the kids in absolute silence, the sea of heads stuck in their respective books. He supposed that it was the first week it ever happened with these students. They had partner study and quiz times, they had choral practice, they wrote and wrote and studied and studied. They didn't even want to go to lunch.

"Learn it, gay boy!" said Juan to his study partner on one occasion. Miguel was growing irritated by that kid, yet hesitated calling his attention to it. Lots of boys used derogatory gay slurs with each other but this kid had been pushing it. Would he be outing himself if he was the first person to call him on it? And then what would they think of him?

It was Thursday afternoon class time when the Directora came in. Her face was serious, as always, her arms folded across her chest. She would administer the test, she said, and grade it herself. The children's eyes widened. Never had the stakes been so high. She told Miguel to have a seat and distributed the papers herself. "I don't want to see any copying. I don't want to hear a word." Children swallowed hard. She looked over at Miguel, whose hands began to sweat. Her mouth turned up for an instant and she winked at him. Then she continued to pace the narrow aisles, her solid work shoes hitting the concrete floor with a thud at each step. When they were done, she collected their papers and left to her office. The children collapsed on their desks.

At four o'clock the students still sat in the room as if awaiting Santa Claus. When she arrived, she no longer carried the papers in her hands. "I have bad news for you," she stated.

Their hopeful eyes lost their sparkle.

She continued, "I won't be wearing my bathing suit."

They looked to the floor.

"But you will!"

As if on cue, they arose in a giant wave, arms in the air, embracing one another and screaming. They had done it!

This time, the students in the other classes didn't gather at the windows to watch them go by. They looked at them in the courtyard from their seats and went about their business. The hike was more casual; the students seemed more relaxed than on the trip to the cross. Miguel, walking beside the Directora, felt at ease. She, like him, came from a distant place, albeit many more years earlier, and had found her place in the mountains with the vibrant life of the mountainside. She watched the children walk down the river's bank, a mother hen and her many chicks. In over thirty years at her post, the job hadn't changed a bit. Miguel sometimes saw her like a reverend mother, as if sworn to duty and celibacy, but she seemed unregretful of her life alone.

The swimming holes were like the dormitories, two genders separated by a grand stone barricade. The water poured between two rectangular stones, light-colored on top,   black like tar at the bottom and perhaps five meters in height, that seemed to have been placed by the hand of God to build a natural dam.

On either side of the dam was formed a swimming hole. The boys would undoubtedly clamber up and jump from the stones' heights. However, they were not to cross over to the girls' side. They made their promises, and when the Directora's head disappeared behind the rocks upstream, their clothes were rapidly strewn upon the shore. Miguel found a shady seat amongst their clothes beside the ponds where the normally rushing water was stilled by nature's engineering.

Miguel watched the boys, their awkward bodies making up in agility what they lacked in grace. Most had a year or two to go before puberty would meet them, but some of the older of the noisy bunch had traces of musculature and body hair indicative of manhood. Some had round protruding bellies and rolls of fat, while others had undeniable physique and enviable curvature. The cold had already caused the testicles of those who had them to ascend into the warmth of their bodies. This left their little penises dangling like dead worms in birds' beaks.

Miguel's glance veered away when the boys looked at him as if they suspected, as if they knew his secret. But in reality, he found them to be not lacking in sexuality, for no one could deny their humanness, but utterly unappealing. On the contrary, he felt their innocence to be sacred. Even the most mischievous and devious of them was only a child trying to survive, pure at heart, susceptible to impulse, and naïve to adult wickedness. Corrupting that innocence was not within him, though he worried they might believe it was. He was attracted to *men* in all senses of the word.

"Jump you pussy, you faggot!" he heard. Miguel knew that voice and breathed in deeply before he looked over. It was Juan, as he had imagined, upon the boulder behind Abi, who crept to the ledge of the largest stone and peeked at the water below. Chubby Abi knelt down atop the boulder, intending to approach the water on his butt.

Juan shook his head. "What a sissy! Butterfly boy!"

Miguel watched Juan as he stepped toward Abi. Miguel stood up in his place and screamed. But Juan didn't hear. He was too focused on kicking Abi off the ledge. Abi shouted, his angry face shifting between the water far below and Juan's oncoming foot. Before Miguel knew it, they both had fallen with a splat into the green water. He lunged a few steps into the cold water before he could see that the kids were fine, as evidenced by Abi's sputtering of profanities at his attacker.

"Juan," Miguel yelled, "Come over here now!"

Juan paid him no mind.

"Juan!" he yelled again with greater fervor.

Juan looked over at his teacher in disbelief. "What?" He shrugged his shoulders and raised his skinny arms as if oblivious to his wrongdoing.

"Come here right now."

Juan walked to where Miguel was standing on the rocky shore. "Yes?"

"Are you crazy? You could have killed the both of you!"

"We were just playing," he responded.

"Just 'playing'? I told you to be careful! You are not to push anyone like that!"

"He was just being a pussy girl. Didn't you see him? Little faggot wouldn't jump!"

Miguel's blood began to boil. He tried to contain himself but his finger came out of his hand and shook at the boy's face just like his mother always did when she scolded him. "You are never to call anyone a faggot or gay or pussy or sissy as long as you are ever in my presence or the presence of any other person who deserves far more respect than you seem capable of showing. Now, you are to sit on this rock," his finger swiftly pointed downward, "until I tell you otherwise."

"No, Maestro," he whined in protest. Finally, Miguel had found the boy in him that could be controlled. And corrected. "I won't do it again, I swear."

Miguel stayed firm. "The Directora is right upstream... would you like to talk to her about it?"

He plopped his naked butt on the rock and then his head on his hand. "No."

Miguel calmed down a bit, too. "What is it with you and the words 'faggot' and 'pussy'?" His tone changed to an inquisitive one.

Juan just shrugged his shoulders as he watched the boys

who continued to romp in the water.

"Well, we won't hear that again, right?"

"Right," he said, defeated.

In ten minutes he was in the water again.

In three hours the lot of them were back at the Internado, exhausted and fulfilled. They went straight to bed after the dinner chores and clean-up.

Miguel lay in his bed in the darkness, listening to the rhythmic chirping of the crickets, a stark contrast to the hollering of the children all day. It was an even greater contrast to the craziness back home in Mexico City. He reflected on the steps he had taken, large and small, in these short weeks, and the anxiety he had endured throughout. He hadn't expected the responsibility of teaching to feel this heavy.

Then he recalled the incident with Juan, the throbbing pressure it had caused in his temples, and the rush of anger that had jolted him into action. Yet, after all, he thought, Juan did respond to his corrections. In fact, it was probably much less stressful for Juan than for it was for him. Perhaps it was a small step for Juan in his journey of growth, and Miguel realized that he had been part of it, as if it took a conflict to get beyond the obstacle. He let out a sigh in the darkness, and then smiled to himself, before he drifted off to sleep.

Eight

THE WATER REDDENED as the old man, Juan, washed the blood from the long-bladed knife. He cleaned his blackened hands next. But the stains on his white linen pants and shirt would never wash out. There were years of stain after stain on those same clothes. When his wife was alive, she would take his clothes down to the river after each slaughter and steep them with soap from a one pound bar and then scrub them on the washboard till they looked as clean as the day she made them. But Juan had no need for clean clothes; he was ignorant of the work of women. He always had been and always would be. He even resented hauling water up the hill to his shack. The reddened water, still and dead, would sit there a while longer.

He pulled the cloth hanging in the doorway to one side and stepped outside the hut. His one intact eye surveyed the surrounding hills from his grassy patch. With a single movement his arm swung down and stuck the knife in his tree trunk chopping block. It would be dark soon and he'd be up at dawn to see his son, fulfilling the promise he had made to his ailing wife to look after their boy.

He recalled the predictable scream of the sheep as the knife pierced its throat. His recollection was not of horror or distaste, or the guilt of one who committed some immorality, but rather the way one peruses the happenings of a workday, like an electrician recalling a socket. He still preferred to shoot them—one loud bang, a quick fall to the ground, no scream—but it splattered the brains too much for those who liked to eat them.

If anything had stuck in his brain over the years, it was their frightened eyes. Despite their stupidity, they always seemed to recognize imminent peril. He had seen it in their eyes. Even he

46

could see the irony that he had shot his own eye out, although he had few words to describe such things and even fewer people to whom he might describe them. His private thoughts made him chuckle at times. He still preferred to shoot them.

Slaughtering was the only talent he had for which people would pay him—not much, only one hundred or two hundred pesos, but enough to keep his propane tank and sack of beans full for the month. He did not know that modern times were naturally de-selecting him. By the time he was dead, so would be the neighbors scattered amongst the hills who currently required his services. They needed him more for the butchering and the preservation of the hide than for the simple slaughter, though many folks saw him as they saw the undertaker, somehow enveloped in a cloud of death. No, when he was gone, no one would take his place; there would be no need.

Inside the wooden shack, he lit a single candle and shoveled a big spoonful of crusty brown beans into his mouth from the pan that sat on his metal stove. He lay back on the hammock beside it and rested his sandaled feet, as black and dirty as his hands had been, upon the plaid blanket. With a sigh, he tilted his hat down over his eyes, not to keep the light from his face, for there was little of that in the shack, but the flies. It was a long journey to Comalticán, and he would need the rest.

In the dark morning, he dumped last night's bloodied water into the grass patch a few paces from the front door. He drank black coffee from a kettle and yanked a flap of dried meat from a line in the patio. He then donned a red serape and slipped on his sandals, hat, and a sheathed machete on a rope strap. He headed down the hill in the light of the rising sun.

A little past midday, he arrived at the gate of the Internado. The sign at the front said "Enter" with an arrow pointing toward the office. But he could not read the word and ignored the arrow. He tapped on the metal with his machete till someone came to answer. If anything, he respected territory.

Miguel answered. "Come in, Señor." He opened the door cordially.

"Juanito?" asked the man, standing still at the threshold.

"Are you here for Juan?" Miguel clarified.

"Yes."

"Are you his father?" Miguel inquired.

The man's working eye just looked at Miguel seriously. He nodded his head slightly and then looked up toward the sky, his one eye squinted in the light.

Miguel left to find little Juan.

Juan was in the dormitory and happy that his father had come. He always hoped to feel his mother's love extended through his father. It was her hands that he remembered that touched him gently, stroked his hair, and cared for him; it was those hands that he missed.

"Juanito, what happened?" was the first thing his father said to him. He stooped to see the shiner on his cheek.

"Nothing, Papá. We were just playing yesterday. Wrestling."

Father's strong hand grasped his son's arm. He put his face close to the boy's. "Don't you be a faggot," he said. "Faggots lose." Little Juan only looked at him, staring at the eye. "Your Mamá wouldn't want to see that I brought up no faggot who can't stick up for himself."

It was as if the entire background of a painting had been created with but a single stroke of the brush. Miguel stood like a silent juror as the man pulled his son away. He recalled from some pedagogy class back at the university, "Whatever you do, don't do any harm." *This applies as much to parents as to teachers*, he thought. He felt a pang of guilt at the distaste he often felt for little Juan. *It's true what the Directora said*, he thought. *We're the only chance these children have.*

Nine

MARKET DAY IN ARBOLITO, the second and fourth Saturdays of each month, brought people in from all the surrounding provinces like cattle at feeding time. They brought with them their goods for sale, counting on the pesos that they would earn to buy those essentials they didn't have at home. All along the three parallel roads that comprised the village, from one side of town to the other, vendors spread their goods on blankets. There was everything from red chile powder to brown mole paste, leather sandals to handcrafted jewelry, brown or white rice to colored corn, razor blades to hammers and machetes, papayas to lemons and roasted coffee beans.

Miguel watched as brown, round women balanced baskets on their heads and carried turkeys hand-cuffed at the feet like suitcases. The birds contorted their long necks to keep their heads upright as they were walked to market. They looked like tourists quietly taking in the sights as they were transported through the streets.

The town was a-bustle with bartering, weighing, and packing. Women in the street cooked *huaraches*, oblong tortilla-like snacks made from blue corn dough with grilled steak, cactus, shredded white cheese, and spicy salsa on top. The bells of the *raspado* carts called attention to the numerous bottles of colored syrups to be poured over shaved-ice cones, with whole fruits in them like snakes in bottles of Chinese potions. Bees maneuvered to procure samples for the hive. The familiar smell of pork skins being fried in large sheets in huge vats of boiling oil reminded Miguel of home. He strolled along the streets, dodging the throngs of people, looking for a few personal items he needed and perhaps some cheap treat for his adoptive chil-

49

dren or some ideas for the upcoming Day of the Dead.

He spotted Teresa, the crazy soda seller from up at the cross. She wore long striped socks visible beneath her pleated skirt and a San Diego Chargers cap on her head. She smiled and waved at Miguel as he passed, her other hand supporting a long wooden staff from which red candied apples stuck out like branches. She pointed at her apples and smiled. "What else can you do?" she laughed from across the street to him. "Gotta sell what you can get, right?"

As he passed the candy shop, now somewhat quiet because of the competition, he saw Ruben, the store attendant, chatting with an elderly white-haired lady who was clinging to a walker. "Maestro! Come inside!" he said to Miguel.

The lady slowly turned her head to measure him. "Doña Conchita," said Ruben, "this is Miguel. Miguel, Doña Conchita."

"Oh," she nodded. "This is the new teacher at the Internado?" Everything she said, she said slowly.

Doña Conchita had lived in Arbolito since it was as small as Comalticán. She ran the two-room museum, or rather sat in it, since running was a pastime she had left behind seventy years before. The museum was in the city hall building, along with the one-room police station, the one-room public records office, the mayor's office, and a single jail cell mostly used as a drunk tank during New Year's festivities and September Fifteenth celebrations.

The memories in Doña Conchita's head easily outnumbered the files in the records office, although they were far more jumbled and even less accurate. She normally would doze away the days in the cluttered museum that held what looked more like a garage sale than a display, waiting for an outsider to stumble in. She'd tell them some version of her childhood and some version of the town history, and always spent considerable time on the lacy and discolored wedding dress in the center display case which lay beside an equally faded black suit. The dress was her own. Her grandmother had made it. Now the dress and suit lay beside photos nearly sixty years old of her and her husband, a man who had disappeared under mysterious circumstances only a year after the wedding.

Her current inspiration was found in the local gossip. She heard it all and even began a few rumors of her own. Thinking of some tales she'd heard whispered about town, she turned to Miguel. "You took the naked boys to go swimming in the river, no?"

Miguel smiled and looked at Ruben quickly before answering her. He noticed a sly, almost devious look in his face that he hadn't seen before. It made Miguel wonder.

"Well yes, Señora. The Directora and I took the students to go swimming at the river. The children had a great time."

"Yes. I'm sure you did." She paused. "They say you've fallen in love with those children who were swimming naked with the Directora."

He smiled bashfully as Ruben shook his head. "Yes. I am very fond of them. They mean a lot to me."

"I'm sure they like you, too. Viviana says you're a natural."

"I'm not sure how she'd know," said Miguel. Doña Conchita's eyebrows perked up. "Her being so busy with the Christmas festival and all."

She nodded slowly. "Right. Christmas festival." She pulled up on the walker to aim it toward the street. "Well, I'd best be on my way. They tell me there are four Canadian tourists in town who will surely want to stop by the museum. Do be sure to bring the children by some time with their proper clothes, I mean uniforms, on. It was a pleasure to meet you, Maestro." And she moseyed out to the street and made her way sluggishly toward the museum.

In truth, Doña Conchita had never been noticeable as a child. She had grown up among many siblings in their quiet home and she had been ordinary in almost all respects. As her kin moved away or to the next life, she earned notoriety simply for being the last De La Torre from a long line of De La Torres in Arbolito. She had taken the job in the museum two decades before because there was no one else to do it. She had promptly filled the place with her own memorabilia. Luckily for her, people respect their elders in small towns.

Her wedding, so long ago yet so precious in her mind, was

the only time in her youth that all of the attention was focused on her. The church ceremony, the flowers and the band, feeling important and alive. She preferred to tuck away the fact that they pressured him to marry her. She believed that he was in love with her deep down and that he would learn to express it sooner or later. And she preferred the words "mysterious circumstances" to his having simply left her. There was no second husband nor children, and now there was no family. So she savored the power of her position, the first walker to which she steadfastly clung. It was better to have bad breath than no breath.

"Don't worry about her, she's harmless," Ruben said as he put his hand on Miguel's shoulder. "I hear you're doing a great job. Everyone knows how lazy those local teachers are. Viviana was just as lazy as a student when we were in school together, always trying to get others to do her work."

"It's fine. I prefer being independent."

Ruben just nodded.

Miguel looked around the store and spotted some morbid remains that were just what he was looking for: sugar skulls, chocolate eyeballs, gummy organs, and skeleton suckers. Ruben was glad to give him a discounted rate.

Then he offered, "So...you should come horseback riding with me some time. There's not much else to do around here but drink beer."

Miguel looked into Ruben's brown eyes. He noticed a small mole between the eyelashes on his left eye. He liked the way that Ruben combed his hair, spiky in the back, as if molded by a strong headwind, fashionable but masculine. His forearms and biceps were strong and defined, perhaps from lifting boxes. His shoulders were square and upright, and a small patch of thin brown hair showed above his unbuttoned polo shirt. "Sure," Miguel said. "Any time."

"Hey, and say 'hi' to the Captain for me."

They shook hands again before Miguel headed back to the Internado, but not before seeing Juan munching one of Teresa's red candied apples. Juan walked silently at the side of a father who understood duty to his late wife far more than fatherhood.

Death was not to be feared; it was a normal part of life. For that reason, the Day of the Dead had a light side. The students built life-sized skeletons of newspaper and paper tape that they propped about the room or sat in someone's chair sacrificed for the occasion. Miguel took advantage to discuss the skeletal system and the students labeled the names of the bones before clothing them in everyday garb. They found an old janitor's suit, a worker's hard hat, and a donated floral dress. Students made a paper chef's hat, a red bandolier, and whatever else they could think of to dress their skeletons in lively costumes. Each of the skeletons was different but each bore a happy face. All the while the students munched on the death candy that Miguel brought in. Death is among us; do not be afraid.

The shrine was not as cheerful, though, for it represented those who had passed on. Miguel had cleared his tiny desk to be used as a shrine, and the children placed items upon it that symbolized someone who had died. There were photos of famous people and of loved ones, some leftover foods that children brought in from the cafeteria, games and poems, and other random things. In the middle of the table, the class respectfully ceded a large spot to Jesse, upon which he centered the only portrait that he had of his mother, a wallet-size picture, and a carefully written phrase on colored paper: "I Have Faith."

Outside the colors were changing and the green leaves turned to brown. The summer heat had subsided and the air began to cool. For Miguel, the newness of the Internado diminished; for the children, the newness of their teacher subsided also. The cycle of life carried on.

Ten

MIGUEL LOVED TO WATCH the enthusiastic hands of the children as they created their papier-maché masks. At his request, the Directora had purchased brand new paints and paint brushes for his class, tossing one more log on the fire of growing envy among some of the school's staff. Had their instincts led them to actually be competitive, or at least moved them to try and provoke some kind of creativity or motivation in their students, they might have warranted some of the Directora's largesse. But instead their instincts led them to dwell on superficial inequities and personality imperfections. They would be more content to see him fail than expend energy on the chance that they might actually succeed.

This mattered not to Miguel, who was aware that their politeness was hypocritical. He had never been a real achiever, either, and was more familiar with their train of thought than he cared to admit.

The children giggled as they painted age lines on the pink masks, and bumps and spots on the long noses. They glued clumps of white string for hair on top of the decrepit faces. The masks would be featured prominently in the dance of the old folks, a favorite not just in these parts but all over the country. At least Viviana would teach them the choreography, for Miguel had no idea.

Abi and Johana were the first to finish. He helped her into full costume and she did all she could do to contain her laughter as she crouched with her cane, hump on her back, crusty face pointed down to the ground. When she stood up straight again she swung the long white hair around to her back with a single movement of her neck and this wiped the grin from Miguel's face instantaneously. She reminded him of his mother.

Not once had she attempted to call him in his three months at the Internado. Nor he her, for that matter. Just as well, for she would not have known how to encourage him nor how to bask in any accomplishment of his for a moment. No, she would ask about his pay, complain about her bills, tell him the bad news of his sisters, his absent father and step-fathers, and his "faggoty" brother. He would not expect anything different, he could not. Sometimes, the best way of improving a family situation was by leaving it.

Johana's joyful scream woke him from his stupor. He watched those two kids and then scanned his realm, his ocean of children that were teaching him to flourish despite his up-bringing. He was able to create a new kind of family, perhaps even a better one.

It was dark after dinner, crisp outside in the November air, when Miguel brought the bread trays up to the bakery. Captain was cleaning up behind the counter, the inevitable accordion and tuba noise from his banda music in the background.

The Captain was startled by the sight of Miguel at the door. "Hey! Maestro! Seems like we sleep together—you don't even say hi anymore!" He laughed gruffly.

"I've been busy, Captain, with the children and the Christmas fair."

"Ah…Christmas, Christmas."

"Oh, Ruben sends his greetings, by the way."

"Who?"

"Ruben, from Arbolito."

"Ah…you met the little candy boy…" His voice died down as he mumbled some words to himself. He turned his attention back to cleaning.

"Well, I'll let you finish," said Miguel.

"Finish? Huh, nothing's ever finished," he said abruptly.

Miguel paid little attention as he turned back to the door.

"Maestro." Miguel turned back once again. "Why don't you come over here and help me finish then?" He looked at Miguel's face and then down below.

"I can't, Captain, I have to go back to the kitchen."

"Come on, Maestro. It's been a long time. You know you came up here for something."

Yes, Miguel thought, *to bring the trays*. He wanted to take a step back to the door, feeling more repulsed than excited. He had better things to do than be this street dog's bitch any time his desire or need called for it.

"Maestro," pleaded Captain, "you're turning me on just standing there." He grabbed at his crotch. "You know I can't resist a pretty butterfly boy like you."

The seduction ended. "What?" Miguel asked.

Captain didn't catch on. "Come now, I'm all horned up and you're a faggot. You know you want it."

"No!" Miguel startled the Captain again. "I know who the faggot is and who you'll be thinking of tonight when you jerk yourself off!" He left the door open as he marched out.

"Fine, you pretty boy," Miguel could hear from behind him, "and tell that faggot Ruben to fuck his mother!"

Miguel just snickered as he walked back in the cool night air.

Eleven

HORSEBACK RIDING WAS AWKWARD, the back and forth swaying that was not jerky like the buses in the city but unstable, like riding a see-saw for the first time. His hands were like those of a school boy at his first dance, unsure where to be, because there was no place to grab at the saddle and no way to hold on to the horse's rump beneath him. Ruben's waist was a most tempting handhold and, because of that, forbidden. His hands settled onto his own thighs, his lower legs clinging ardently to the creature's ribcage. Unexpected jolts caused his hands to grasp at Ruben anyway. Miguel was not convinced that the equestrian life was for him.

Much of the rocky river bed was still dry and the horse's hoofs slid on the smooth boulders at times before finding solid ground, but it plodded on without complaint. Ruben looked at the canyon walls on either side that not long from now would be wet with the winter's rain. Random logs, branches, and dry vines littered the river bed, testaments to last year's storms that flushed them down from the hills above and left them like bodies on a battlefield.

In Ruben's silence, Miguel focused on the fine hairs on Ruben's neck. He imagined his muscular back shirtless and the feel of his forearms on his palms. He was quietly aroused, but embarrassed, too, for thinking only of sex at a time like this. Perhaps it was the liberty of the canyon, empty of people and garbage, loud children and watching eyes. The moving air refreshed him as it passed through his hair. He felt as if he had escaped. Then he reflected on the irony—his coming to Comalticán had been the escape. He had already escaped. What was he escaping from now?

They must have been ten kilometers from town by now. Ruben pointed into the trees. "Do you see the power line?"

Miguel followed his fingers and saw where a heavy black wire was hidden in the thick of the leaves.

"It's the only sign of people out here…and the only source of electricity for all of Comalticán. They're always worried about it going down in the winter storms like it did a few years back."

"I hadn't noticed," replied Miguel. "You'd think they'd have put it in a better place, then."

"Yeah, but they put it up in the summertime when the river bed was dry. They found it easier to use the river bed than building a road for it. Maybe they'll fix it next election." He shrugged his shoulders. "We'll stop up there beyond the bend. There's a small beach that formed this spring where I like to rest."

Ruben had always tended toward tranquility. He hadn't fallen into the bad crowd at school, hadn't hung around at the park and gotten shit-faced at parties like the rest of the guys. He hadn't enjoyed talking about fucking this or that girl or arguing over which was the best soccer forward or which was the fastest four-wheeler. Mostly he had hung around with the studious school girls. He had had a serious air since early childhood.

Perhaps it was his Christian upbringing that set him apart, at first, or at least the dedication that his mother had to it. She would read him Bible stories and talk about the greatness of God. She would pray with pathos and sing with eyes closed and hands raised toward the heavens. She preached honesty and sincerity, and challenged others in tight spots with "What would Jesus do?" She was a good woman, Ruben knew, and he loved her dearly. But he didn't believe what she did. He found her religion dogmatic and, at times, self-righteous or simply unbelievable. He had acquiesced through his adolescence to keep the harmony at home, however.

Indeed, he had been the perfect child—quiet and obedient, not easily led astray, always striving to achieve in school, help around the house, and save his money for a rainy day. He was his mother's pride and joy. He had been afraid for a long time that he might destroy that pride and joy. He knew he was different from the other kids in another way.

Once he had finished preparatory school and began having serious feelings for a long-time friend, there was no more denying. His mother had instilled honesty in him, so how much longer could he ignore what had to be said?

The worst part was that he was right. His mother had been devastated when he told her he was gay.

The roof caved in and the storms came down. It was a good thing that Ruben had saved some money in anticipation of disaster. When a friend's parents were selling the candy store in nearby Arbolito, Ruben was ready to start anew. It was the perfect opportunity, a godsend, for studying at the university in the big city held little interest. Despite the problems with his mother at home, he was a small town guy...and a Mama's boy, after all. He believed she'd eventually find a way to rationalize loving him. He believed in love.

The rift hadn't been entirely healed. Until it was, his horse Micha would be his solace. Ruben loved the solitude and solidarity he found with her. She was also a symbol to him of his modest financial success, and the tranquility of being alone with her was a luxury, a short-lived vacation on lunch hour.

Recognizing the little beach, Micha stopped at her resting place beneath the tree at the river bank. The two men dismounted. Then Ruben took the blanket from where Miguel had been sitting and pulled sandwiches and sodas from a knapsack. After eating, they lay together on the blanket in the cool November afternoon, watching the gray clouds sweep across the sky, and chatted awhile.

"Captain sent you greetings," Miguel said, finally finding the confidence. "I think it was 'Fuck your mother!' to be exact."

Ruben looked over at him and laughed. "Typical macho man! He's so pathetic."

"I guess you know him pretty well?"

"Are you kidding?" Ruben shook his head. "He started suspecting that I was gay and would come to see me at the candy store. Starts grabbing his cock and looking at me in his 'sexy' way, as if I'm gonna stop what I'm doing and suck his dick right there." Miguel's confidence began to waver as Ruben continued. "He thinks any queer will fall for that. I have more dignity than to let some fat slob fuck me who just wants to blow his load. I told him he'd have better luck baking himself two buns and drilling a hole in between them."

Miguel nodded and chuckled in agreement, silently relieved that he had rejected Captain's last come on.

"He's probably put the make on you, too, huh?" Ruben asked.

"Yeah, something like that."

"What a pig."

"So," Miguel shifted. "You're gay?"

"Am I gay? Yes. Why did you think I asked you out here?"

"Okay…I just wasn't sure."

"I figured *you* were," Ruben said, "you know, for taking naked boys down to the river and all." He laughed and elbowed Miguel in the side. "As you can imagine, there are not that many open gays out here. And when they are, they're usually practically drag queens or hair stylists. I don't have many friends like me."

They lay silently, reveling in the moment, the liberty and solidarity. Miguel thought of the Captain and of his students. What if the world knew the truth about him? What if Ruben knew about him and the Captain? What if his students knew about him? Then where would he escape to? He thought of Abimael, whose warts were displayed for the world to see. Those warts didn't affect his usually happy disposition. Why couldn't it be so easy for him?

On the way back, Ruben put Miguel in the driver's seat. He instructed him on the use of the reins and the kick of the heel. "You have to show the horse who is in charge," he said. But Miguel could hardly concentrate as he felt Ruben's arms firmly wrapped around his waist and his body pressed against his back.

The bread pans sat in their usual spot on the counter in the kitchen. Crickets chirped in the darkness outside, as always.

Most of the students had finished their meal and were on their way to the dormitories. Most of the dishes were washed. Years of black and brown residue showed on the pans that, like the entire school, were once shiny and new, many years before. They were waiting for Miguel to carry them up to the bakery. They would wait, he decided, for he wasn't going to take them.

They would not wait long, it turned out. As he finished cleaning in the kitchen with another Normal student, they heard the cafeteria door bang open. The noise echoed through the cool concrete cafeteria and immediately drew the attention of the score of children who lingered over their meals. Their chewing stopped as they looked at the Captain in the doorway and then in unison looked over at the teachers in the kitchen. Abi, sitting beside Johana, was close to the kitchen, a shiny ring of grease around his mouth like clown makeup.

"Where are the fuckin' trays, Miss Teacher?" Captain slurred loudly as he pointed at Miguel from afar. He walked in, staggering, and Miguel recognized instantly his inebriated state. He did a slow three-sixty in place as if to assess the audience. "This little gay butterfly doesn't do his job!" he explained to them emphatically.

Except for their blinking eyes, the audience was absolutely motionless.

"He thinks everyone should serve him! Him and the other gay boy, Ruben." He stepped ever closer to the kitchen where Miguel stood incredulous. Miguel began to sense the aroma of liquor with the Captain still six meters away.

The Captain looked over at the brown bread trays, then at the other teacher. She snapped into motion. She grabbed the trays from the counter and pushed them toward him. "Are these what you're looking for?"

He approached the counter and reached for the trays, mumbling profanities to himself. "Give me those dirty trays," was the only intelligible phrase. He glanced over at Miguel again, angry eyes in a wobbling head. "Fuckin' faggots think they can tell everyone what to do."

Miguel felt paralyzed, frozen, more shocked than scared.

Captain picked up the trays and walked back out the door

without looking at the children. They watched the Captain's white t-shirt as he made his way up the sloping field to the bakery. They looked at each other, stealing quick glances at Miguel, who by now was leaning against the kitchen wall, mostly out of sight of anyone but the other teacher. She approached him, unsure what to say in consolation, but he walked out toward his own room before the first awkward word could even be pronounced.

Twelve

MIGUEL'S MOTHER had her first baby at the same age as her mother, seventeen. She had hated proving her mother right—that she was going to get pregnant. How many times had she nagged her? In a way, though, she was spitefully satisfied to fulfill the low expectations that had been repeated by her mother so many times. It probably made her mother content, too, both for being right and for not being the only one who had made that mistake.

Having a baby confirmed her role in life—a single mother stuck at home—and allowed her to avoid having to try hard at an occupation to become something. At least this way, she didn't have to worry about failing in any job aspirations. She wasn't dumb by any measure, but never felt that there was true opportunity for her. Jobs in Mexico City were notoriously demanding and poorly paid. People who were rich had money because their families had money. There was no hope of changing classes when you lived hand to mouth.

And yet her children were a letdown, too: while one daughter was running around with the wrong boys, her yuppie-wannabe son, Miguel's brother, was telling off teachers at his school. Her so-called common-law husband was never at home, yet he failed to bring home any money either. Now Miguel was off in Puebla with illusions of teaching country kids. All the teachers she had ever known were lazy, poor, and worn out. How was this going to be any good? Since he had been gone, he had never even called her, his own mother. Her children were simply ungrateful, she concluded, for the effort that she had exerted throughout the years and the stress of motherhood that she had endured.

She recognized sometimes that she seemed bitter, that she was self-righteous, even hypocritical. Being a mother was too much pressure and she had no idea how to handle it. She reminded herself of her own mother sometimes. She had the same harsh lines around her mouth from trying to muffle her reprimands. Yet some things had to be said. If she didn't tell her children what was best, who would? It wasn't going to be their father.

She remembered the time that Miguel's history teacher in the fifth grade called her for a conference. "He never did his workbook," he told her, "Never, never, never, though I reminded him everyday." Then Miguel had the nerve to talk back to the teacher. What an embarrassment! He never learned to respect his elders, neither his teacher nor his mother.

Miguel had told a different version of the story. He knew how the teacher talked about students and humiliated them. When he told the teacher that a classmate stole his workbook, the teacher called him a sissy. He was told that there was no proof that it was his workbook and that he'd have to buy another. But his mother complained so much about money, how could he ask her to buy one when it wasn't even his fault? He was afraid she wouldn't listen and she wouldn't understand.

Her resources were limited. Poverty stretched far beyond money. She didn't know how to handle these situations any better than her mother did. It was as if Miguel were trying to draw water from a rock. She knew she had to pay for his books…but with what? Then the only tool she had in her toolbox was anger, so once the screaming began, there was no end to it. Besides, it was his fault, too. The teacher was right when he called Miguel a sissy. He never knew how to stand up for himself like a real man. His eyes would well up with tears and his spirit would cower. Her being tough on him was the only way he was going to learn to fight for himself.

Miguel now lay on his bed in his small room at the Internado with that sensation that he recognized from his growing up years. He recollected the screams of the Captain like he remembered the screams of his mother: "Faggot!" He remembered the way that they looked at him and judged him and made him feel so small and helpless. He was afraid that all those children who had loved him would never look at him the same way. Now they all knew his secret. He dreaded seeing them. He'd have to leave.

He was pathetic, he thought, a transparently gay boy running from his past, keeping secrets in the hills of Puebla. He knew that all his success had been too good to last.

The students sat quietly in the classroom the next morning, the news having traveled faster than Aztec hunters in the jungle. They faced forward and waited for Maestro Miguel to enter, uneasy with the break from the routine—he was always the first in the room. Now he was nowhere to be seen.

Jesse told the impatient ones to start on their math practice and he settled two Nahuatl Indian girls who were new to the school in a shared desk by the window. They followed his hand gestures, not speaking any Spanish, and they sat as inconspicuously as possible in their traditional Nahuatl clothing. They did not have uniforms yet. They'd whisper to each other occasionally some question or comment, completely ignorant of the situation into which they had arrived. Their chatter sounded like nothing more than a series of clicks and "ch" sounds to the rest of the students but it was at least a distraction from the tension otherwise obvious to all. Abi, anxious and bored, propped up his head on his hand while his fingers tinkered with the warts below his lip.

The Directora finally arrived thirty minutes after class began. Miguel still had not. The students immediately inquired about him. Only Juan's questions were squelched by disapproving looks from his classmates, for Juan had somehow become the scapegoat of the morning's tension. Nobody knew anything. Maestro Miguel was not in his room nor had he reported ill. Viviana was not to be found either, but that was to be expected. She was rarely at work, always on an "important errand" and wanting her student teacher to get "independent practice."

Without further delay, the Directora dismissed the children to their dormitories, where they were to study their workbooks independently. Gossip about the situation was not to take place, as speculation was no substitute for information.

Miguel was concentrating on the sand between his toes at the little beach that he privately christened the Ruben and Miguel Beach. He watched as the yellow leaves fell into the trickling water from branches high above. Dragonflies rested on dangling vines beside a mossy tree trunk on the river bank and little fish busily darted between rocks beneath the water striders whose outstretched arms kept them comfortably on the surface. Here nature existed so harmoniously, unlike the slamming doors of kitchens and wounding words of bitches. He'd probably regret walking away from it all. But what difference did it make now? The roof had already fallen in or, more accurately, blown off. Everything would be different. He needed out.

He had an out in Mexico City, too. It was a quiet grove in Chapultepec Park where the absence of garbage proclaimed the absence of people. When things would heat up too much at home, he'd make the long walk to his grove where the sturdy trees were like wise old friends who knew that their simple presence was more powerful than even the most thoughtful and well-intentioned advice. They somehow absorbed the scolding of his mother, the wrath of her resentment, and the pain he felt at her ever-present displeasure. He was grateful to the trees.

It wasn't his fault that she became a mother at an early age or that she quit school early and was left alone by his father and his subsequent so-called stepfathers. Many people had to work in jobs they hated and had to travel far to get there. Many people were far from family and far from love, it was part of the Mexican reality, the deprivation of the masses. What good did spreading her hopelessness to him and his siblings do? He hated her for that.

He also hated knowing that she had done the best she could. She had had so little to work with, and even less time. Nobody meant to fail. He knew so many people just like her, hoping to miraculously solve their problems despite increasing bills, constant inflation, and rapidly passing time. What kind of change could she have ever really expected?

He had chosen to study. He had chosen to come out here. He had chosen to take a risk. He had even chosen to walk out on the school and come out to the Ruben and Miguel Beach, but he hadn't chosen to be in this predicament. He hadn't chosen to be gay.

———————————

Was he losing? Would he develop the same bitterness his mother had in a world that would always reject him? Why was destiny so cruel? He thought of his students' eyes, his beautiful ocean of bobbing black heads that now made him sea sick. The ocean was becoming stormy. The clouds above were moving and swirling, darkening. A drop of rain hit his hand. Then another on his cheek. It seemed there'd be another storm.

Natural enough, he thought. The dragonflies and fish and water striders would weather it out. They'd be back and thrive. This very beach might be washed away, yet the river and trees would survive. Were they unafraid of the coming storms?

He took a deep breath. He would choose to face the thunder. He would choose to not be like his mother. He, too, would weather the storm and thrive.

———————————

Miguel was soaking by the time he got to the candy store. Ruben could see that water wasn't his only problem, though, by the solemn look in Miguel's eyes. He stopped what he was doing to walk Miguel up the stairs at the side of the shop to his apartment.

It was a simple place, one bedroom to the rear, a small kitchen in the middle, and a living space in the front, where he could look down at the street and at the passers-by who inevitably would be looking back up. It was furnished basically with a wooden bed frame and a hard mattress in the bedroom and a living room set built by a local, with plaid cloth covering foam on a rustic pinewood frame. The home's lighting consisted of a single light bulb in a socket in the middle of each room. The small refrigerator buzzed above the music from the clock-radio that Ruben had left on since the morning. He hadn't made the bed, either, not expecting any visitors. It was a humble place, yet it was his, a step in the right direction for a patient soul.

He plopped Miguel, who was uncommunicative and visibly tired, on the couch, but then realized that bed would probably be the best place for him. The thought of sex crossed Ruben's mind as he peeled the wet clothes from Miguel's brown and hairless body. His skin was smooth and enticing, the small black tufts of hair from his armpits erotic and tempting. It had been a long time.

It would be longer. Now was not the moment to take advantage of a troubled heart or to consecrate a relationship that might someday be. It seemed decent to offer only comfort. He went downstairs to close the shop. Then he returned to the bedroom, turned out the light, slipped off his clothes, and held Miguel throughout the night.

Thirteen

MIGUEL WOKE UP in the early morning light, his head still on Ruben's chest, the palm of his hand against the light mat of hair. He didn't recall ever awakening like that, and found it somehow relieving that they hadn't had sex, more genuine. It was not like returning to the womb, for he'd never connected a sense of relief with his mother. Rather, it was an unfamiliar tranquility in the presence of another.

He dreaded having to leave, but he knew he'd have to hurry to make it to school on time. He wasn't usually one to neglect his responsibilities and, thinking about it as he hurriedly dressed, he could hardly believe he hadn't reported for an entire day. Imagining the looks of the children produced far more anxiety than that of the Directora. She'd get over his one day absence. Would they get over his secret?

"Thank you, *Bebé*," was all he said on the way out. Ruben looked up at Miguel, waved his hand, then fell back to sleep. *Bebé*? Miguel asked himself. *Where did that come from?* It didn't matter now. He closed the door and slipped down the stairs.

He ran down the road toward the town square and startled the dozing taxi driver with his first fare of the day. As he entered the school, he ran into the Directora in the corridor outside her office.

She said nothing at first, as her dark eyes studied his face. He felt like such a child before her. He could only imagine the excuses her stern and weathered face had absorbed in all her years. He awaited her reprimand.

"Now," she finally said, looking up and down the hallway and continuing in a low voice, as if implying confidentiality in this vacant place. "You're not going to let the ramblings of a drunken old soldier deter you from your work, are you?" She raised her brown hand to his cheek. "Remember, these children need you, whoever you are."

She continued to study his eyes as if checking for understanding until he finally nodded back at her. His eyes started to well up until her brown hand moved down to clutch his throat. She raised her voice and cocked her head. "And if you ever skip out on me again, I'm going to hunt you down and kill you."

He only smiled and wiped his eyes, knowing that her beautiful and welcoming smile was to follow. She waved her head as if to say, "Now, get out of here," which he promptly did. He wanted to beat the children to the classroom.

He began the day as routinely as possible. He put the date on the chalkboard and straightened the desks. Students were making their way over from the cafeteria, now slightly bundled up in autumn's cool morning air. He opened the door, expressionless, subtly studying their eyes before determining his next move.

He didn't need to read too deeply. The children were outright joyous. They all smiled at him, save the two new Nahuatl girls, as they walked through the door calling "Maestro!" or "Doce!" and finding their seats. They were quick to pull out their pencils and workbooks, waiting not so much for an explanation as for his direction.

He chuckled at himself, at his fears. That was it?

The day went as smoothly as it could have ever gone. He reveled in his teaching...and his learning. He realized now that children were different from adults—they recognized love and didn't care about much else. So there was no confirming or denying the Captain's accusations. Somehow the kids sensed it would be better that way. There was enough reasonable doubt to keep the status quo.

The Captain was suspended for a week. The Internado would have to do without his lard-ridden bread for a short time. They missed it more than they ever imagined they would, but they didn't miss his grotesque visage or his constant vulgarity.

Fourteen

THEIR EYES LOOKED FRANTIC. The six or seven kids who ran into the classroom, scurrying about desperately, sent adrenaline through Miguel's body instantly. He arose quickly from his chair, confused. Everything had been fine before the break.

"What is it?" he asked them.

"Cups!" they said, without so much as looking at him. "We need cups!"

"What is it?" he repeated. "What's wrong?" His mind listed the possible emergencies.

"It's Don Coco!"

"Do you need water?" Miguel asked. "Is somebody hurt?"

They continued to look around the room, but they could not find what they were looking for. A cry was heard from outside. "The Directora has cups!" Then the room emptied of children as fast as they had arrived.

Miguel walked out in the courtyard, confused at the sight of running, desperation, and laughter. White shirts poured from classrooms all over the school. Then he saw the point at which the crowd converged. It was an ice cream cart with the words "Don Coco" lettered diagonally on the side. An old man scooped round balls of ice cream into the plastic cups that were handed out by the Directora to the children at his side. Miguel held his pounding heart in relief.

Don Coco only made the walk from Arbolito a few times a year. The homemade coconut ice cream was an exceptional delicacy, appreciated even in the crisp air of a December morning. The children would eat it whenever they could get it. After the Internado, Don Coco would go on to fill the plastic containers of the neighborhood folks until the cart ran out, collecting a bag full of coins along the way. His supply of cups had never kept up with his supply of ice cream, so his customers had become accustomed to bringing their own containers. Now he didn't even bother.

When they all had their fill, he'd wave goodbye till the next time around. Nobody could resist, not even the two Nahuatl girls, who sat on the ground beside half a dozen new friends holding their nearly empty cups and smiling in delight. For them, this had been a small contentment in a turbulent transition to their new environment.

A lot of the students thought they looked the same and acted just alike—identical twins! If anyone back home had heard that, they would have burst out in laughter.

Xochitl was the first born. It had been a hard birth; the spirits of health and motherhood had held the fate of the woman and her baby in their hands. The screams of her mother could be heard far from the oval hut as smoke from the incense burned by the birth maiden seeped out through the stick walls. It was an especially bloody birth that left her mother weak for months. And she was a constantly demanding baby, the kind whose desires are quenched not always for love but for appeasement. Her crying never seemed to stop.

Xochitl was like the flaming yellow petals of the flower she was named after. She became a rebellious and energetic girl, impatient and funny. She was slower to learn the art of her family, beadwork and yarn-work of bright designs and heavy symbolism, because of her short attention span, but her combinations of color and symbols, her pitting strength against wisdom, her contradictions and insight, earned the respect of her elders.

Misol-Ha came into the world as if she had been waiting a lifetime in the rain clouds to come down to earth. She slipped out like the water in the cascades after which she was named. She absorbed the lessons of her parents as if she already knew them. And she sat contentedly with her grandmother for long hours and listened to soft melodies that her grandmother's grandmother had hummed to her many decades before. She was tranquil and little and kept the same face from the day she was born. She looks young, they would say of her, but she has an old soul. Her needlework reflected the balance between day and night, earth and water, snake and eagle. She was one with the ways of her people but knew little of the outside world.

Their parents grew up in a village far west of Puebla and the Internado, deep in the mountains of Central Mexico. They were of the few who still spoke only the native tongue, educated by their parents in their homes. They sold their art at rock bottom prices, unable to negotiate with merchandise-movers from faraway tourist towns. Yet it seemed everyday that those towns were less and less far away. Change was looming. They did not want for their daughters to be defenseless in an encroaching new world.

The girls grew up so fast. It seemed that one day they were infants, sleeping sacks in the cloth wrapping at their mother's bosom. The next day they sat up in the same cloth, which was arranged differently and tied on their mother's back. Then the next day it was they bearing weight on their backs—firewood gathered daily from within a few miles distant from home, strapped in bundles, supported by a rope around their foreheads. If they had been boys they would have been of the most esteemed for their toughness and solidarity, but girls were not as publicly recognized.

Finally, things couldn't wait any longer. The girls could not learn Spanish from their parents, and they had to be ready for the world. Though others were in disagreement with such a forward-thinking attitude, their parents were of like mind. The new conquistadores would not vanquish their daughters like the Spaniards had done to the Aztecs so long ago. It was better to know the ways of the new world, even though they hoped their daughters would return to the village and continue their family traditions in harmony. In the meantime, monthly visits would have to suffice. Schools that were closer had reputations of discrimination and abuse. Their parents' decision would lead them far from the village, far from the mountain's womb.

Although they were more than a year apart in age, the Directora had thought it best to keep them together and place them in the classroom in which they'd have the best chance of success.

Miguel could tell them apart from the start. It was Xochitl who looked him in the eyes first. Xochitl said the first word, "ice cream," in Spanish. Then Misol-Ha would look in her eyes and copy the same word. Xochitl was more inquisitive, quicker to try a math problem, likelier to get it wrong, and faster to forget it. Misol-Ha, hunched quietly in her seat, toiled with a problem until she mastered it and continued until the page was complete.

They had a lot to teach, too. From the most simple items they crafted intricate works of art. Small balls of excess string were braided into bracelets with complex designs. Before long, many of the students in the class sported necklaces and rings, headbands and hair pins in the proud Nahuatl style. In exchange, it was this new band of brothers and sisters that taught them more Spanish words and playground games than any teacher might ever hope to teach. Miguel knew it would be best to set up situations to make the students interact, and let the magic of the camaraderie take its place.

And where is the camaraderie amongst the teaching staff? he found himself wondering. While the whole school was attempting to put the finishing touches on the Christmas festival, he smelled the not-so-subtle aroma of rivalry, envy, and, now, homophobia, as if some teachers needed only the accusation to use it as a weapon against him. They seemed to snicker behind his back, comment emphatically about students' masculinity and femininity, and generally avoid conversation with him whenever possible...or was he being paranoid? Thank goodness he had the help of Ruben as he prepared for the teacher pride festival...or, rather, the Christmas festival.

As the festival date approached, the school seemed one-dimensional—more and more time from class was dedicated to the event, as children rehearsed and painted and sewed and stitched and sang and danced, ever more focused on this culmination of effort and talent. The importance of class starting times and ending times diminished; break times and lunch times, even dinner, melded into this one great work.

Even Ruben began leaving a friend to tend the store to help out more at the school. He spent more and more time with this new pastime, and it became like an addiction, at first started for Miguel and then continued for the kids. He was another beacon amongst the black ocean as the children sought him for assistance and encouragement. Of course, he and Miguel also became closer, more accustomed to each other's presence. It wasn't something discussed explicitly. Rather, their connection began to grow quietly and deeply; they worked together as effortlessly as two birds tending a nest.

The students didn't ask a lot of questions about Ruben's presence. When Ruben came to class, the obvious reward was the caramels or chile-covered watermelon suckers. The hidden reward was the attention of another adult, for which the now forty-four young beings competed like trees competing for light beneath the canopy.

A Saturday afternoon horseback ride was a much needed break from the festival which was now just one week away. And then the two snuggled on the bed beneath Ruben's only wool blanket in the cold night air of the last days of fall. Their first time happened as naturally to them as everything else had.

They were laughing as they undressed, eager to find warmth under the covers. Then they hugged and rubbed each other for body heat. The laughter changed to smiles. The smiles turned to quiet stares into open eyes. Then the kiss, with eyes still open, a union of intentions, trust, and the rich flavor of one another. It was a stopping of time, a light speed ride to a distant planet, a bending of gravity. There were only two people in the world at that moment, though they had a mutual feeling of oneness. One was in the other, who was himself possessed, not invaded or penetrated but shared in common desire. There was no necessary climax, but a satisfaction somehow more primal and complete. Then finally sleepiness overcame them and they passed from this dream-like state to truly dreaming, never letting go their embrace until orange morning light hit the white walls and the new day was a new song.

Fifteen

IT SEEMED AS IF THE ENTIRE TOWN OF ARBOLITO had been evacuated to the Internado, along with hundreds of mountain families. A single line of people formed at the entrance gate, stretched past the crooked wooden electric post and the cemetery, and down the twisting highway as far as the eye could see. They brought their young ones and old ones, relatives and friends, to what had effectively become over the years a regional beginning of the Christmas holiday, the New Year season, and winter break.

The Internado was converted from a humble place of living and learning to an enormous fairground. The school's courtyard became the center ring where people would gather and watch the performances in the evening. The rocky soccer field became the commerce area where each class, as well as many private parties, sold a variety of food items and holiday knickknacks from rows of tables that lined the perimeter. Lines of people began forming at the dormitory bathrooms and masses of litter began accumulating all about the campus almost immediately.

Wedged somewhere between the crepe table, the cut fruit stand, the grilled corn vendor, the cake table, the ceviche tostada stand, and the fried banana sellers, Miguel and Ruben stood behind their own table with a host of children from Miguel's class. They beckoned at passersby to purchase coconut bars and pecan brittle from their table of colored candies and sweets. Ruben had offered to sponsor the class's fundraising drive.

"What will they use the money for?" he asked.

Miguel shrugged his shoulders. "Next year's Christmas festival," he replied.

Near their table was a craft table that sold handmade Christmas dolls like Santa Claus, Mrs. Claus, reindeer, and elves. The little boy behind the table was more of a draw than the cloth dolls. Not more than four years old, he stood on top of the table with his sandaled feet between the red Santas. At the top of his lungs, he screamed, "Bring Santa home! Bring Santa home!" Then, when people grabbed the merchandise for a look, he quickly demanded of them, "And your pay, lady?" It gave the people at the other tables a chuckle, this boy, this assertive little man, alone in the world of capitalism. How much longer till his parents came back?

The school had been specially cleaned for the occasion. Even the dirt floors of the art room and storage shed had been swept out. Crepe paper banners were strung from post to post and building to building, depicting Christmas scenes and celebrations in green and red and white.

As the day wore on, people left the soccer field and the mechanical bull, the boxing ring and the beer stands, and began moving toward the courtyard, from where cheery music was loudly played from meter-high speakers brought in from town. Miguel looked out across the crowd at these hundreds of faces that now seemed so familiar to him. Though there were many he had never met, he still felt like he was among family.

The Directora stood at a microphone to one side of the speakers. She introduced the mayor with her warm smile. It was only once or twice a year that the mayor would come out to greet the people of Comalticán, and he was used to a royal welcome. He proudly stepped up in his freshly shined alligator skin boots and his best scorpion belt buckle and began to address the crowd in the language of the politician, words that made the people instantly search for other topics on which to focus.

Miguel's gaze fanned the crowd. He saw Johana smiling from where she stood between her parents. Her father held her hand on one side. Abimael stood at her other side, dazed by the many sights and sounds. His shirt was stained at the top of his round belly where hot sauce had seeped from his bag of pork skins. He bore the happy smile he so often wore when he was around people who liked him. Out of pity, and because of Johana's pleas, her parents would take Abimael with them back to the coffee plant, acting as surrogate parents until his real parents returned.

The parents of Xochitl and Misol-Ha also stood at the edge of the courtyard in the same traditional dress—white clothes with flowery borders typical of the Nahuatls. They clung closely to their children and smiled politely at those around them, certain that their own discomfort with the unfamiliarity justified the reason they sent their girls there in the first place. Nevertheless, it was worth the fifteen-hour bus ride to see them and to be there.

Doña Conchita stood beside Maestra Viviana, who offered the old lady incessant editorial commentary in her better ear. As Doña Conchita leaned to one side of her walker, Viviana leaned toward her. The old mind of Doña Conchita worked overtime, compensating for her less functional legs, while her eyes shifted from target to target amongst the crowd. Miguel had the privilege of more than a couple of their glances. They'd have more than enough fuel to keep a winter fire aglow, he decided.

In the far end of the courtyard stood the Captain, on relatively good behavior, next to Juan's father in the same linen clothes with the same machete strapped around his shoulder. The two men shared no communication save an infrequent touching of liter-sized beer bottles and manly grunts, at best. Juan, for his part, was making his rounds of the school with Jesse and Orfil. They'd play teen pranks on the girls for lack of actual words that might woo them. Pranks didn't work much better, however.

"Sweet nuts," Miguel heard, as he turned to the outstretched hand of the father of a student. Miguel thought twice about the comment, and with a chuckle concluded that he referred to the candied peanuts which he was munching. Tomas was his name and Brenda was his daughter. She was a quiet girl, uncommonly studious and adept at pencil portraits. A computer technician who traveled a broad region of the state to service accounts, Tomas looked unusually young for his age and unusually fair-skinned for a Mexican.

Miguel had already shaken his hand at the vending table

when he bought the nuts but actually found the exaggerated attention of parents to be quite commonplace, their way of making up for their months of absence from the school. It was the father's blue eyes, as well as the mannerisms of an obviously university-educated man, that were not commonplace in these parts. He almost seemed overly nice.

Ruben did not notice the interaction.

The mayor's speech ended and the performances began. The crowd, now tired from standing, sat on the bare concrete and hunkered together in the cooling night. Their breath was white when they exhaled. Their eyes were transfixed on the performing children.

First, a dozen boys stood in a line from shortest to tallest and strummed traditional favorites on well-used guitars. Then two of those boys showed off choreographed roping techniques, jumping in and out of spinning lassos.

One of them, David, was from Miguel's class. He so often seemed incapable of learning even the most basic of ideas. As the boy concentrated, coordinating mind and body, his tongue popping out from his mouth from time to time as he moved, Miguel reflected. *Kids, it seems, learn much more than we might ever expect.* He felt a pang of guilt for having lost hope in little David, who was exhibiting a joy for life that Miguel had scarcely seen. *We teachers*, he thought, *have no right to stop believing in them. We have to just keep looking for ways to reach them.* He applauded loudly as the pair of boys skipped off the courtyard.

Following them were girls in long dresses and pineapples in their hands that they held up at their shoulders. It was the famous Oaxocan dance celebrating the harvest. Several other songs and dances kept the crowd animated until the Dance of the Old Folks came up. Johana and Abi had snuck off to change while Miguel's stomach churned nervously for them.

Their performance was exceptional. Their masks were a hit—pink faces with black moles and heavy lines and scraggly white hair. They looked and moved alike, stepping to the music, bumping feeble hips, smacking canes like swords, bending over in feigned decrepitude. They hit each of the steps that they had so ardently practiced for the last few months.

Miguel watched them proudly and smiled, sure that they too were smiling behind those pink masks, and sweating. Miguel knew that Johana danced for her parents on the far side of the courtyard while Abi danced for Miguel...and for Abi. His class was responding to his challenge to contribute to the festival and not allow a second embarrassment like that of September Fifteenth.

The final performance ended with a traditional seven-pointed piñata, seven cones with dangling streamers that protruded from a colorful, spherical core. The children from the school and others from the audience gathered around as it was batted down, the seven deadly sins no match for the stick of faith from the blindly faithful. When the treasure was spilled, the fruits and nuts and candies spread about the floor and the children leapt at the bounty of the pious.

Then the mayor, now visibly tipsy, gave a closing speech. He entertained his constituents with a humble fireworks show as his aides passed out meter-long sparklers to the children in the crowd. It was nearing one in the morning, but few people had actually left. Several buses and taxis waited at the gate of the school, the drivers leaning against the hoods, chatting amongst themselves while enjoying the night air, the chance to make an extra peso, and, of course, beer.

Ruben was at the table, packing up the unsold goods with a couple of the kids. Miguel was near the front gate, bidding farewell to those of his students who were leaving for the break with their parents. As Brenda walked out of the gate with her father, Tomas unmistakably winked at Miguel and their eyes followed each other for an odd moment.

It was long enough to get Miguel's pulse up momentarily. It was unbelievable, this man acting this way as he held his daughter's hand. And, yes, it was a bit arousing.

Nothing doing. Miguel refocused on the task at hand. He needed to pack up his things; Ruben and he had agreed that Miguel would stay with Ruben for the break.

As the exodus of people diminished, Miguel made his way toward his bedroom. He walked down the corridor, passed the

Directora's office, then turned at the corner. His bedroom was one of six. A decades-old rose garden, unkempt, was at one side of the walkway and the teachers' doors on the other. A shared bathroom was at the far end.

As Miguel approached his door, he noticed it was slightly ajar. Miguel had a habit of closing doors securely. *Might someone have entered?* he wondered. Possibilities flashed through his mind—Ruben, other teachers, the students, the Directora, Tomas—but none of these possibilities made any sense. No one would enter without permission. And for what? He had nothing to steal. He reached in and turned on the light from the walkway. He peered in and saw no one. The room was empty, the area was quiet.

As he stepped in, he saw something on his bed. It was red. He then recognized the Santa doll from the little kid at the vending table. Someone left him a present. Strange, he thought. Why not give it to him personally? Why intrude in his room? He didn't mind, he had nothing to hide there.

As he picked it up, he saw that it was not one Santa Claus doll but two. They were lying beside each other, head to toe. Then, when he picked them up, he noticed that they were not separate but tied tightly together with a sort of shoestring.

What? This was no present. His feelings suddenly changed to a suspicious insecurity. It wasn't over.

As he turned the dolls, he felt a prick on his finger. His mouth went agape as he saw it—a single wooden stake through the torsos of both dolls.

Sixteen

CANDLES CREATED A SOFT LIGHT in every part of the house. There were dozens of them, maybe even a hundred. Some were tall and skinny, others were simple votives, while others were grandiose, but they were all white or off-white and all lit.

It wasn't for the heat that she lit them, for they truly didn't help to warm up the cold place. It was His spirit she felt, as if God Himself were here in the well-groomed living room and in the daily-scrubbed bathroom and in the bedroom with the perfectly made bed. He was so present to her.

And that was good, for she was otherwise alone, save the rare visits of her church friends for prayer circles and tea. They would sit some Tuesdays, demonstrating their utter piety, their deep faith, and their handmade clothing. They'd then leave, having been quite unfocused on each other and, had they thought about it, they might have realized that it was as if they'd never met at all. They were like perfect chocolate truffles with a flavorless filling, never to be eaten but one day to be placed in a most beautiful box.

They were in Molino, named for the centuries-old mill on the river, where Ruben's mother Dahlia lived. Miguel had never imagined himself in such a dreary place. He thought of that first noisy bus ride through the hills to Comalticán, that random bouncing hither and thither, the great foreboding of the unknown. It seemed so long ago, and he was such a different man now, as if years of development had occurred in just four months. When he stepped onto that bus, he had known that there would be no turning back.

Here he was in the unknown again. It was not as unfamiliar, though. This day, Christ looked down upon him—literally. Di-

82

rectly in front of the couch on which he sat hung a large painting of Jesus on His dying day. Blood from where the crown of
thorns pierced His scalp ran down His miserable face. His
droopy eyes looked, not up into the sky at His Father, but directly down at Miguel. On either side of the picture were oil
smudges on the peach-colored walls, leftovers of the house
blessing process. There was an oil smudge on nearly every wall
in the house. Miguel sat with straight posture and his hands on
his knees, attempting to disguise his sins that he sensed were
entirely transparent in this judgment chamber.

Ruben sat equally erect on a matching chair to the far side
of the couch. He was conscious of both Miguel's discomfort
and his mother's demands for dutiful respect. He had assisted in
everything—the pouring of the tea, the wiping of the table, the
careful placement of the coasters. She was visibly more uncomfortable than either of them as she struggled for conversation as
much as she struggled for some way to accept their presence
here before the Lord. *Love the sinner, hate the sin*, she repeated
in her brain silently as she clamped her hands together for
strength. *Love the sinner, hate the sin.*

Is this a test for me? she wondered. God had given her a
beautiful boy nearly thirty years ago. The sparkle in her eyes,
the pride of her life. Was this the punishment for pride? Was it
a taste of hell? Was she not good enough? After all those times
she had prayed, was she still not forgiven? Was this the Devil at
the door, a wolf in sheep's clothing? Or was he a good soul,
lost upon his way, a sheep in wolf's clothing? She could not
judge. She *should* not judge. She must not be afraid. She
straightened the ruffled black shawl upon her shoulders and
looked up at the painting of Jesus as she sat.

"So, Miguel," she asked, attempting sincere curiosity,
"What type of church does your mother go to?"

Ruben glanced at Miguel, apologetically. Miguel smiled
politely. It was going to be a long week.

It shouldn't be any worse than Christmas at home. What
Miguel had once thought of Christmas, the holiday of joy and
excitement, had changed over the years. Though his family
generally attempted to be more pleasant during the holidays, the

concomitant pressures of Christmas gifts, decorations, expensive groceries, traffic congestion, nasal congestion, and cold weather were always a challenge. There were not always solutions to these pressures, and so he was reminded that life, holidays or no holidays, was not all it was cut out to be. Maybe his family could have used some faith in some greater being on whom to hang their hopes. Maybe believing that this was His strategic design would alleviate their overriding negative thoughts. But that faith would never be part of the picture. It was far too late.

She had prepared them separate beds. Ruben would be in his old bedroom next to hers and Miguel on a cot in her sewing room. She was concerned for their comfort, both of them. And she could not deny the pleasure she felt at having her beautiful boy home. *Even Miguel is a nice-looking young man*, she thought. *If only...* He was respectable enough being a teacher and seemed rather proper. His mother must have felt so proud of him, she imagined. She wondered, too, if she knew. Had she felt the same disappointment? Was she being punished, too, for some drift from the Lord's path? She forced a smile as she showed Miguel his room. It would only be for a week. She could endure.

She turned to pull the blankets straight one more time and then winced in secret pain. It was not emotional distress that she was responding to this time but a pain that had reoccurred for more than a couple of months. It came from deep within her thigh. It was part of being older, she knew, and a reminder from God to be thankful for health and her ability to do everything that she could do.

If Ruben were rich, he'd have rented a motel room. When he had left this house, he'd known that, as much as he loved his mother and she loved him, living apart would be for the best. Ever since his father had left, he had had to accept her extremely religious life style. He looked at his single bed and imagined the night alone with Miguel down the hall. Was this the only way that she would accept his lifestyle? Never had he considered this situation before, never had he been in it. It had been obvious in the past that he would sleep alone; he always came alone. But now he had a partner, from whom his mother separated him by what seemed like leagues.

He looked down and felt the coldness of the concrete floor. It would be unfair to expect his mother to change abruptly. But it was equally unfair to Miguel and himself to quarantine the only love they knew. It was ironic, he thought, that the fact that he paid most of her bills was what made him unable to afford a motel. He sighed. It would only be for a week.

The sharp crack of the cue ball in a single moment split the neat triangle of fifteen colored balls into a random scattering of colored asteroids. They bounced and banged around the table till they came to rest on the green baize. Ruben looked up from where he was leaning at the head of the table. He smiled at Miguel, feeling relaxed in this respite from the pressure of home.

Miguel studied the balls on the table. They were dull and nicked. The green felt on the table was ripped near one corner of the table and folded over to form a sort of hurdle for the balls. He studied the placement of the balls and calculated with mental algorithms. Solids or stripes? He aimed at an imaginary bull's eye. The white ball moved slowly toward the red one and knocked it toward the side pocket. It rolled within millimeters, teasing the newbie, but did not fall in.

Ruben sank it easily and sent the white ball spinning off, and then he blew at the tip of the stick as if it were smoke from a gun. He smiled wryly at Miguel and then cocked his two-meter pistol for the next shot. Bang! The balls exploded about the green table like startled pigeons in the Zócalo. He stood up again, conceding that it was Miguel's turn.

"Solids or stripes?" Miguel clarified.

Ruben's head tilted sideways at the question. "You're the big ones."

"The big ones?" Miguel replied, "They're all the same size." He grabbed a brown beer bottle from the counter where he set it, leaving a ring of condensation on the formica. He took a long swig and looked up at the swirling cigarette smoke in the fluorescent light. It felt good to sin again. It felt good to be alone with Ruben again.

"What are you stalling for?" Ruben prodded.

Miguel looked down again at the fourteen balls that waited on the table. His hands grabbed the pool stick like a spear. The beer had gotten to him faster than he had imagined. "Well, am I solids or stripes?"

"I told you…you're the big ones!"

"I'm telling *you*, they're all the same size!" he retorted, quietly suspecting there was some secret he hadn't uncovered. He took a second look at the balls. They *were* all the same size.

"Not size…" Ruben said, "number."

"Ooooh," Miguel said. "So I'm the striped ones and you're the solids?"

Ruben shook his head in disbelief. "Miguel," he explained, "they're all solid."

It was nice to worry about the little things. Miguel exhaled smoothly and looked for the easiest big ball to sink. Funny how people could look at the same thing in such different ways.

Seven blocks away, beneath the painting of Christ, knelt Ruben's mother. Among the candles and perfectly placed tablecloths, artificial flowers and lace curtains, she was both tearful and afraid. She had faith that He would lead her through. Didn't she? The pain was pulsing in her leg as she looked up to Him. Why did He seem so distant at times? His face was so expressionless tonight, as if He didn't even see her. Was He telling her to have faith in others too? Something inside her, maybe it was Him, was telling her to let go.

Chiles en Nogada were her specialty, and she had laboriously and meticulously prepared them while Miguel and Ruben were in town. They were served with fresh cut flowers on the table. Ruben was surprised by the chilled white wine, a rarity for his mother, who only sipped a glass on special occasions. Miguel had heard of this dish and had seen it in photos, but had never tasted the green chiles stuffed with a sweet mixture of ground meat, raisins, other fruits, and spices. It was topped with a walnut-based white cream sauce and red pomegranate seeds. The aroma was most unique but it was the colors—green, white, and red—that made the delicacy symbolic of Mexico and, incidentally, perfect for the Christmas season.

It wasn't just the food that was special but the demeanor of Ruben's mother. She seemed so much more relaxed at the table, with a natural laugh and a genuine interest when she asked, "So, how did it go?" She looked at Ruben and Miguel for equal durations as she inquired about their work and lives and even their time together. She commented on Micha, the horse, and the beauty of horse rides through the forest and down by the river. Though she seldom made the two-hour trip to Arbolito these days, she was quite familiar with it through her sixty years of living in the region. In fact, though few might suspect it now, she had had her day of popularity and influence, but that was many years ago.

"I hadn't planned on it, since every day is God's day, not just Christmas," she said. "But since you two have come down, let's decorate."

It was a splendid idea, they all agreed. And both Ruben and Miguel were eager to take advantage of her change in attitude and to pass the week more pleasantly. This truly was a godsend.

For Dahlia, Ruben's mother, it also came as a relief. Somehow she had tucked away her righteous instinct, her self-doubt, and let the love she felt for her son and the world in general flow from her heart. It was so easy to get stuck in constant thought of how to live correctly. It was a hard coating that those thoughts created. Yet she knew inside her that Christianity was, in the end, about love. Everyone must make their own decisions and she would choose to not lose her son. She would love the sinner. And she would remember that we were all sinners and yet, somehow, all created in God's image.

For Ruben and Miguel, it felt good that she was approachable, whatever her reason. Miguel had noticed a tightness in his body since they arrived. He hadn't slept well on that cot, but not because of the cot itself. That night would be different. He lay by himself and thought of his mother. As all of us, he thought, she was a person who had faced hardships in her life. She must have struggled, too, in her own way. She must think about that, and think about him. Didn't she?

The door creaked open in the darkness. Miguel saw

Ruben's silhouette in the moonlight. In a moment, he was savoring the taste of Ruben's tongue and the feel of his hand on his chest and stomach. He had missed the heat of his body next to him, the curve of his back and the hard ridges of muscles along his spine. He touched his face and recognized the supple form of his lips, the stubble on his chin, and his soft eyebrows. Ruben's hands moved up and down the length of Miguel's body. They were hard hands but tender, too. They were strength to which he surrendered.

It was a short moment they shared but, under the circumstances, more powerful than entire days of passion they had shared together back in Arbolito. Ruben pulled away after a final kiss and left sleepy Miguel and his intoxicating aroma. He crept back down the hallway to his bedroom and closed his door with a quiet click.

Dahlia heard his footsteps as she lay awake in her own bed. The pain in her leg had subsided that day but had not disappeared. Sometimes it got worse in the nighttime. She heard the click of his door. She asked God to guide them all in whatever might be His path for them. She knew, after all, that she would not always be on Earth and she prayed that Ruben might be happy and live with love in whatever way He thought best.

From surrounding hills, they collected long, thin branches, fresh enough to bend and weave into wreaths. Dried cones and various sorts of seeds or berries, in addition to some store-bought figurines, would serve as adornments.

The handcrafts reminded Miguel of his students whom, up until now, he had removed from his thoughts. As much as he cared for them and enjoyed his work with them, he also realized that they demanded a great deal of energy. He missed them when he thought of them, the cheerful warty face of Abimael, the macho posturing of Jesse and Orfil, the intellect of Johana, the creative spirits of Xochitl and Misol-Ha, and the competing yet beautiful personalities of the rest of them. He missed their joy and only hoped that they missed him, too.

As he sat beside Ruben and his mother, who were chatting away with each other, his thoughts began to drift. A small wooden reindeer reminded him of his grandmother and the tranquil times that he would sit with her and make decorations for the holidays from cloth strips and knickknacks. She would tell him of her childhood on the north side of Mexico City, twelve blocks from the city dump. Nowadays, people who didn't get to the dump during business hours or who didn't want to pay the dump fee left piles of garbage on sidewalks and empty lots all over the neighborhood. More than a few fistfights broke out over such junk. There were not enough police to do anything about any of it.

It had been more peaceful in her day. Boys and girls would run and play in the street, with never a thought of cholos or stray dogs or junk. Her mother would have her cut newspaper rectangles for toilet paper that would later frustrate those who were concentrating on reading the cut-up pieces while in the bathroom—they could never find the ending of an article. Tortillas and beans were the staples, occasionally accompanied by some meat product in hot chile sauce, but oftentimes not. Men worked the days they could, but drank beer every day; not everything had changed. And the family went regularly to mass on Wednesdays and Sundays, sure to take confession before any important event. She got new shoes once a year or so and passed the evenings stitching clothes, mending socks, and scrubbing floors. Somehow seven children and two parents fit into three small beds in two small bedrooms. They were used to physical closeness.

Emotional closeness was another matter. As much time as her family spent together, she often felt anonymous and unknown. She left home to marry, and she began a new family with the ways she had learned from her parents. For that reason, she was as distant emotionally from her children as her parents had been from her. Sometimes, she just didn't know what to say. When situations arose that her parents had never shown her how to handle, she just closed her mouth and waited for them to pass.

With Miguel, it was different. He forced himself into his grandmother's heart as he forced himself onto her lap. He never had been much of a Mama's boy—she knew that his mother was bitter and that she was herself to blame, at least in part. She had been negative to her daughters; she had been so young, with so many responsibilities. Her children's father was in and out of the picture until, like so many of their acquaintances, she got tired of waiting and threw him out. But she learned to live happily single again and then forgive herself, in time, for all that might have been but never was. She became more affectionate and caring, knowing that it was what was inside her that would matter in her life, not what was outside.

No wonder Miguel became a Grandma's boy.

As the trash from the garbage dump spread and the neighborhood grew more violent, Miguel could no longer visit her with the same frequency. Time and space might have separated them, but they felt a mutual closeness. She hoped to one day leave the city; her asthma was ever-worsening, as were her ability to get around and her financial situation. She would just end up another poverty statistic.

It was difficult for Miguel to not regret the separation between them, or to keep from feeling guilty for not being able to make things better for her. But he had so little control over her situation. What could he do? It took all his power to do well at what he was doing in the present. It was up to him to build a life in a world of challenges, he knew. People from his world were neither able nor willing to hand anything to him. He shook the thoughts away and focused back on Ruben and Dahlia.

By the end of a long day, the house had been converted from a humble and respectable home to a Christmas shrine. On every wall and empty table space, a Christmas decoration made of branches, pine cones, and needles conjured holiday happiness and harmony in the little abode. Though Dahlia detested Santa Claus, reindeer and snowmen as pagan idols, Christmas trees and wreaths made up for their absence. For that matter, Miguel and Ruben preferred not to see Santa, for they didn't want to remember the token left back on Miguel's bed at the Internado. This was not the moment to worry about that, but to celebrate a moment of joy and the building of the bond between the three of them. Dahlia hadn't been so cheerful since they had arrived. Her face was absolutely aglow.

Bing Crosby sang "Do You Hear What I Hear?" in the background from a decades-old cassette tape, in the absence of any Mexican Christmas carols. A turkey browned in the oven and dark green, spinach-like romeritos steamed in a pot beside the spaghetti in a cheesy cream sauce. Dahlia flattened tortillas in a metal press from fresh corn meal that had been prepared at the tortilla store on the corner that morning. Beans simmered in boiling water on the busy stove. Who didn't love the traditional Christmas menu? She felt blessed this year for the company and the holiday cheer, able for the moment to let morale beat out morality, as she hummed along with the foreign words from the speakers; she had no idea what they meant but was reasonably sure that they were about Jesus, which was good enough for her.

After dinner and a single glass of cold red wine, Dahlia rose from her seat below the Jesus portrait. She looked up to Him as her leg throbbed. She knew that He would watch over her as He had done during this entire visit of Ruben and Miguel, as He had done during the economic crisis and the devaluation of the peso back in 1994, and even as He had done when her husband left her for the secretary at his job in 1998. Her husband used to scream at her about how she "couldn't see the forest for the trees!" She never knew what he was talking about but just trusted in God that he would repair the marriage. It was not re-paired. She was no stranger to suffering and sacrifice, and didn't think she could make it without Him.

She went to her room to retrieve the presents that she had found for the boys. Christmas gifts were not a necessary part of their family tradition, but the pain in her leg had reminded her about her own mortality and about the short time that people have in this life. She wanted to show them that, although she didn't entirely approve of them, she respected them and His decisions. She felt inclined to give them something.

"Ruben," she said. "I want to give you a present." She set a small gold box in his hand.

He was silent, not finding the words to express his gratitude and humility in the moment. He could only smile as he felt a lump in his throat that wasn't there before.

He opened the box and was instantly delighted at the shininess of the silver bracelet. It had a small band with an engraving that he turned to read: "RUBEN TQM, MAMA." *Te quiero mucho*, I love you very much. He felt the swelling of tears as he read it and held it. He imagined, too, the number of weekly payments, *abonos*, that this was going to cost her with the local silver peddler.

"Well, put it on," she told him, at which point he snapped out of his sentimental trance and obeyed her orders. It fit perfectly on his wrist, though it pulled a bit at the hairs on his arm. He didn't mention that, of course, and thanked his mother profusely.

"Miguel," she said as she turned to him, "I didn't know what you might like, but I hope this present comes in useful. It is to help protect you in harsh times."

"Yes, señora. Thank you." He smiled politely, wondering what she might have chosen for him. It was a rare occurrence to receive a Christmas gift, let alone from his boyfriend's mother.

From behind her chair she lifted her arm in a motion, as if she were drawing a sword. But it was no sword, he could see; it was a long, black umbrella. He smiled again politely as she handed it to him.

"I hope you can use this, Miguel," she said. "And here," she pointed, "Read the engraving."

This, too, had a metal band, though this one was gold-colored and glued to the wooden handle of the full-sized umbrella. He read the words out loud: "For Maestro Miguel and his journey." There was a small cross after the final word.

"It is wonderful," he said to her. "Thank you very much for this present and this wonderful Christmas."

"You are welcome," she answered. "I wasn't sure if you already had one, but I know you're not from around here," she explained. "You do know, Miguel?" she looked at him seriously and then, when he looked back at her, she continued. "The rains are coming."

Seventeen

IT WAS TIME to get back to Arbolito. The candy store was swamped with business, and inventory was low. It was never easy to leave a business in the hands of employees. Miguel had to start preparing for school again and Micha hadn't been tended to for a long time. Though she was getting fed, she was sure to have missed Ruben's brushings and their long talks. It had been hard for Ruben to pull away from Arbolito at this time of year. Now, it was hard to pull away from his mother.

"Why don't you stay a few days longer, Ruben?" she said to him when Miguel was waiting at the door with the suitcases, out of hearing range. "We can be together for New Year's."

He just shook his head. He didn't like to say no to her but he had responsibilities to attend to. He held her hands in his. "Mother, we had a great time seeing you. But it's time for me to go back. I'm sorry." Her eyes welled up a bit. She seemed pretty sentimental, he thought. "We'll try to come back at Easter break when Miguel is off again."

"Very well," she said. She looked down toward the floor. "I do have something to tell you, Ruben."

He didn't like her tone. "Yes, mother. What is it?"

"I don't mean to startle you. I don't want you to worry about me."

"What is it, mother?"

"I am sure the Lord will see me through."

"What is it?" He felt his blood pressure rise.

"Well, I've been having pain in my leg. I'm sure it's nothing. But it has been some time now."

"Why are you telling me this now, Mama?" he exclaimed. "We could have gone to the doctor. But now I've got to get

93

back to the store right away."

"I know, Ruben. I can take care of it. I don't want you to worry about it, I just wanted to let you know."

He sighed. He wanted to reprimand her. She should have told him. He knew, though, that her way of doing things was different from his. "Okay," he told her. "Go to the doctor. Let me know if you need money." She nodded at him as she looked in his eyes. "And tell me right away when you find out what is causing your pain."

"Yes, son. I will." She nudged him to the door. "I will take care of it and I'll call you right away. Now, you two go and do what you have to do. There is no need to fear, for we are in His hands."

He gave her a final hug. "I'll be waiting for the news."

A chill set in every morning that made it hard for Miguel to get out of bed and feel the cold tile floor on his feet. Even getting up to go to the bathroom was distasteful to Miguel while he was lying next to Ruben's warm body. But, as was the case with everyone, routine naturally evolved between them. What at first was new and exciting, unfamiliar and scary, became commonplace. Nevertheless, Miguel knew he had arrived at some kind of golden time in his life, feeling a brightness he could not readily remember having experienced. Despite the gray sky, the threatening clouds, his world felt like...well, a candy store. Soon his work routine would return and he'd go back to school, back to the children's faces, the lessons, the Directora and the Captain, the rest of the staff, and the bedroom with the single bed, the place where he had found the impaled dolls.

A rooster crowed. The day called. "Come on, *Bebé*," he said, stirring Ruben, who lay beside him beneath the wool blankets. He couldn't resist his square shoulder blades and planted a kiss between them. He breathed in deep to fill his lungs with Ruben's aroma and sniffed at his underarms, an act he found most enticing—he loved the smell that he recognized, he loved to feel that it was his. Though some part of him was cautious, aware of the dangers of falling in love, a bigger part of him had already yielded. His hand wandered down Ruben's back to his butt; he shook him again to and fro. "Come on, *Bebé*, it's time to get up."

Ruben let out a groan. Then, as was habitual for him, he flung his legs up and kicked his feet down to stand up in a single motion. He was instantly awake and ready for the day. "Let's do it, *Bebé*."

Women, the matriarchs of the town, were the majority of Ruben's customers. The store was just another stop on their list of things to do, one more errand in their New Year's preparations. They were bundled up against the cold but were cheery nonetheless, always ready to greet acquaintances and share the neighborhood news.

It was past midday when Doña Conchita wandered in, lugging her walker, which seemed to be as great a nuisance as the fact that she could hardly walk. She came when Ruben was out; he had slipped out during the slow supper hours to see Micha. His horse needed as much attention as people do. Doña Conchita was sniffling and looked more worn out than most days.

"Maestro Miguel," she said in a subdued but inquisitive tone.

"Doña," he responded.

"I see you two are back in town," she said as she looked him up and down.

"Yes, Doña."

"I trust you had a pleasant time on your visit with Ruben's mother," she said, as her eyes wandered the shelves.

"Yes, Doña. I had a pleasant time," he responded, wondering how she knew about his trip to see his mother.

"Very generous of Ruben's mother to host his *friend* for a whole week, no?" she asked wryly.

"She is a generous person, Doña Conchita. Can I help you with something?"

"Well, since they put Teresita in jail, I can't find the caramels that she sells me for the museum."

"Jail? They put Teresa in jail?" he asked.

"Maestro, even you know that people can't sell whatever they want in the street without a permit."

"Ah." He nodded. "The caramels are over there," he pointed to a shelf behind her. "Would you like me to get some for you?"

"No, I can do it." She turned around and began to pull at the candies.

Just then Ruben walked in through the back door. "*Bebé?*" he shouted from the back of the store.

Doña Conchita's head perked up.

"Did you remember to pull down the Christmas cups?" he continued as he walked in from the back. He then saw the old lady by the shelves and looked over at Miguel. He clenched his teeth at his mistake. "Did you remember to pull down the Christmas cups, Miguel?" he repeated.

Miguel confirmed with a nod of his head. "Have you finished with Micha already?"

Ruben returned the same nod.

Doña Conchita made her way to the counter between the narrow aisles. Frustrated by her walker and her cold, she didn't even attempt a smile. "Hello, Ruben. Aren't you two getting along just…beautifully? You seem like a pair of happy hummingbirds."

"Hummingbirds don't travel in pairs, Doña," said Ruben.

"I didn't come for nature lessons, just caramels." She put coins on the counter, laboriously tied the plastic bag to her walker, and then made her way out to the street.

"Thank you, Doña," said Miguel, moments before she disappeared down the street. "I hope you feel better."

Her crooked hand went up in dismissal and the noise of the plastic wheels faded. Then, as if on cue, Teresita walked by clad in a thick fur-like coat with a leopard pattern and a short denim skirt on top of black pants. Pink legwarmers encased her lower legs and a green knit cap was pulled down over her head to cover her ears. Her arms held a big basket above her round stomach. She walked by quickly but took the time to wave in at them as they watched her. She smiled as she shouted in a raspy voice, "Chocolates! Walnuts! Caramels!"

As in almost any place, the approaching New Year brought to Arbolito the stresses of preparation, the endless lists of things to do, the waxing anticipation of a new beginning, reflection on things past both exhilarating and disappointing, the hopes for triumphs on the horizon, and farewells to difficulties now past. The town was a-bustle, rogue firecrackers popping, the work of children who couldn't contain their enthusiasm, more cars than usual plying the short town blocks, people everywhere with full bags weighing down straining arms.

Miguel and Ruben had little time to concern themselves with anything besides business. For the three days prior to New Year's Eve, they did nothing but get up, work the store, grab a quick meal whenever they could, and crawl into bed near midnight.

Yet the sense of prosperity was more motivating than the work was tiring. Nothing kept a businessman's smile wider than the feel of crisp currency on his fingertips. The sheer quantity of product moved was astounding, and even the ugliest of piñatas, a dusty yellow Pokémon, got pulled from where it had hung at the back part of the store since summer.

It wasn't until eleven o'clock on New Year's Eve that the pair finally closed the store, despite the pleading of last-minute shoppers still hoping to bring home the family favorites, wondering how the time could have passed so quickly again this year. The two were worn out and a bit grubby from the week's work. Miguel had the impulse to just throw himself on the bed and stay there till Cinco de Mayo. If it hadn't been for Ruben pulling him to the shower, he would never have made it to the festivities in the town square.

The public park at the town center was at least as crowded as it had been at the last Independence Day celebration, when the president of this region had shouted "Viva Mexico!" from the small balcony of the municipal building. Townspeople, old and young, came from every alley forming a great gathering, waving and hugging, screaming and drinking. Food stands were at full tilt, selling steamed tacos, fried bananas, and crepes. The town's mariachi band took center stage in the octagonal kiosk that was characteristic of all town squares. The scene was probably the same as in thousands of towns all across the country.

Miguel saw many familiar faces, cheerful ones who screamed, "Maestro! Maestro!" and he remembered that his tiredness was only from his second job. He still had a mission to complete. *How*, he wondered, *will my life change? Will I be able to return to the routine of teaching after having grown accustomed to life with Ruben?* He thought of the great plaza in Mexico City, the Zócalo, between the historical government palace and the centuries-old cathedral where hundreds of thousands of people might be gathering right now. His mother, of course, was not part of the picture, since she deplored throngs of citizens. But he tried to imagine his old friends there. He realized now that many of their faces had begun to fade from his memory, like the photos in dusty albums of times gone by. He had taken so many steps from his original path that he hardly remembered his starting point.

Ruben's eyes flashed in the colored lights of the fireworks. His arms were strongly around him in a hug as he screamed, "Happy New Year!" Miguel looked down at his watch—11:57 p.m. Well, nothing was perfect. He hugged back and looked up to the sky beyond the exploding fireworks and their smoky clouds to the twinkling stars that sat still above the commotion, unmoved by the planet's completion of another revolution. Ruben let go to hug those around him; any two arms would do to spread goodwill and wish luck to others.

Not long after, they both staggered back exhausted to the store. They could not hold out till dawn like many of the townsfolk would. The uneven road felt hard and cruel on Miguel's pounding feet and the brisk breeze stung his uncovered ears. The noise behind him, all around him, was penetrating and the only solace was Ruben's shoulder beside him and the thought of a warm bed and a closed store tomorrow.

As they approached the store, Miguel looked toward the stairs in the back, but Ruben stopped in the middle of the street.

"*Raros*," said Ruben, "Queers."

Yes, queer indeed, smiled Miguel. Why was Ruben stopping now?

Glancing at the metal curtain of the closed-up shop, he answered his own question. "Queers" it said, in thin letters of sloppy black spray paint. Some fucking kids, he imagined, and their idea of a good time.

Miguel pulled Ruben, whose jaw muscles were flexing and whose breath was huffy, toward the stairs. "We'll paint it over tomorrow, *Bebé.* Don't worry about it now." His sleepiness drove him, but he still saw something in Ruben that worried him, a quiet fury he hadn't seen before.

Fatigue overcame their righteous anger for the moment, hiding the will to fight. It would be a troubled sleep for both of them in this time of paradox—prosperity, sincerity, bigotry, and absurdity. Happy fucking New Year.

Eighteen

THE PHONE RANG some time on New Year's morning. Neither of them wanted to answer. Not even the roosters had awakened them. It wasn't till the second ring that Ruben picked up.

"Mother?" Ruben said.

"Tell her 'Happy New Year,'" Miguel managed to utter.

But Ruben's tone changed noticeably. "What?"

It was the kind of tone that stirred a person from slumber. Miguel propped himself up on one arm.

"A tumor?" Miguel's jaw dropped as he heard the word. The t-word was as bad as the c-word. "What kind of a tumor?" Ruben asked.

"Yes. Mm-hm." The information came to Miguel slowly like Morse code. "And they're going to operate. They want to take it out." He continued listening. "How much money do you need, Mom?" Miguel sighed at the news. What a new year. "Is there someone to help you?"

Why is life such a struggle? Miguel thought. *Just when things seem to swing toward the positive, they always get knocked back again. How can anyone endure it? Is it even worth it?*

Moments of significance flashed through his mind— stepping off the bus, the beach on the river, the life in the river that overcame the storm, the impaled Santa Clauses, the "Queers" still painted on the door, their first kiss. Life was a mixed bag. Yet somehow he felt he had advanced beyond the drab misery in Mexico City. He had taken more steps forward than back and was much the better for it. *Two forward, one back*, he thought, *two forward, one back*.

"Besides God, Mom. Is there someone to help you?" Ruben

paused. "Okay, just tell me whatever you need, Mom," Ruben finished. "I love you, too."

All the words that needed to be said had been. The two sat together on the bed in the cold room, Ruben in the arms of Miguel, as they stared silently at the walls.

When Miguel recollected his mother, it wasn't good things he remembered. The bitching voice from the snarling mouth, the constant comments that would burst his rare happy moments or remind him that failure was what she expected— "That'll never work! I told you so! I knew you'd do it again!" His brave attempt at the secondary school choir was squelched after his first day of practice: "You sound like a dying dog," his mother told him. He never returned to the lessons. He wondered, at times, if he had inherited that same disposition to always see things through negative lenses. Was he using those same lenses on her? Or was he simply seeing her as she was? He didn't have a negative view of the rest of the world—he cheered his students on, he believed in people, he had hope.

But now was Ruben's time to reminisce. Unlike Miguel, he had let go of the bad times, not really recalling them. Rather, he remembered snuggling up with his mother on the couch to Sesame Street episodes. He remembered how she'd save for him the largest and most beautiful strawberry before she sliced them. He remembered the time his ice cream scoop dropped clean off the cone onto the dirty street and how she picked it up with her bare fingers and wiped off the pebbles. He remembered how she would prize his crayon drawings and hang them in a frame in the living room. He remembered her pushing him down the street on his bike for his riding lessons.

They had grown apart in some ways, he knew. He had taken his own road in his adolescence. She needed her own ways of coping. But they had come to accept their differences, it seemed, and had grown close again. He sent her the lion's share of his savings without a second thought.

For his part, Miguel stood at the ready. He volunteered to work the store, cook the food, clean the house, paint over the graffiti on the metal curtain, whatever seemed to ease things for his partner. Inside, he hoped for some recognition, but at times, Miguel got the feeling that Ruben didn't even notice that he was there or, frighteningly, secretly wished that he wasn't. He felt now that he hardly knew this man who had become so introspective and muzzled these days, and so troubled. Miguel knew that this wasn't about him, and that this wasn't a time for selfishness. But did he really have no part to play here at all? Ruben's face was like a cold metal door...with a big lock on it.

It gave him a chance to start focusing on school again. In just a week's time, it would be back to normal, back to the routine. Those tiny minds now dispersed throughout the rainy hills would come back and make demands of Miguel once again. It would take his full concentration to steer the ship. He was like a captain awaiting sail and soon enough his crew would be at the embarcadero. This was no time for doubt. The children still needed him.

When Miguel stepped off the bus from town in Comalticán, it was like a homecoming. He felt he was back in the place that he belonged. He had not been certain he would feel this way and was relieved, in a sense, to feel good about it. Perhaps he had become overly dependent on Ruben for a sense of vitality, a sense of importance. But he knew that nobody could give that to him, that he'd have to find those within himself. Wasn't his mother so bitter about life for having expected that others would give her life meaning? For her, that expectation was never met. That would not be his destiny. He would find his own way of creating meaning; he couldn't count on others for that. "Be with people because you *want* to be," he remembered from some TV talk show, "not because you *need* them. The former is a statement of love, the latter a statement of fear." If Ruben needed his space then he would have it.

The weather was constantly cold at this time of year. Miguel's feet were always cold; the tip of his nose seemed bitten by the frost. Yet it was so normal that he didn't even notice anymore. He did notice the sprouts of green grass that grew in the rocky soccer field. Bushes by the main gate seemed especially lush. It reminded him that this was still a new year and there was still much new growth yet to happen. It was time again for him to lead; it was time to be a teacher.

The school seemed strangely desolate. He remembered the first time he ever laid eyes on it. It seemed like a hundred years ago. The school looked as it did back then but his memories of it now held a permanent place in his heart. It looked the same but it would never be the same. Funny how a place, so inanimate and concrete, could have such an impact on emotions. It actually conjured in him the faint yet profound urge to cry.

He opened the gate, whose padlock sat rusted on its useless perch on the fence where someone must have left it years ago. Apparently no one had ever seen the need to secure the gate again. Or perhaps they had lost the key.

He entered his bedroom quarters which conjured in him another memory—the distasteful and yet unsolved mystery of the Santa Claus dolls. He had stored that memory in some back cabinet for a while, but it was time to take it out again. Miguel left his backpack on the bed. He had brought with him his essentials for the night. He'd let Ruben be alone that night. It would be their first night apart in nearly a month.

Fog slipped down the hill and covered the peaks of the mountains. In the cold morning, Miguel couldn't even make out the cross where, on the day they climbed up to see it, they'd been wishing for relief from the heat. Stray dogs huddled together in the patches of grass near his classroom. Neighbors' chickens quietly pecked at the ground. And Miguel made his way to his classroom like a sole sailor on a great ship.

Soon the ship would be filled with life again and would set sail for distant shores. It would hit lulls when the wind would rest and the only hope for movement would be sheer force of long oars. It would hit stormy seas and great swells. Someone would fall overboard. All these perils would only be overcome by a crew that acted as one, that met the challenge head on and had the same goals in mind. Dissent from the team would be tantamount to sabotage.

Yet Miguel wasn't even sure of his own place on the team. At times captain, it seemed. At times, inexperienced crewman waiting for directions. At other times, he felt like a stowaway, secretly along for the ride. At still other times, he felt in jeopardy of being ostracized and thrown from the ship as a traitor.

But what had he done? Besides put his soul into the job? Besides follow his heart? Maybe he had slipped up at times, but he was only human. He knew he wasn't perfect; his mother's words always reminded him of that. He did the best he could (and far more than many others). Should he be punished for that? He passed the day alone in the classroom, searching inside himself for answers, and for a feeling of stability.

The night was ice-cold and merciless. He shivered beneath the blanket, clad in all the clothes he had brought. Before too long, the stars in the black sky were covered by clouds that began dumping water down in torrents. It banged on the roof and on the windows, dripped rhythmically in one corner of the room, and formed, behind the quarters, a gushing river whose sound was as relentless and grating as the pressures in his life. Both seemed strong enough to make the walls fall in and the roof come down. Why did everything seem so perfect in one instant and then so sour the next?

Miguel did not speak with Ruben for three days in a row. Not long ago, they hadn't even met and now Ruben was a huge factor in Miguel's life. Three days seemed like forever when Miguel thought about it. Yet paradoxically, he didn't miss him or yearn for him as he would have thought he would. It was as if Ruben and their love was all a dream or some sweet movie he had once seen that had touched him deeply but was somehow temporary and unreal.

But he doubted himself, too. Perhaps, he thought, he was merely defending himself against Ruben's recent distance, as if minimizing the relationship or bracing himself for pain. Or was he overreacting, he wondered, simply not giving to Ruben the space he needed? Was he being selfish while Ruben's mother was unwell? He only knew that he was tired of having so many questions and so few answers.

Like factory workers back on the line, familiar faces in familiar uniforms came through the gate and took their places. There was dutifulness about the workers, and sleepiness in the eyes of the children, who were also happy to be back. The Directora walked from classroom to classroom and welcomed the teachers back. The Captain walked across the field, down from the bakery where he had started early on the morning's bread. He avoided even the most superficial greetings from everybody. Maestra Viviana didn't show, which was no surprise to anyone. It was actually only Miguel who noticed.

Miguel stood at the door as his black-haired bunch found their way from breakfast to the classroom. Their cheer alleviated Miguel's preliminary anxiety and instantly restored his sense of vitality.

They trickled in at first, then streamed in. Xochitl and Misol-Ha in their new uniforms looked almost like the rest of the kids. They took their usual seats beside one another, Xochitl greeting one of her new friends in Spanish. Juan came in without looking at Miguel, as tired from the trek down from his father's hut on the hill as he was indifferent to school. Orfil entered right after Jesse, of course, whose voice was the loudest, and went directly to Miguel in a macho embrace. Rebeca, the little one, had passed through the door unnoticed with a number of other students, who began right away to gossip about their times well spent, or not, in the last four weeks.

Johana walked in nearly last, accompanied by a boy who looked vaguely familiar. He had grown a bit and was grinning proudly. His double chin and baby fat had noticeably diminished, calling attention to the fine mustache of a young adolescent. Most striking were his good looks and the absence of warts on his face. It was Abimael.

The noise from the class suddenly ceased. Even David, wedged between desks and lost in his guitar strumming, stopped at the silence and the children's stares. Abimael was gleaming, his smile so broad it must have nearly made his facial muscles cramp. They had never even noticed the light color of his eyes, brown and clear like fresh honey, and his thick eyebrows beneath his rectangular forehead. "Good morning," he said in a deeper voice, soaking up their gawks. It was Jesse who applauded first, and soon there erupted the most genuine clapping that Miguel had ever heard. It was a true metamorphosis, a miracle.

It took Miguel a minute to calm the crowd. He smiled like a proud father as he ushered the shining Abi to a seat. "Where are your warts?" someone asked from the surrounding desks.

He turned to the kids behind him and simply said, "They're all gone. They're all gone." As if all the cells in his body had had enough, and had turned those nasty warts black and expelled them from his face, although a few still remained on his fingertips. The teeth in his smile were like freed hostages. Even his walk and posture had changed, and the whole room shared in his victory. Yes, it was a new beginning and all felt inspired to step forward.

By day's end, everyone's energy diminished, for the students were not used to the strain of a full day's work. Brenda was the last one remaining in the classroom. Miguel shuffled through his memory to recall her name. She pulled an envelope from her backpack and handed it to him. "My dad said to give this to you." Then she promptly left the room.

Miguel opened it without a second thought. *Most likely a New Year's card or a request for additional tutoring.* His mind wandered as he read it: *"Meet me at the Hotel Arbolito. Room 17. I'm here till Sunday."*

His hormones raced in his groin and his heart thumped in his chest. He swallowed hard at the temptation. He thought of Ruben, unsure that Ruben thought of him. He tucked the note back in the envelope and buttoned it safely in the back pocket of his Normal uniform.

The metal curtain at the candy store was shut, bolted to the ground on either side. Miguel looked at the gray spot where he had painted over the graffiti. The apartment door was locked. Standing at the top of the stairs, he knocked, knowing that there would be no answer. He had folded, couldn't stand not making contact, not seeing Ruben. He wanted to share with him the happenings of the day. He wanted to feel Ruben's skin beneath the sheets and rub his lips between his shoulder blades.

There was no note, no sign, no bread crumb to follow. He

was angry at having taken the bus ride in vain. He was alone in the cold evening wind that pecked at his face like a black crow. It must be that Dahlia was sick, he reasoned. But that did not mean that he no longer counted, he argued. He knew what advice he would give his students if one's partner had slammed the door on him in the cold. No, he must be patient. The dissonance in his brain was driving him mad.

He thought of calling Ruben at his mother's house. But then he laughed off the thought. He didn't have a phone, let alone her number. He even thought of calling a hospital, but didn't know which hospital, or clinic, or doctor's office. Anyway, Ruben should have called him. It couldn't be that hard to get through to the Internado.

Numb, he walked down to the cantina. The same two whory waitresses were at the bar. A stiff shot of tequila burned its way down his throat where it joined the already rumbling lava of his insides. There sat those same men at the plastic tables, their voices tamed by the temperature. They were despicable. He had no need to stoop this way.

He walked back to the Internado, too riled to wait for the bus, not even sure it was coming. The night was dark and indifferent and had him frozen to the bone by the time he crawled into bed past midnight. He hoped that he was wrong, that the worst was not to come, that everything would be okay, but he knew better.

Miguel passed the days that week dutifully and, despite some moments of being jolted into the here and now by the students, was mostly distracted. Just as a person can drive for hours to a destination and not remember how he got there, though presumably he drove satisfactorily, Miguel did his job, minded the students, and dwelt on Ruben. The mere fact that Ruben hadn't called was gnawing at him.

It wasn't till Thursday that his arms dressed him for the cold, his hands grabbed the umbrella for the rain, and his legs took him once again into town to face the steel curtain. He didn't agree with the decision his body had made to break down and go to see Ruben again. He believed that it was Ruben's turn to look for him. But there was no reasoning with himself. He would never sleep if he didn't go find out for himself. For all he knew, Ruben had found someone else. Maybe Ruben's mother had nothing to do with it. Perhaps Ruben was the hypocrite. Perhaps, for all his self-righteous talk, he was with someone else.

He mindlessly arrived in town unaware of the swaying bus, the drip from the window that was soaking his pants, the glances of the bus driver. He walked directly toward the candy store as if with blinders on. When he turned the final corner, he was afraid to see it, afraid to see the light on and two shadows through the window frame. Or to find Ruben alone, at home, simply uninterested. Or even to find the candy store closed and locked down as it was the other day, as if abandoned. He was afraid to be right about this and hear the voice of his mother over his shoulder, "See! I told ya!" His head could hardly conjure a positive outcome, and he was disgusted with himself for even coming.

He looked up from beneath the sprawled umbrella with the slightest trace of hope still in his blood. He was right. He could see it from a block away. The place was as dark and alone as he had left it, the curtain closed like a stubborn mind. Why was he right all the time?

He pulled down the umbrella and prodded the metal curtain with it like a spear. He kicked at it and gnashed his teeth. Then he walked up the stairs to the apartment door by force of habit. He stood in front of it without even knocking. "Ruben," he said, "Fuck you!" And then he propped the umbrella against the door, the umbrella that Dahlia had so sincerely given him not a few weeks before. This change in Ruben seemed as drastic as the one that had led Dahlia to give him the umbrella in the first place. *Like mother, like son*, he thought. Hands free, he headed down the stairs at a swifter pace, prepared to never see that door again in his life.

He heard a metallic banging from below, the same sound he had made when kicking the metal curtain a minute before. A sudden blast of adrenaline opened his eyes wide. Who was there? Was it Ruben? Why would he pound on his own store?

Had he lost his keys? It took him only another instant to reach the street level and see who was at the door.

She was in zebra pants that stretched tight against her wide thighs where pockets of fat bulged out. Beneath a red checkered tam, she wore dark sunglasses as large as a fly's eyes. Her tennis shoes were surprisingly white considering the mud and foul weather. One hand held a large black plastic garbage bag at her feet while the other banged again on the curtain. It was Teresita.

She looked over to Miguel where he appeared. "Oh, good! You're back!" she said smiling, her momentarily desperate look replaced by her usual peaceful smile.

"Yes, I'm back," he responded.

"I need to stock up on gum and chocolate. I haven't been able to get it from any place," she explained.

He shook his head at her. "Ruben's not here, Teresita. I don't have the keys. I don't know where he is."

"No kidding. Too bad. I've been coming by every day this week."

"I don't know what to tell you. He's not here."

"Well," she said as she pulled up on the plastic bag to show him. "You always got to have a plan B, right? You never know what's gonna happen."

"Yeah, right."

"I've been selling these shoes instead." She held the bag open so he could see several contorted shoe boxes in the garbage bag. "I figure, I can't sit around and wonder what's going to happen. I got bills to pay. I got a life to lead. I gotta move on. If he comes back, fine. I'll sell candy. If he doesn't, I'll sell shoes. Can't stop life just because things have changed, right? Can't always count on someone else, right?" She hoisted the bag over her shoulder, winked at him through her dark glasses, and turned down the street. "Good night! Tell him hi for me if you see him, Maestro."

What a crazy old bat! he thought. *How does she manage to be happy all the time?* She was right, though, you couldn't always count on others. You had to move on sometime.

He stood there beneath the small overhang in front of the

store, protected from the rain. His hands, now empty, were perched on his hips as he contemplated the rain. His left hand moved from his hip to his pocket, hoping to find a handkerchief for his face. He found a folded piece of paper instead. He unfolded it in the dull light of a faraway streetlamp. *"Meet me at the Hotel Arbolito. Room 17. I'm here till Sunday."*

It's still only Thursday, he thought. *I got a life to lead. I've got to move on.*

Nineteen

THE HOTEL—a small, Spanish colonial-style establishment built around a courtyard, and containing perhaps twenty rooms in two stories—was a short walk from the town center. *Everything* was a short walk from the town center. Water fell on the dark streets, and Miguel entered the reception area sopping wet. He heard the sound of a TV behind the desk where an elderly man sat, barely seeming to notice him enter.

Finally, the old man looked up from where he sat, his body faced more toward the TV against the wall than toward Miguel. "Can I help you?" he said with little interest.

"Um, room seventeen, please." Miguel imagined he'd be recognized as the teacher from the Internado.

"What about room seventeen?" the man asked, not about to recognize anything but the soccer game on the television. "It's already rented."

"No. I came to visit," he explained.

"Well, visiting hours are over. But you could rent a different room."

Drops ran down Miguel's face from his hair. "Can I at least go see if my friend is there?"

"Young man," retorted the old one, "I said visiting hours are over. It would be best if you came back tomorrow."

Miguel walked out the door. The old man again barely noticed.

Once on the street, he turned the corner toward the town square. "Maestro," he heard whispered in the dark. He looked over to see Tomas from behind a barred window.

"Over here," Tomas said, waving at him to approach the bars. He shook Miguel's hand through the grate. "Meet me over there at the service door." He eagerly pointed toward the end of the building.

Miguel only nodded, now as interested in staying out of the rain as he was in a one-night stand. He walked over to the door and heard the heavy thud of a century-old bolt unlock.

The door creaked open, and Tomas quietly led him to his room. "He'll never notice, the old geezer," he said.

Tomas seemed like an expert at this and, in reality, it wasn't his first time.

He had a wife someplace, the mother of Brenda, with whom he had lost contact a few years back. They had married in the city of Veracruz, not far from Puebla, but a slow stretch through the mountainous regions of eastern Mexico. He hadn't wanted to disappoint his parents nor embarrass his family. Marriage was the *normal* thing to do. Soon after, she became pregnant and Brenda was born.

It wasn't long before their constant bickering drove them both apart. Aside from that, she thought of him as sex-crazed and he thought of her as frigid. Deep down, though, he was more of a prowler, a hunter. He was in it for the catch. And he preferred to catch young boys, late teens or early twenties, who thought of themselves as straight. A couple beers later and he could have just about any guy on all fours, especially the open-minded guys from Veracruz. Most of the time he could get them to go bareback, too.

His wife was probably off with other guys, too. At any rate, she had certainly met her current husband before they ever separated. The marriage between Tomas and her being only a religious ceremony, there was no paperwork to worry about. The only uncertainty was Brenda.

"I am just not ready to be a mother," his ex-wife told Tomas' mother when she dropped the two-year-old off at her house. That was the last time they ever saw her. It didn't make much difference to him; he wasn't ready to be a husband, either.

He did love Brenda, of course, but his job as a computer programmer was the perfect pretext for leaving her at the Internado, and, incidentally, it left him available for his other pastime. He had a regular trick or two in almost all of the towns that he frequented due to his work. Brenda's teacher would be another feather in his cap. He was one more piece of evidence that showed he still hadn't lost his charm, one more person that allowed him to deny his irrelevance.

For Miguel's part, he couldn't help but compare him in every way to Ruben. After nearly two weeks of no sex, it was good to simply feel flesh, like eating meat after a vegetarian diet. The intimate smell of nakedness, the primal moans and groans, the forbidden pleasure, they all played a part in his arousal. Even the feeling of independence and liberty from the chains that kept him distracted all week. Why should he let Ruben control his emotions? He would surely feel guilty once this was all over, but for now the taste of freedom restored his sense of power, his self-determination. Maybe being single again wasn't such a bad idea. Perhaps after all the changes he'd been through, he'd find more doors open than ever before if he were alone. Perhaps this was meant to be.

He didn't like the way that the hairs on Tomas' stomach fanned out across his belt line and stopped before they ever reached his chest. They were dark on his white skin. Ruben's lighter hair was thicker, high on his chest and narrowed to a V down his stomach and across his bellybutton to where it disappeared at the button of his blue jeans. Miguel didn't mind Tomas' smoker's breath as much as he did the bitter taste of oily skin from the years of smoking that saturated Tomas' very pores. And he was quickly reminded of the Captain by the attitude of Tomas, a dominant and selfish kind of you-please-me perspective. Miguel had graduated from strict subservience months ago. But it was better than nothing for that moment, a last-ditch effort. It was a sort of sexual stupor, a temporary binge, that was better than the gnawing, constant pain of having lost a love.

It was the shame and indifference of a burgeoning depression that kept him from work the next day, Friday. And it was pure desperation that kept him the whole weekend. Tomas' strategy was a scarcely disguised attempt at spoiling him with cheap food from the corner taco shop, a tooth brush from the pharmacy, two bottles of white tequila in plastic bottles, and half of a small brown bottle of amyl nitrate—poppers—the vapors of which would get them in the mood. His charm didn't work that well with women, either, but Miguel didn't require much enticing. He stayed enclosed in the hotel room the duration of the weekend, declining maid service for fear of discovery. Miguel knew the whole thing was utterly irresponsible but, for the moment, he felt like he just didn't care about the consequences. If it was a subconscious cry for help, no one was going to listen.

Twenty

ON PHYSICAL EDUCATION DAY in secondary school, Miguel wore his navy blue sweat pants like all of the other students in the entire Federal District. He could only imagine the humiliation of changing in a locker room like those he saw in the subtitled American high school movies on late night television. Those boys were so nonchalant about showing off their private parts and pubic hairs. He, on the other hand, had nothing to show off, a lanky and completely hairless body. He was definitely a late bloomer if there ever was one. Even if his body had dispersed its ration of testosterone as soon as the other kids had, he could hardly imagine flashing and grabbing at others like they did. He was aware of the way these scenes aroused him, in some curious way, and hoped this was some phase that would pass away. Wasn't it normal for pubescent boys to get erections for any old reason?

His mother had convinced him that he would never succeed at sports. She was probably right about it, too. So when it was time to enroll in a compulsory sporting activity, soccer was out of the question. It was either swimming or gymnastics. He wasn't getting in the filthy public swimming pool water. Actually, the filth was the perfect pretense; the real reason was the aforementioned biological concern. So gymnastics it was. After all, how hard could tumbling on the floor be?

The first day was an eye-opener. Simply getting there was difficult enough, south for over twenty stations on the metro and then two bus routes to Colonia Libertad where the closest public recreation center was. There was nothing like that in his part of town and, if there had been, it would probably have been replete with cholos and graffiti by now. Then there was the

115

locker room, larger than he expected, smelling of fungus and sweaty linen. A few basketball players were just leaving as he began getting ready for his night course. If they had seen what he was about to put on, he might have ended up bleeding and crawling on the shower floor. He lingered around the toilets to stall for time, reading the lewd messages of disgusting old men.

His mother reminded him of his terrible ungratefulness when she handed him the required tights that she found at a hole-in-the-wall neighborhood sporting goods store. Soccer was the preferred sport, of course, and the gymnastics tights, whose gender design was questionable, was the only pair that store had seen in years. "There's no taking them back to the store, and I'm not going to spend my hard-earned money on another pair. They're fine," she said to him.

He was dying to get the initial embarrassment over with and crossed his fingers, hoping that all the boys would be wearing similar garb. Somehow he didn't look like those gymnasts he'd seen in the summer games.

The gym was large and he entered from the men's locker room amidst a host of giggles from the circle of girls already stretching on the blue mats. What were they laughing at? They were wearing the same tights. Only one other boy was in the entire class of thirty or so. He stood directly across the circle from him at about twenty meters. He, too, had been warming up and seemed rather agile, judging by the near splits he performed. He hardly looked over at Miguel during the entire session of neck cracking and back bending. Maybe swimming wasn't such a bad idea.

Back in the dressing room after the session, the two were the only people amongst the rows of metal lockers. The other guy was in the same row as Miguel, but way down toward the far end. Miguel looked over frequently but attempted to seem uninterested in his fellow gymnast.

"This was your first day, wasn't it?" the kid yelled from where he was changing.

"Yup," Miguel answered, his judgments about the boy's unfriendliness quickly subsiding.

"You did pretty good. But where did you get those tights?"

"My mom got them for me," he answered loudly enough to be heard. His voice echoed in the expansive room.

"You should get some like these." The other boy pulled them off and walked over, barefoot and in his underwear, black tights in hand. He passed them over for Miguel to see. "These won't make you look like you raided your grandma's old clothes dresser. Here, you can have these. They should fit you," he said. "My mom just got me two new ones."

"Thanks," Miguel said. "What's your name?"

"Giovani." He walked back to where he had left his things.

Miguel watched him till he got there. He was as hairless as Miguel but was in better shape, presumably due to the gymnastics. His torso made an inverted triangle, broad shoulders tapering to his narrow waist.

Giovani dressed quickly. "See you Thursday," he said.

"Yeah, see you Thursday. And thanks for the gym clothes."

The gym class was over before Miguel knew it. Three months of rolling on the floor and swinging on the creaky bars. He actually developed a liking for it, mostly because he and Giovani became best friends. They were the same height and same age, Giovani an entire two months older than Miguel. They lived about ten metro stations apart and went to separate schools, but started hanging out together outside the gym class.

Giovani was an energetic and assertive kid who filled the time with stories of triumphs at school, fights with his sisters at home, and his obsession with Batman. Miguel never had much to say but became the perfect buddy because of his ability to listen. Though Miguel felt entirely inferior, Giovani was too busy thinking about his next yarn to even consider such an idea. And Miguel was the only person to whom he confided his stories about masturbation.

Giovani seemed a bit compulsive about it, maybe three or four times a day. He sometimes asked permission to use the bathroom at school just to jerk off quickly. He was an impressive ejaculator, too, prompting his mother's inquisitiveness about the refreshments he must have spilt on his headboard.

Miguel was far too shy to discuss such intimate behavior of

his own, though he was secretly aroused by Giovani's confessions. Of course, he masturbated, too. What fourteen-year-old didn't? But he'd never admit to the details. He didn't choose to have those images of Giovani appear in his head. He couldn't resist holding those tights that he gave him, knowing that Giovani had worn them. He knew it was bad, but he began to idolize him.

It was Giovani who took the next step. They had been alone in that locker room so many times, horsing around in its emptiness. Then one night he got a mischievous look in his eyes. "Want to watch me?" he asked.

"What?" Miguel said. "Watch you what?"

"Masturbate, you idiot."

Miguel sure as hell did. He didn't have to say anything. Giovani stood up on the bench to check for company and then, as if it were no big deal, pulled it out and did his thing. It was over in ninety seconds though, for Miguel, that first image lasted forever.

Then Giovani took another step when sleepovers became a common pastime of theirs. They were always at Giovani's house. Miguel couldn't imagine inviting him over to his house in the slums, with his mother bitching all night. They would crowd together in Giovani's single bed. Before too long, Giovani wouldn't resist any more and he'd begin his nightly ritual. Then one night he said, "You want to touch it?"

Miguel never responded with words but his enthusiasm said enough.

Before much longer, he went a step further: "Put your mouth on it. I swear I won't tell anyone."

To anyone else, it might have been normal adolescent sexual exploration. For Miguel, it was his first true love.

He took a chance for the first time one night in the darkness of the bedroom, in the heat of the sheets. "I want to kiss you," he said.

"Are you serious? That's gross," came Giovani's reply.

"No, I mean, I've never kissed anyone before. It's just to try it," he said.

"Well, I guess just to practice, then."

After nine months, they had tried it all and had practiced and practiced and practiced. They found hiding places during the daytime on neighborhood playgrounds and in restaurant bathrooms. They found reasons to be together every night. They drew the suspicion of their parents, who would surprise them with mid-evening door openings and third-degree interrogations. There was no stopping them. They fought due to teenage jealousy and fits of anger, they wrote letters from their cross-town classrooms, and they gave small presents to one another—very best friends.

It was a time of bliss for Miguel who, for every milligram of extroversion that Giovani had, matched him with introspection. He saw himself in the mirror, a year older and slightly hairier, matured and practically married to this boy, his best friend. And there was no denying the truth.

"Giovani," he said one night after a steamy session, "I am more and more certain that I'm gay."

His partner was still in the darkness. "What? You're gay?" he asked.

Miguel laughed, believed he was joking. What could be more obvious, right?

"*Guey!*" continued Giovani, "Why didn't you tell me that? I'm not gay. This is just for fun, I thought. My parents would kill me if they thought I was gay. Besides, I'm Catholic. We don't believe in that."

Miguel was perplexed. "Look at us," he said to Giovani. "It's like we're boyfriends."

"Are you kidding? I'm your friend but I am not your boyfriend. I like girls, Miguel. I don't know *what* you're thinking."

As if a drive belt had broken, the engine stopped cranking. Giovani went his own way. Miguel found himself alone with his illusions. The friendship was over. No more hanging out, no more phone calls and letters, no more passion. Where had he gone wrong?

He returned to the gym where it all started. He went back to that bathroom with the lewd messages, where he ran into prowling men who were more than enchanted to meet him. He

discovered the dark alcoves around the outdoor track and the
cruising bushes where overhead light bulbs were constantly
burst. He found emptiness in the anonymity, and safety. He
didn't want to go wrong again.

Whatever became of Giovani? he sometimes wondered.
Married? Family? Or has he come out of the closet? Did he
find out he was in denial? Did he ever wish for Miguel again
and think, after all this time, that *he* was the one who had gone
wrong?

Twenty-one

THE NORMAL SCHOOL in Mexico City was surrounded by a wall composed of thick blue cylinders positioned closely together, so that one could clearly see the school but could only get in through the security gate and turnstile. As if there were anything to protect. The school was as humble as any other public school—featureless classrooms, decrepit furnishings, not even seats on the toilets. What was anyone going to steal? Or who would they rob or kidnap? Anyone with any money would have been at the Pedagogical University down in Tlalpan…but, then again, anyone with money probably wouldn't have been studying to be a teacher.

Monica, Miguel's friend from down the block, was a Normal student. She had entered two years before he did. She had left for the rural parts of Zacatecas up north for her student teaching and had never returned. The prospect of leaving was part of the allure of the Normal school.

In those years, Miguel's mother had been particularly acidic, after having lost what might have been a decent boyfriend and what might have been a decent job. Miguel was only twenty-two but he was far too old to still be putting up with her contempt for everything about her life, including her children. Perhaps her insistence on seeing the world so negatively kept her from being disappointed, yet being constantly discontented was a heavy price.

Not long before that, Miguel had screamed at her in an argument, "I'm gay! So get off my back about attracting girls!" It had been his counterargument in the moment, and so "faggot" became her word of choice, at times under her breath and at times not, to put the finishing touch on her arguments. She could not resist capitalizing on the perceived weaknesses of others. It helped her to concentrate on anyone else but herself.

Salvador had the perfect name. It meant *savior*.

Miguel and he were introduced at a party, a little shindig to which neither of them had been invited, brought along in true Mexico City fashion by friends of friends of someone who actually was invited. Salvador seemed as sturdy as a dump truck. He was in his mid-thirties, with a neatly trimmed goatee, a broad, gym-generated chest, fashionable yet conservative clothing, and a sweet, confident smile. He was good looking in part because he believed he was. And he was a contrast to Miguel, who still looked like a school boy who wore pirated name brands with imperfect logos as prominent features on his jeans and tees. Miguel's demeanor was a somewhat transparent exaggeration of personality designed to gain the respect of others—his laugh was a little too hearty and his comradely shoulder-punches a little too contrived. He was a college kid.

Salvador's apartment was like the rest of his life—it was like a safe, protected by thick metal on all sides and a heavy padlock on the iron gate that sealed the front door. The gate shut like the echoing door in a monastery hallway. His décor was practical and conservative, like his clothing, and everything was placed in its perfect location. It boasted heavy-duty luxury appliances like an espresso machine and a stainless steel bagel toaster, things that Miguel had seen only in movies or peering through windows of upper class restaurants. Salvador became just that—a savior—as well as a prized possession, a safe house, and a lover.

Miguel's mother was opposed, of course. She met Salvador when the two drove over in his pickup truck for Miguel's things. He had timed his arrival so she wouldn't be there but things didn't work out as he had planned. "Ungrateful! You never help around the house! You don't know what it's like to pay the bills! You should get your own place!" she would always say. Now that he was leaving it was: "Ungrateful! Now who will help around the house? How can you just abandon your family?" She even looked Salvador in the face and said, "And you're no spring chicken. What do you want with a young boy like this? Just to quench your desire?" He'd no reason to respond to her as she followed them down the stairs and to the car like a hungry bitch.

"You'll be back, Miguel. It's never going to work out!" were the last words from her mouth as she stood on the curb and cursed them. He hated her for those words. And he feared they were true. He wanted so badly for them not to be. At that time, anything was better than what he had. He was saved!

Miguel began to learn what the rules were by breaking them. He was not to change the order of the shirts that were hanging in the closet nor the placement of the shoes on the floor. He was not to leave garbage in the garbage cans. He was not to use more than one light at a time. He was not to use Salvador's exfoliating soap nor his scalp-moisturizing shampoo. He was not to leave the toothpaste next to the sink, for it belonged label-side up on the second shelf behind the mirror. He was not to touch the condoms, which were counted, of course, for Salvador was the only one who could properly put the condoms on himself. Miguel would never have the need to use one, since he was the bottom and Salvador was the top. By the same token, he was to perform oral sex whenever expected, though it would never be performed on him, for hygiene reasons. Items in the refrigerator were placed according to expiration date and used specifically in that order. Finally, there was no talking to others in the building, or on the phone, or at school, or in the store, definitely not on the internet or in any place of social gathering—no talking to others at all. Infractions of the rules were sure to beget belittling lectures.

Not all rules applied to both equally, though. Salvador paid the bills and could use the phone and lights and food as he pleased. "I'm a grown man. I won't be told what to do by some young Normal kid." It was he who was caught cheating on Miguel, some unfinished business with his ex and then a chance rendezvous with an old friend from the preparatory school. Yet it was Miguel's "suspicious behavior" that forced them to move one day, seemingly out of the blue though, in reality, carefully planned by Salvador.

"Pack your things right now. We're moving," he said matter-of-factly.

The new place was already paid for, fifteen minutes by car but two additional bus routes to the Normal school for Miguel. It was equally as secure, the same metal-encased box, and it quickly began to feel more like a jail cell than a safe house. Going back to his mother's house would be more like transferring jails, yet it was still the worse of two unpleasant choices.

The arguments escalated and Salvador's responses became more and more extreme. Miguel would never forget the first time he was slapped across the face for using too much laundry detergent for a small load...and then arguing about it. Each of the five fingers of Salvador's heavy hand stung his face separately. They woke him up to a new world as if he had not been born, but instead had been shit out into an ugly toilet bowl. He hadn't known that there was such a thing as spousal abuse in the gay world. It was hard enough to be gay, and now he was the poster child for domestic violence to boot.

He was still too proud to return home. He had used too much detergent, it was true, for so few clothes. Salvador was stressed out with the pressure of bills and safety and taking care of Miguel. Each bout of abuse brought on apologies and sweet spells, the gentleman Miguel had met over a year before. Nobody knew about what was going on. Indeed, there was no one to tell.

The final exam of his requisite history class had been on a Thursday morning, one Miguel would never forget. It occurred after a typical Wednesday night argument about a lunch he went to with friends. Salvador had risen early, as always, and left for work. He had not said goodbye. Miguel prepared for school and the big test on an otherwise normal day. But the door was jammed. He shook the metal grate of solid bars. It did not budge. He saw the padlock right away like an iron fist in his face. That same lock that would keep the villains and danger out was a sentry that kept him in. He had felt incarcerated at times, figuratively, but this time he was literally confined. His pride was not worth this.

He said nothing to Salvador when he returned home in the early evening. Miguel had packed his things in a cardboard box and a backpack and left them in the closet, awaiting a single lapse in Salvador's control. When the perpetrator was in the bathroom, the victim slipped out. He quietly descended the stairs with his things in his arms, not so much afraid of Salvador as wanting to avoid the conflict or the apology or the explanation. Salvador always had a way of convincing him, but this time Miguel was leaving no matter what.

He caught a green taxi at the sidewalk. "Where to?" said the driver.

"Away from here," was his only response.

Salvador made it to the sidewalk before he pulled out. His arms were raised. "Stop!" he yelled at the taxi driver.

"Go, go," said Miguel desperately. The reign was over.

Not much longer until he could leave for his practicum, his student teaching, he thought. *Any place but Mexico City. To hell with this city. To hell with family. To hell with men and to hell with love.*

Twenty-two

BY MONDAY MORNING, Miguel's head was throbbing from the tequila and his Friday clothes reeked of debauchery and idleness. The skin on Miguel's nose and upper lip was blistered from the poppers, something new to him. It was the closest he had ever gotten to drug use; they had relaxed his butt muscles enough to endure the weekend of bottoming for Tomas and his insatiable sex addiction. His butt was raw and sore nonetheless.

Leaving the hotel was a relief. Early in the morning, he passed the old man who had fallen asleep crookedly in the wooden chair by the counter, the television on full blast. He walked fast, with not a single urge to look back at the hotel, ever visit it again, or even remember the entire weekend. It seemed reason had returned and guilt was about to set in. What had he done?

He spent the last fifty pesos in his wallet on a taxi and slipped into the Internado unnoticed. There was ample time to take a lukewarm shower and find a reasonably clean uniform. He reported first to the cafeteria for his kitchen duty…and to test the waters. Kids were eating beans and some slop of meat chunks in brown salsa with the usual lard-topped bread rolls and hot chocolate on this dry but muddy morning.

"Maestro!" the children screamed when Abi and Johana saw him. Their voices were an elixir that gave him a momentary return to grace. They smiled at him brightly and inquisitively. "Where were you? We missed you." And then: "What happened to your face? You look terrible. Have you been sick?" Drunks and children always tell the truth, so the saying goes. "You'll be in the class today, right?" they asked.

He nodded.

"Because we don't want to have Maestra Viviana again," they added as they walked off with their trays.

When he walked back to the kitchen, he saw a woman at the sink washing a steel pot the size of an ice cooler. She turned to him without a smile. It was Viviana. She had worked up a sweat scrubbing the crusty salsa from the sides of the pot with hands gloved in blue latex up to her elbows. "The Directora wants to see you right now in her office," she said monotonously before she turned her attention once again to her cleaning. Miguel swallowed hard and left the kitchen.

The hallway to her office was cold and narrow; the floor was shiny. He remembered her hand around his neck not long ago and the look in her eyes when she said: "…if you ever skip out on me again, I'm going to hunt you down and kill you." She had entered into his soul through his eyes and read the footprints of his history. *She understood*, he thought. He swallowed again. He knew he had passed the limits this time.

She looked up at him from above her reading glasses and the paperwork she was doing at her desk. She pointed at a chair where he was to sit. She breathed in deeply in preparation. He did not find the warm motherly smile in her face, but the stern look of a school administrator.

"Do your students know how to count?" she asked, looking him directly in the face.

"Yes, Directora."

"They count on you, Señor Hernández." She paused for reflection. "You have let them down and so you have let me down. You have shown them that they can't count on you. This is not some unimportant hick town hideaway. This is real life, the lives of children and their families depend on you in order to succeed in it. You are good, Miguel. You are a gifted teacher and have a true heart. But if we cannot depend on you, then we are better off with lackluster locals who will at least be here." She was still looking at him in the face. "Get your things and get out."

His mind reeled. He couldn't believe what he just heard. "What? Excuse me?" He tried to shake it off. "You're kicking me out?"

"Miguel, we all have problems and difficulties in life. Part of our job is to show students that despite the problems, life goes on. We will continue to do our part even when life gets tough."

"I know, Directora. You are right. I blew it. I am sorry. I made a mistake." His hands were emphasizing his sincerity. "Please don't get rid of me. I love it here. I need this place. I need my students."

"I'm not getting rid of you, Miguel. I'm suspending you. Take your things. Get away from here. Think about what is going on with you. Reflect. You'll report back to me after a week and you'll receive no stipend in the meantime."

"Directora, I don't have any money to live on. I've no place to go."

"Like I said, life goes on. You got yourself into this problem, now you deal with the consequences. You wouldn't have it any different for your students, would you?"

"No, Directora." He bowed his head and made his way for the door relieved, at any rate, that he hadn't lost it all. He donned his backpack, as full as the day he arrived, said goodbye to no one, and left through the rusty metal gate that he previously thought of as his entrance. There was only one place he could think to go.

Thick clouds rolled along hills and through the streets of the town. The only people who could be seen were those who had no choice but to be outside; the cold was prohibitive of any comfort. Miguel walked again down the familiar road to Ruben's place, expecting to find nothing in the dwelling that once had so quickly become home. He tried not to think about the next step. He had no other place to go. Even Tomas had left to some job in some other town. For all Miguel knew, he was already with some other trick.

He reached the closed candy store and then the bottom of the staircase. He looked up to see the black umbrella exactly where and how he had left it leaning against the door. He didn't even have the will to go up and get it.

He sat down on the cement stairs and let the wetness work its way through his thin pants to his bare ass. Everything had been going so great, and now look at it. He had really fooled himself this time.

Drizzle began to fall but Miguel remained motionless.

"Hello?" woke him from his slumber; he was still sitting on the wet stairs. It was Teresita again, this time dressed in a long camel-colored overcoat about as thick and rough as a fiber doormat. Her sunglasses were spotted with drops of rain but her smile persisted as usual.

"Teresa," he said to her, "You sure have a way of popping up in my life."

"I guess so," she snickered. "What are you doing here? Is Ruben back yet?"

"I don't know what the fuck I'm doing here." Her head retracted in surprise. "And no," he continued, "Ruben is not back. How are you?"

"I'm okay. Didn't have breakfast this morning...ran out of beans. I was hoping to see Ruben this morning. I've been checking every day. Even the boy who takes care of Micha has no idea where he's at. I guess his mother's real sick, huh? Anyhow, good thing I'm a little chubby, huh? For hard times and cold weather." She let out a hearty laugh whose contagion even Miguel couldn't resist.

"Yeah, Teresa, good thing. I guess we should be prepared for emergencies."

"So, are you just going to sit here and wait for him all day?"

Miguel shrugged his shoulders. "I don't know, I've no other place to go. I had to leave the Internado for a week."

"Oh," she replied, not with the sinister mischief of Doña Conchita but with genuine concern. "Well, why don't you come over to my house?"

"What? Are you kidding?" he said.

"We always have room for one more. What's one more mouth to feed? I'll hustle up some beans by early afternoon. Come on, we'll get you out of the rain, at least."

The pair walked down the slippery stone street together. Miguel was more relieved than he let on. She was like a serendipitous angel sent from some kind of tornado cloud, appearing in her disheveled yet propitious way. He thought of Jesus on the wall of Dahlia's living room who, at the time he'd seen Him, didn't seem like a guy with a sense of humor. Then he wondered how Dahlia was doing. Perhaps she was on her deathbed at that very instant, and here he was creating all this drama like a child with a tantrum. It was time for him to get back on the road.

They passed by a corner market for a ten kilogram bag of beans which Miguel purchased before they left town. It was the least he could contribute. "See," she said to him. "I told you I'd hustle up some beans before the afternoon."

Her house was about fifteen minutes from the candy shop, reached by walking to the end of town and down a wide trail that led to the river. The water level was at least a meter higher than before and it spread along the banks. Surely Ruben and Miguel's little beach upstream had washed away long ago. The house had a view of the rushing river, which moved now about fifty meters from Teresita's front door. There was another house in either direction; both were within yelling's reach.

Hers had been built long ago as a single cinderblock room, to which had been added, over the years, a few plywood rooms in the back with sheet metal roofs and an unfinished cinderblock room upstairs, accessible only by ladder from the outside, with rebar sticking up like a steel skeleton. The main room had a poured concrete floor that was far enough from level to be immediately noticeable. The workers' curved tool strokes could still be seen like an artist's brush strokes on a canvas. It was notably warmer than Miguel's room at the Internado and even Ruben's apartment above the candy store, for there was a wood-burning heater at a side wall of the main room. Its black tubular chimney disappeared in the ceiling.

The main room was over-furnished—the two vinyl couches and the coffee table left little room for walking and the large entertainment stand held crooked pictures in broken frames, tall candles in glass vases with the Virgin Mother painted on the exterior, various papers and souvenirs, books and children's toys, and a large dusty television that probably hadn't worked since it was given to the family four or five years ago. Bedrooms in the back could be seen, strikingly darker for the wooden walls and lack of windows, with clothes strewn all about. Children's voices could be heard from there. The smells in the humid air were a mixture of cooked chilies, burnt wood, and dogs. The home felt cozy due to the clutter, the chimney, and the unexpected hospitality.

"This is your house," she said to him in true hostess form.

One more adjustment, Miguel figured. He was given the choice between sleeping in a hammock in the bedroom where four others would share the bed or the green vinyl couch, much closer to plastic than to leather. He took the couch.

The entire family of husband and wife, five children aged from toddler to teen, a dozen wandering chickens, and half as many dirty pawed dogs had easily assimilated his presence. It was as if he were another family member. Not one of them seemed uncomfortable with his presence nor with the fact that they didn't know him at all.

There were only four chairs at the dinner table, six dinner plates in the house, and five forks of varying designs. That was just as well, since Teresita could only serve so many people at once. By the time the first person was done eating, they could pass the chair off to the next person and have the plate washed for a new serving. They insisted on Miguel taking the sturdiest chair and keeping it for the entire duration of any meal. The first night, Teresita served tostadas with refried beans and sliced hard boiled eggs with spicy tomato salsa. Breakfast was a plate of bean enchiladas and dinner the next day was bean burritos with grated white cheese. Miguel was no stranger to cuisine made creative by financial necessity. The strangeness was the happy and grateful attitude with which this family accepted it.

The jovial smile of Teresita was constant and her cheerfulness permeated the house, her husband, their children, and even the dogs who came in from the cold and lay on the rough concrete floor hoping to receive some morsel but thankful, nevertheless, for the covered dwelling. One or two of the dogs had names but they were mostly just called "Dog" by anyone who had reason to address them.

Miguel was in another world. Again. First removed from Mexico City, then removed from single life and the Internado, then again with Dahlia and Ruben in Molino, and now this. He was wandering this world like the first day he got here, still trying to figure out what his place was in it. He stayed awake in the dark night and listened to the rain fall and the wind blow. The trees rustled and animals howled and squawked.

How this life was filled with contradiction! He was a teacher who was most certainly learning. He was in a place so poor, yet rich with joy. He had found the perfect love, but it was forbidden and feared by society. He wanted to be close to Ruben, yet he was so far away. He loved his students, but left them hanging. He was in a simple place with such complex problems. What was he to do? He peeled his face from where it stuck to the vinyl couch.

He could hear the river flowing outside. He had been on his little beach where he found the valor to proceed when things had gone bad. The fish and insects weathered the storms; the river just flowed whether the land could contain it or not. How could so many things exist without conscious thought?

The answers to the most important questions were simple. Did he want to continue in the Internado? Yes. Did he want to stay with Ruben? Yes. Did he have control over everything? No. He had never considered himself insecure, but perhaps he had not let himself get into situations where his insecurity showed. He had been such a non-achiever before coming here. He had never had anything to lose, or even anything he'd fear losing. Now he could see what made him fearful and vulnerable.

Wherever Ruben was, he would be worth the wait. Sooner or later, he'd have to come back. Maybe he was no longer interested, but maybe his mother was so sick that he had had no other choice. Maybe, Miguel thought, he had found his own vulnerabilities. In any case, Miguel knew he could not control the situation or Ruben's actions. He could only control his own.

He had lost control but he could find it again. Ruben was worth it.

If it didn't work out, though, Miguel knew that he was worth it, too. In the end, he would choose the path of his life and the people who would accompany him on that path. If being with Ruben didn't work out, then something else would. Lightning flashed through the living room window like a comic light bulb illustrating a great idea. Finally, something was not a contradiction.

The morning routine in Teresita's house started early. Hot water had to be boiled for bathing, the makeshift chicken coop checked for eggs, the youngest children tended, dishes washed, coffee percolator started, breakfast made. Three of the children went to school in town while the eldest stayed home with the youngest. They were enthusiastic about school, although two were thought of as hyperactive, attention-deficit types by their teachers.

Daffne, the middle of all five, was an exceptionally intelligent and promising student who worked diligently on her schoolwork till late hours in the night. Provided she had lighting, she would lose herself in borrowed books and laugh at things that only she would understand even if everyone else had read the book, which they wouldn't have. She aspired to go to college one day, to live the fantasies like the stories she read in her books. She hoped to be the different one, have a house in town, her own business or practice, maybe be a university teacher or a writer, and spoil her parents with things they never had before. She was afraid she might get pulled from that dream by the need to work. Her only chance was to be so great that everyone would see what a shame it would be for her to leave school. She loved her family and she understood the pressures of the world. She was hoping to outsmart them.

They were all thrilled to have Maestro Miguel in the house. They were all raised with a dutiful respect for teachers much like that reserved for priests. Their respect for policemen wasn't the same, however, and probably rightly so. Both Teresita and her husband, Luis, had been hustled by the police for bribes over minor infractions. Luis had even been thrown in jail once on suspicion of burglary when items in a house he was working on disappeared. They assumed him guilty by association, treated him poorly in the town jail cell for the three weeks he was there, and his freedom was stalled for a couple of days when the missing items showed up at the house of a friend of that family. The man hadn't been arrested though, because he was a policeman, too.

Miguel got up in the mornings with the rest of the family and tried to make himself useful. He charged himself with trying to keep the floor clean. As people and dogs came in and out from the bathroom in the rain and wet, the chicken coop, and the garden, they inevitably tracked mud inside. He didn't mind, though, as it gave him something to do. More than anything, he was busy in his head thinking of the Internado and Ruben, his mistakes, and the way he intended to repair them.

On Miguel's last day with Teresita and her family, Luis left early. Carrying the plastic-wrapped firewood he'd gotten from a neighbor down the canyon—the most expensive item on the dinner menu—he came back down the hill near the house and to the final twenty or thirty steps, which were made of stacked used tires stuck in the hillside along the grade, the cheapest form of stairs. Miguel had watched the water pour from them like a champagne fountain and then find its way down to the river. He imagined the thousands and thousands of inlets to the river, the places where water accumulated and fed the fattening flow. Maybe it would get too high, but Teresa's family seemed not to be worried.

Teresa made fried chicken for his farewell feast, a true sacrifice for the family. For a while, two nests would be vacant in the coop. Soon, however, there would be new chicks scurrying about the ground again.

He'd never known a chicken before he ate it and found it awkward to hear its deathly squawks, to see its feathers pulled by savage fistfuls, to smell the boiling of its carcass for tomorrow night's broth, and to taste its gamy flesh. He was able to stop thinking about it enough to enjoy its flavor, though, and the tribute which the entire family was making to him.

It was Sunday night. A whole week had passed. Tomorrow

he would return to the Internado. He had taken a trip, more psychological than geographical, and had traveled most unexpectedly to a land of basic values: love, harmony, thankfulness, work, and simplicity. The Directora was a wise woman to whom he felt grateful the way a child might be thankful, deep down, for parental discipline. God only knows what would have happened had he returned to his family in Mexico City. Not many basic values to be found there. No, he was here for a reason, he thought. This was meant to be.

He didn't sleep as well as he had hoped that night, but was quick to rise and bathe. He thanked the family profusely, feeling some urge to cry. He would see them again, he knew, but wasn't sure that they understood what a profound effect they had had on him. That was the effect, after all, of those basic values and of true friendship.

Twenty-three

"YOU WERE RIGHT," he said to the Directora, "to suspend me. I let the children down and put aside my responsibilities."

She looked at him without saying anything.

"I want to thank you, in fact, for doing what was best for me and for the children. I was not myself and needed to sort things out. I wish that I had discussed this with you beforehand instead of just not coming."

She sat in silence during his pause.

"You had warned me the first time and I did it again. I will not let it happen a third time. If I did, I would not expect to come back at all. I wouldn't deserve to."

She stayed quiet, for he said what she intended to make clear.

"I apologize and thank you for letting me come back. If you will excuse me now, I have work to do."

She was delighted inside the way a teacher feels when her students learn, the way a mother feels when her child grows. The corners of her lips pulled up in the slightest of uncontrollable smiles but she would not let on completely. "I will excuse you, then," she said.

He felt undeniable joy to be back, and the children responded with smiles and cheers of glee. He stood at the classroom door and hugged each one as they walked in.

Maestra Viviana was happy to see him, too, only not for the same reason. She smirked as she greeted him. "Welcome back, Normal student," she said. "I suggest you be more careful of the things that you do. People are watching you and won't tolerate deviations from the rules."

He looked at her through squinty eyes. "Of course,

Maestra," he returned, "I will be most cautious." *Basic values,* he thought. If others didn't have them, *he* still would.

He was in his ocean again, and he began to swim in it as if it were the last time he'd ever be there. *You don't appreciate what you've got till you lose it, or almost lose it, anyway,* he thought. It was clichéd and ironic, so obvious yet so easily forgotten. *We have to be reminded, at times, of the fundamentals, as if we had to remind our lungs to breathe.*

That afternoon, Misol-Ha fell down in the mud and soiled her white uniform shirt, like a soccer player in the February championships. Her sister, Abimael, Johana, and Rebeca led her into the classroom after lunch. Abi had her in his arms, as she was shivering from the wetness and the embarrassment. She had chipped one of her front teeth. Her sister tried to calm her by cursing at the other boys in Nahuatl. She screamed at the top of her lungs to the pack of boys who, like hyenas, couldn't resist the hilarity, and her face became ugly with anger. Then her voice reverted to that of the sweetest of mothers as she comforted her younger sibling.

Abi was the knight in shining armor. He seemed to translate into Spanish the words of Xochitl in a macho tone as he cursed at the other boys who pranced a few paces behind. He knew what it was like to be the butt of the joke. It was the first confrontation between the alpha males.

"Leave her alone!" he said. "How would you feel if it happened to you? Idiots!" His fuller chest was swollen high and his fists were clenched at them.

Miguel brought them in to the desks, where he tried to regain calm and assess Misol-Ha's wounds.

"It would never happen to me, you faggot!" heard Miguel. It was Juan again, with Jesse and Orfil and a bunch of other kids from his class. Miguel only shook his head.

Little Rebeca pulled Miguel's shirt. "They'll pay for what they're saying, right Maestro? Things will go bad for them, won't they?" she pleaded, hoping there was justice in the world.

"Of course, Rebeca," he answered. "They'll pay, sweetheart."

The rest of the day was damage control. It was as if the savages had reverted to their old ways. The demons had come out.

Miguel sat at his little desk at the end of the day, face in hands, defeated. His head throbbed and it seemed he could actually feel his hair graying because his scalp hurt. Between these childish acts, half the kids forgetting their times tables, only a handful finishing their readings, and one student who occasionally misspelled his own name, he felt like they had taken more than a single step back; it was more like reverse evolution.

"They are only re-establishing themselves," he heard from the door. It was the Directora, who stood today in the school's uniform sweatpants, the kind that made swishing noises as she walked. She came inside and put her hand on his hand. He couldn't help but let a tear fall onto error-filled papers beneath his face. He couldn't believe he was crying. He couldn't answer her and only imagined that she lost respect for him. He couldn't control a class and obviously wasn't teaching them anything.

"They are children, Miguel," she said in a tender voice, almost a whisper. "They twist and change like the river. They rise and fall. They will do it again. Sometimes we get so used to them that we forget what they are. They are children and they need you. You are the bedrock beneath the soft sand. Show them the way and keep them safe."

He looked up at her as he used to look up at his grandmother, so kind and patient and loving.

She gifted him with her soothing smile. "Welcome back," she said, "and get over to the kitchen for dinner duty." She squeezed the back of his neck softly and pulled him to his feet.

The next day it was as if none of those things ever happened. Most of the students finished their work, they impressed him on the spelling test, and they sang the national anthem together for their civics lesson like a seasoned choir, smiling and harmonious. Misol-Ha came in a clean uniform, her chipped tooth barely noticeable. Abimael, Jesse, Orfil, and Juan armwrestled like bosom buddies. Miguel chalked the whole thing up to a lesson for a neophyte and sighed; he exhaled the tension and convinced himself as he breathed that he was inhaling gratitude, simplicity, and love.

What was supposed to look like a chubby pink cupid was looking more and more like a cross-eyed pregnant sow. It had been Miguel's idea to get the class working on a group project as a kind of team-building exercise. Each was to use a saying about friendship, write it correctly, explain what it meant, and then stick it on the giant cupid piñata as a tribute to the Day of Love and Friendship the following week. Maybe if they heard enough about friendship, he figured, it would start to run through their veins a bit stronger than inciting adolescent hormones.

They tackled the project with great enthusiasm, and their work was promising. Too much enthusiasm, in fact, because they were nearly finished and there was still a week until Valentine's Day. Nothing could get them working better than the prospect of candy.

They came to the front one at a time with their slips of paper. Each child read a saying aloud, then pasted his or her pink crepe paper to the spherical contraption.

First student: "If you want to have the perfect friend, then be the perfect friend."

Second student: "Only your real friends tell you when your face is dirty."

The sayings went on: "Friends are God's way of taking care of us." "To know me is to love me." "Friendship doubles your joys, and divides your sorrows." "A friend is someone who is there for you when he'd rather be somewhere else." "Everyone is a friend, until they prove otherwise." "The best way to destroy an enemy is to make him a friend." Each saying begot a short round of applause.

Slowly but surely, the words were sinking in. Or perhaps it was just Miguel who was absorbing them. He began feeling sentimental, thinking of long-lost friends in Mexico City, and thinking of Teresita and her family. He tuned the children out for a moment until their voices grew more animated and excited: "A road to a friend's house is never long." "A friend is a person who knows all about you, and still likes you." "A real friend is one who walks in when the rest of the world walks out."

As the last student shared her words and was gluing her paper to the pig's face, the children began chanting in unison: "Candy! Candy! Candy!" There was only one acceptable ending for a piñata. Miguel shook his head. He knew the pig was still empty. He wasn't ready yet. And where was he going to get the candy?

Ruben. The image of him was now firmly in his mind. Damn. Perhaps he subconsciously had known that this activity would bring him up. What else could he expect from the Day of Love and Friendship? He felt that tension again that might turn his hair gray. *No, think of something else*, he told himself. There was still a week, still a way to fill the pig without counting on Ruben.

February seventh. It was exactly a month ago that he had seen Ruben last. One day he had been there...and then he was suddenly gone. And that was the end of that. Exactly one month. He never thought that he would be recognizing an anniversary of *not* seeing each other.

And he worried that he was transparent, that the children could see right through him. It was as if they were tormenting him. As they continued screaming: "Candy! Candy!" they might as well have been shouting "Ruben! Ruben!"

"No," he said coldly as he stood up and turned to them. They were suddenly silenced. He looked out over the ocean and came back to his senses. They weren't seeing through him for they looked confused. "No," his voice changed and he forced a smile as he waved a finger in the air. "It's not yet Valentine's Day...you'll have to wait."

"Maestro!" they whined, playing along with his game.

"We must wait." He made his way to his desk and changed the subject. "Now, take out your Spanish workbooks and turn to chapter seven."

"Don't you mean chapter four, Maestro?" one asked.

"Yes, Damaris. I mean chapter four."

Two days later, Miguel hadn't figured out from where he was going to get the candy. He had been living from hand to mouth since he had come to Comaltícán. Well, for his whole life, really. What difference did it make to spend the few pesos in your pocket instead of saving when so few pesos took so long to add up to anything anyway? Couldn't even keep up with inflation. He found more joy from treating for a dinner here and there, buying a present, and keeping a fresh uniform and clean socks. Asking students for money was not an option, either. They didn't have any. He wasn't about to hit up the Directora for any extra funds right now, either; he didn't want to push his luck. He needed to keep his record clean for the time being.

They saw him come to the classroom door before Miguel, whose face was to the chalkboard. He was drilling away at state capitals as he wrote. "Sonora!" he said.

"Hermosillo!" they chanted.

"Jalisco!" he said.

"Guadalajara!"

"Michoacan..."

He waited for the response but only a few gave it in a quiet tone: "Morelia."

"Michoacan!" he repeated.

"Morelia..." even fewer voices.

He finally looked back at them. They were not looking at the chalkboard but at the doorway. The Directora?

But more like Santa Claus, it was Ruben, and he had a great burlap sack thrown over his shoulder. The kids could only imagine what was inside it, or perhaps they imagined the two had planned a surprise for the piñata. In his other hand he held Miguel's black umbrella.

"Ruben!" the children shouted.

He stepped through the door where he saw the pink pig hanging against the bricks above the windows by a twisted coat hanger. It was the only item of color in the classroom now, as everything that Miguel had attempted to hang had fallen from the moisture and weather. It was lifeless there, as if indifferent to the beating it would soon receive.

"Will you be needing these?" he asked the class as he hoisted the sack in front of him.

"Yes!" Their smiles heated up the chilly classroom like a bonfire.

Then he turned to Miguel and raised up the umbrella. "Won't you be needing this?"

Miguel's smile was feigned. Though something at his core was jumping for joy, his skin had toughened and remained poised. He did not respond with words.

"I'll leave it in your quarters," said Ruben, sensing the distance.

"Very well." Miguel then turned back to the class. "Quintana Roo!" he shouted at them.

"Chetumal!" they replied. And Ruben disappeared from where he had stood in the doorway.

Miguel couldn't wait for the day to pass. He needed to get to his quarters to see that umbrella, to feel Ruben's presence again. He couldn't deny how much he wanted to grab him, tear his clothes off, hear the news, reunite. But his body admonished a balanced response and would allow him to proceed merely on tip-toe.

When he finally got to his room, he literally took smaller steps, finally approaching the door and pushing it slowly open. He had no idea what to expect. In part, he wished to see Ruben sitting on the bed waiting for him. Of course, he did not. It was the umbrella he saw in the middle of his bed. It looked as if it was carefully placed there, not thrown, and there was a single red rose on the pillow beside it. He snatched up a small square note beneath the rose and read the words hungrily: "Come see me, please. I miss you."

He was angry, in a way, as he quickly gathered a few things for the trip to town. He was angry *because* he was so quick to gather his things and give in again. It was like the way he had given in so easily to the Captain and to Tomas, pathetic attempts at feeling needed. He knew that Ruben was not a pathetic choice as a lover, but should he forgive so easily?

The metal curtain of the candy shop was still shut. That meant Ruben had come to see him at the Internado before he had concerned himself with the store, Miguel thought contentedly. When he knocked on the door, Ruben answered right away. Miguel's impulse was to jump at him and hold him tight but he restrained himself, standing at the threshold, exploring the open eyes of Ruben, who stood there patiently.

Ruben moved first and lifted his arms to embrace him. But Miguel pulled Ruben's arms down. "No," he said without knowing his next sentence. He could control himself now. Why couldn't he do the same when Tomas was pounding him violently and incessantly? Tomas wouldn't have cared, he could have found himself another. It was easier to reject someone knowing that he wouldn't really lose him. Why did love create a place where it was secure enough to deny the same love that created it?

"*Bebé*. What's wrong?" said Ruben.

"*Bebé*? You don't know what's wrong? You're trying to play it off?"

Ruben pulled him into the apartment and sat him down at the dining room table. "No, I know I fucked up. My mother was sick and suffering. I was going crazy. I thought of calling you at the school or even sending for you, but I was helpless. Do you really believe I didn't think of you?"

"What evidence did I have that you did? A whole month. You couldn't even leave a note? I figured you changed your mind, totally forgot about me."

"Miguel. There is no way. I even talked with my mother about you...all the time." He reached for his hand and was startled at its coldness. "You're freezing," he said. "Come on, let me heat you up. I'm back now and not planning on leaving again."

"How do I know that? You could close down the shop and leave for a month any time you feel like it."

"No, Miguel. I can't. I'm broke."

"What?"

"That's what part of all this is about. I've been pulling out my hair about money. I've spent everything I had in savings on my mother's surgery. She still owes thousands."

"Surgery?" said Miguel. He remembered the phone call from Dahlia on New Year's, of course—but he'd told himself that an operation was unlikely to happen soon, if at all.

"Yes. They took out a tumor the size of a mango from her thigh. There was no other treatment for it."

"Fuck," he said. "That must have challenged her faith in God."

"No," said Ruben. "If anything, it fortified her belief. She prayed to Him a hundred times a day."

"'Friends are God's way of taking care of us,'" Miguel recited from a paper on the pink pig. "I guess you were busy being her friend."

Ruben just nodded his head.

It began to feel just like old times as Miguel's defenses relaxed and his brain began to think normally again. "Maybe I overreacted," he said. "I was actually a bit frantic about it. I must have come down here fifteen times to see you. It occurred to me to go to your mother's house. But it also occurred to me that you didn't want me there. You were quite withdrawn. Then, when I stayed at Teresita's house, I gave up on you."

"Teresita's house? What are you talking about?"

"Never mind. First, I want to hear about your mother's surgery. How is she doing?"

"Well, by the time I got there in January, she was in a lot of pain. There was no time to wait. They had her on a bunch of pain medication, which knocked her out for the bulk of the day. She didn't like being knocked out. But when she was awake, she was in pain. Even when she was sleeping, she would moan and her face would twitch and spasm. It was an ugly thing.

"I had taken her to the hospital in Cordoba. It took us two hours to get there by taxi. And they operated on the tenth of January, a group of young doctors and nurses who seemed like they had just gotten out of the university. One would look at the X-rays and explain it to the others. He wasn't discussing them, he was *explaining* them. I didn't have much faith in them, but she insisted that she was in God's hands, not theirs.

"The cut they made in her leg was nearly thirty centimeters

long. I had never seen such a thing. It's so strange how you can have something so big in you and barely even notice it from the outside."

"I knew she was in pain when we were there," Miguel said, "but I didn't even think it could be a tumor that big."

"It wasn't just the tumor, Miguel. It was the huge wound they left on her leg. They sutured it but it didn't stay closed. It took forever to start healing." His eyes were wide with emotion. "There was this big hole in her leg. You could see inside to the tendons and the muscles she has left. She couldn't walk, she couldn't get out of bed, she couldn't go to the bathroom, she was in constant pain. It was awful...and disgusting."

Miguel winced. He felt almost embarrassed to have acted the way he did.

"Then they were afraid that it would become gangrenous, that she could even lose her leg. So my mother prayed and prayed, saying that God would make the decision for her. 'He will understand that I can't live without my leg.' I spent my time getting her water and medicine, trying to get her to eat. I would undress her wounds, unwrapping the huge bundles of bandages, cleaning up the seepage." He sighed deeply. "I never thought I'd be doing that for my mother. She was the one who took care of me when *I* was sick.

"Aside from that, there was water running in her house during the rain, leaks all over the place. The boiler was on the brink and I'd have to light the pilot outside in wetness. And the cable company kept calling over some bill that she supposedly owes from over two years ago. She doesn't even *have* cable, never did."

"Sounds like you had a blast."

"Oh, yeah."

"So, how's she doing? I mean, why'd you come back if she's doing so poorly?"

"Well, in a way, I did want to stay. Or, more accurately, I felt like I should stay."

"Yes?"

"But, in a way, her prayers were answered."

"In a way?"

"Well, she is still not walking. But a neighbor of hers died, an old guy who knew her pretty well, and the family gave her his wheelchair. By that time, the wound started closing up. We made a trip back to the hospital and the doctors said that they found no trace of the tumor left. The problem for the time being would be the weakness in her leg. She'd need rehabilitation and constant care. The good news was that she didn't and isn't going to lose the leg. She believed that God answered her prayer."

"He might have kept her from getting sick in the first place," answered Miguel.

Ruben only shrugged his shoulders. "What good does it do to refute her? Especially now. It's better that she believes in something, no?" Ruben squeezed Miguel's hand to get his attention. "She asked about you. She asked why you hadn't come and why I hadn't talked to you."

"What did you say?"

"That I would see you soon enough. I mean, I didn't want to leave her alone while she couldn't take care of herself."

"She's still alone though, isn't she?"

"No," Ruben shook his head. "I found her the perfect mate who will never tire of her religious sermons. I got her a Chihuahua."

Miguel laughed delightedly.

"Yeah," continued Ruben. "Its name is Carmelo. He's a little thing that lies up on the bed with her. He's so small that you can hardly tell he's even there. He puts his round head on her good leg and waits for a little affection. At first she didn't think it was a good idea but she's truly fallen in love with him. And now I know that she's not entirely alone.

"Then she told me, 'Ruben, I know you've spent a lot of money. I know you have a life to live and a store to run. I know you need to see Miguel. He must be dying waiting for you. Go back to your own life and let Him watch over me now.'"

"She said that to you?"

"I needed her to say it. I needed her to release me. I'd have never come back if she hadn't. Not that I didn't want to. I just felt too much duty to her. I mean, she was right...but she is my mother. How could I leave my mother with a gaping hole in her fucking leg?"

My mother has a gaping hole in her fucking heart, and I left her a long time ago, thought Miguel. But he shook his head, understanding Ruben's point of view.

"Miguel, I didn't want to lose you. I *don't* want to lose you. All of this got me thinking about being old and being alone. Being sick. We gays need to take care of each other. Lord knows we won't be having any children to do it. A little Chihuahua isn't going to cut it, either."

Ruben reached over to where Miguel sat at the table and put his hand on his thigh. His face became serious. "Miguel, I want you to come and live with me."

It was music to his ears. It was like those Thalia and Christina Aguilera songs he used to listen to back in Mexico City that kept him centered and sane. Juan Gabriel's love song, "*Cosas de Enamorados*," was in his mind and the true words about lovers fighting and getting back together, sharing the little things of love. He enjoyed being lost again in the lofty clouds of early July.

But this was February, and it was cold outside. "There is no way, Ruben. I mean, I would love to, I really would, but I can't."

"Why?" Ruben pleaded. "Are you that angry? I told you I was sorry. This will be a big step for us."

"No, Ruben. It's because of the Internado. I told you that I stayed at Teresita's house. I came here first and you were nowhere to be found. They took me in when I had no place to go. They are incredible."

"What happened? Why did you have to leave the school?"

"Because I fucked up again. I went a little crazy when you left. I lost control and was depressed. Then I skipped out on school again."

"Wow. I'm so sorry. I didn't realize that it would affect you so much. I wasn't thinking much about anyone else but my mother. I guess I went a little crazy, too."

"So," Miguel finished, "the Directora told me to get out. At first I thought she meant for good. My heart nearly popped out of my mouth. Then she told me I was suspended for a week and had to leave the school to think things over. I realized I couldn't depend on you to give my own life meaning."

"Yes, you can, though. I want you to," said Ruben.

"Come on, Ruben. Look at your mother. The reality is that people can go any time. You or I could be dead tomorrow. I don't mean that we shouldn't be together, but there is a big difference between dependence and choosing to be together."

"Yes, that is true."

"Anyhow, so now I'm back at the school. Things are picking up again with the students. And I don't want to fuck up again. The Directora told me: 'No more chances.' I need to keep a low profile for now. Just being with you, it's hard enough to get to the Internado on time every morning when things are fine. Then imagine the weather, those times it's so hard to get out of bed. It's not smart right now. Maybe later."

Ruben thought it over. "What if we got a car?"

"A car? With what money? You said you were broke. Besides, what would people say about us? The gossip is bad enough around here. I feel like some people hate me at school, want to get me out of there."

"Buying the car could take a little while," Ruben agreed. "But who cares what people say? You said it yourself—we could all be dead tomorrow. We only live once. Never mind what people say."

"And do you even have a license to drive?"

"A license? No one has a license around here."

"Well, I think we'll have to wait a while," Miguel concluded.

Without another word, they stood up and walked together to the bedroom. With few words, they reconfirmed what they felt for each other, and renewed their relationship in the way that only love-making could do. Miguel's butt was still a little sore but he didn't think this was the time to say anything. Would it ever be? he wondered.

Twenty-four

WHAT A RETURN TO BLISS, thought Miguel. Not only was Ruben back and their relationship returned to normal, but it was Saturday morning and *not* his weekend to work the cafeteria, the sun was shining through the window, and there was even perfect reception on the radio. It was as if all the planets were suddenly aligned in their great travels through space and time. It was silly of him to have ever doubted the universe.

"Where did this toothbrush come from?" asked Ruben from the bathroom. "It's not your usual style."

"Ah," replied Miguel nonchalantly. "Tomas, the father of one of my students, Brenda, gave it to me."

"A father gave you a toothbrush? That's weird."

"No big deal." This wasn't the time for the big confession. "Let's go get some chorizo for breakfast."

Inside the cleared cafeteria on Monday afternoon between lunch and dinner, Miguel's students gathered around the suspended pink pig piñata that was hanging with a rope around its neck from a steel rafter; the metal hook in the top of its head wouldn't hold the great weight of the sow for the hefty supply of candy stuffed down its neck. It seemed like a lynching. The kids shouted and clapped with eyes wide open. Xochitl and Misol-Ha sat beside their friends on top of tables that were arranged in a circle around the killing field.

As each child took his or her turn with the wooden broom handle and blindfold, the rest of the children sang together:

Hit it, hit it, hit it!
Don't you lose your aim!
Because if you lose it,

149

Then you lose your way!
Now you hit it once,
Now you hit it twice,
Now you hit it thrice,
And your time is over!
This child is very lame!
He's very lame!
He takes after his father!

When they still hadn't broken the piñata by the end of the song, their turn was over. The pig seemed to be made of steel. There was no busting it till Jesse was up, and became infuriated by the enthusiasm by which they sang him the song. He pulled off the blindfold and, in one single motion, jumped at the pig and pulled it apart. Candy flew everywhere and the children scrambled like hungry wolves to secure their spoils. It was a perfectly primal end to the Day of Love and Friendship.

The mountains were like a great funnel that sent rainwater downward to where it accumulated in the creeks and tributaries and, finally, the river. The same rainwater came down on Co-malticán from as high as the white cross and the mountains that surrounded the circular village. It made brooks of the unpaved roads and turned flat places to a stew of earth and water and rocks and mud. Those who ventured out by foot accepted the inevitable mud that caked itself on their shoes. Those who drove were prepared for the slippery roads and the risk of getting stuck in the middle of a mud pot, calling on good friends to help push them out. Just outside of the town, the river was rising. Its surface was half a meter below the bridge that, when the children went swimming a few months back, had stood nearly three meters above the water.

No one was overly bothered by it, most having been veterans of the wet winters that knocked down the bridge twice in the last ten years. The mud was as normal to winter as flowers in the springtime and mosquitoes in the summer. They did not overly concern themselves with the things that they could do nothing about. Like it or not, someone had to go for the tortillas, some folks had to go to work, and some gossip couldn't wait till the dry season.

Miguel braved the weather to go into town at least twice a week during the work week and always on the weekends. He couldn't resist the temptation to be with Ruben. As long as he made it to work on time, he didn't see a problem. He promised to work, but where he spent his free time was his own business. Sometimes it meant leaving town at ungodly hours and sometimes the weather was simply prohibitive. They even rode in on Micha's back once in a while, her hoofs more adept in mud than any taxi tire. It took nearly an hour to get there on horseback.

The children did their best at converting the aisles in the classroom into sloppy indoor roads. There was no way around it. One couldn't keep the students from walking outside, for the bathroom, the dormitories, and the cafeteria were across a patch of muddy field. Cleaning the floor was merely a humorous gesture, for where would the forty students go while they were cleaning, and how would they not track new mud on the now wet floor? For the time being, cleanliness was futile.

The days marched on. The teaching, more than ever, was like trench warfare, each day a muddy battle. Although the students had generally positive attitudes about learning, there were constant obstacles—personality clashes, sicknesses, lack of materials, lack of space, a great range of abilities that varied by subject, monotony, and sometimes plain old bad days. The school year was a lengthy endeavor and much of it was punctuated by holidays and festivals, always something to look forward to and prepare for. Now, however, was a definite lull, and Miguel spending so much energy trying to balance work and his life with Ruben didn't leave much energy left for educational creativity.

This was no longer a new relationship, though, and Miguel was less concerned about winning them over and entertaining them than he was about getting the teaching job done. The students were used to him and his style. They knew that the bulk of the creativity had to come from them. Also, they knew they were accountable for learning. A few students had hit a wall, and Miguel was giving them daily activities to fortify their skills. Brenda, for one, was aloof; she was frequently off-task, doodling in her notebook or staring out into the sky. At times she wouldn't follow Miguel's directions, which was beginning to frustrate him. He was especially careful with her, though, for he was afraid to stir things up and let the cat out of the bag.

On Friday afternoon, she handed him another envelope before she left, this time a bit resentfully, as if knowing she were being used only as a messenger. "My father said to give this to you," she said without looking him in the eyes. Just as he tucked the envelope away as if it were contraband, a bolt of lightning cracked down close to the classroom and water began pouring in a deluge. He rushed the children out of the room so he could make it to Ruben's place before the rain kept him trapped and solitary for the whole weekend.

He grabbed the last bus into town; this downpour was going to keep everyone inside and immobile. He got on the bus after having slipped and nearly fallen on a downward slope of clay at the foot of the power post. He was drenched to the skin. As the bus grunted and fought its way onto the paved highway, Miguel looked over at the threatening river that was lapping at the bottom of the bridge. He was not turning back now. Nobody else in town seemed overly concerned, although it defied logic, so why should he be?

Ruben insisted on keeping the store open. The streets were desolate, doors were shut, homes were sealed up for protection, yet Ruben's store was lit up like a lighthouse in the dark. The wind beat in, the water poured down, and Ruben pushed his sweets farther in from the street. As Miguel walked up to the store, wet and shivering, it gave him a laugh to see the store open. Joy, too, because that open store and Ruben's light were a beacon, a home where he hoped to soon live and a home to his heart.

It only took a couple of phrases to convince Ruben to close down: "*Bebé,* not even the bees are going to come out in this rain," and, "Come on, I'll help you shut down." The metal curtains slammed down and the pair retired upstairs. The apartment was humid and clammy, but the bed was inviting and the body heat they soon generated warmed things up.

By morning, the rain had not let up. It was one of the larger storms that had hit the area for several years, just long enough for the townsfolk to forget the havoc that the previous storm had created. Ruben was the first up in the morning. A quick trip to the bathroom became a chore—they had left Miguel's sopping clothes all about the floor. He started with the socks and underwear, laying them out on the living room floor. The pants and shirt he hung over the chairs. And the coat was hung on a hanger on the doorknob.

Ruben was not distrustful by nature nor was he disrespectful of his lover's personal space. Trust only goes so far for a businessman, though. That was why employees had to sign in, receipts had to correspond to income, and deliveries had to be counted every time they came in. It wasn't distrust, it was practicality. As the saying goes, "Clear accounting, long friendships."

So when Ruben pulled the envelope from Miguel's coat pocket, he certainly wasn't spying. He was merely attempting to empty the wet coat of its contents in order to salvage them. If it had said "Maestro Miguel" or "Docente" or "Sr. Hernández," he would not have been tempted. But what envelope would say "Miguelito"? Even students most fond of him used the appropriate etiquette to address a teacher. The letters were smudged by dampness; the envelope was partly disintegrated. It opened easily, as if wanting to be read. *"I'll be in the hotel this weekend. Come and stay with me again. Tomas."*

Ruben's blood went cold. *Again?* he repeated in his head. *What was meant by AGAIN!*

He tried to calm himself down. He would wait for Miguel to tell him what happened, what this was all about. No. He wanted answers right now. He couldn't wait. He pulled the covers from where Miguel lay so unsuspectingly, so innocently.

The coldness startled him awake. He sat up quickly. "What happened?" Miguel said because he did not recognize the expression on his face. "What's wrong?"

He looked at Ruben and then saw the envelope in his hand. Shit. He hadn't even opened it. He had no idea what it said.

Ruben raised it to the level of his eyes. "You tell me what

happened. You tell me what's wrong."

"Where did you get that?" He was stalling. "I haven't even read it yet!"

"Well, do you want me to read it to you? Or do you want to just tell me what happened with…Tomas?"

Miguel pulled the covers back up. "It was nothing. He's just the father of one of my students. You know her. He's Brenda's father."

"My question is not about who he is."

"Ruben, I told you I was depressed when you were gone. You didn't even let me know what was up. Even before you left, you were distant. It was a whole month! What did you expect?"

"I'm not asking for your reasoning, either, even if it makes you feel justified. Simply tell me what happened between you and Tomas…*at the hotel*."

The words were piercing. He had meant to tell him sooner and to be honest about it. He had been waiting for the right time, knowing that in some cases—like this—there would never be a right time. It had been a mistake; he had faltered in his weakness and sadness. Now that Ruben was back, he had been hoping to just forget about it. Tomas would have disappeared soon enough, and then what harm would have been done? It would have been worse to bring it up, he thought.

Now, it had brought itself up like an ugly weed. Well, he had accepted Ruben for his reaction to his mother's illness, and had forgiven him for it, and Ruben would have to do the same for him.

"I felt really bad when you left, empty and abandoned…" Miguel began.

"Spare the drama, Miguel," said Ruben.

"Let me tell it as it is, Ruben. This is the whole truth. You left me hanging. I tried to understand that your mother was sick but I didn't see why you couldn't have communicated with me. I thought we were over. I came down here, like an idiot, time and time again, knocking on your door as if you were going to answer, but knowing that you weren't.

"This guy Tomas was flirting with me since the first time

he saw me...at the Christmas Festival. I didn't say anything to you because I figured that it was absurd. You and I were together, everything was fine, I wasn't into him. Nothing was going to happen."

Ruben sighed and his head dipped.

"The last time I came here to see you, the night was pitiless. I gave up on you. I couldn't wait forever. I couldn't depend on you. It wasn't your fault, it was mine, I figured. I would have to depend on myself.

"When I got the invitation from him, I thought I'd stop by and see what was up. Then, one thing led to another..."

Ruben inhaled again deeply and brought his hands to his face. "So that was it?" he said. "A one-night thing? Do you have feelings for him?"

"Well, it wasn't a one night thing exactly. He invited me to stay there with him the whole weekend. The weather was bad, I had nothing better to do. So I stayed."

"The whole weekend?"

"It was the day I didn't go to work, the Friday. For which I got suspended."

"Where was this?" Ruben asked.

"At the Hotel Arbolito."

"The whole weekend then?"

"We were together for three days."

"And? You must feel something for him. It was like an entire honeymoon."

Miguel laughed at that comment. "Hardly," he said. "It was a weekend of self-abuse, self-mutilation. It was hardly any good at all. I was only trying to escape the feeling that you'd abandoned me."

"Did you at least use condoms?"

"Of course we used condoms! Are you kidding? He probably fucks a hundred boys a year. He asked to go bareback but I refused."

Ruben walked from the bedroom to the living room and sat pensively on the couch. Miguel threw on some sweats and found a pair for Ruben. He came out to where Ruben sat and put the sweats in his lap. "Put on some clothes," he said, "you'll freeze to death."

He put on the sweats slowly. "This is not some fling we have, Miguel," he said. "Is it?"

Miguel shook his head.

"I know I fucked up. I left you a whole month without even talking to you. I didn't give you what you needed. I left you hanging." He raised his hands to his face, his palms together as if praying. "You fucked up, too. You had no faith in me. I thought you knew that I'd be back. You *should* have known. My mother was sick, I checked out for a while. It was no reason for you to jump off the deep end."

"Yes. You are right," Miguel said.

"We want to be together, right? There will be good times and there will be bad times. Each of us will have to be the strong one at times. We should be together to balance each other out. This time we both fell in, we didn't pass the test."

"I am sorry, Ruben. I shouldn't have fallen apart so easily. When I look back on it, it seems so ridiculous. I guess a relationship like this can really scratch at your vulnerabilities. The more of yourself you give, the more you trust the other with it. I was so mad at you. I was mad for the power that you had over my feelings. I wanted to feel free from that."

"Do you still want to feel free from that?"

"Yes and no. I mean I want to be together. But I shouldn't feel like I am nothing without you. How will I be strong when I need to be if I fall apart so easily?"

"And I fell apart easily, too. I wanted to be closer to you but I was so affected by my mother. I had tunnel vision. I should have talked to you and I meant to, I just didn't know how."

"Your mother was very sick," said Miguel. "I understand."

"It's not okay, Miguel. We have to be better than this. We deserve to treat each other better."

The two lay together on the couch, Miguel embraced by Ruben's arms.

"Here's your love letter," Ruben said, passing Miguel the limp envelope that he still had in his hand.

"Ha ha! Don't even remind me."

"You best never forget."

Twenty-five

THE BENEVOLENT GIVER was angry. High atop the mountain in the shack that Abimael used to call home, his family scurried to remove their most crucial belongings—the cookware, the clothing, the bed mats, the flashlights, and the leather. What used to be a small spring, a trickle in the summertime, now pushed its way through the rock violently, like a ceaseless geyser. The noise of the river was frightening, like heavy bass moans from the very bowels of the gorge below and Abi's family shouted at each other to be heard over the blare.

Had they gone too deep into forbidden territories where only the gods were permitted? Had they been too greedy? Or wasted their profits, the gifts of the earth, on folly? Were they being abandoned now by the powers that had watched over them as they had abandoned one of their own? There was no time for answers. The damage had already been done. This goddess was not about to change her mind. They were grateful even for the trembling warning she gave. They would respect her and leave.

They didn't know as they climbed down the hill that they would not return, that the cave would become inaccessible, that their home would be destroyed, that they would leave this area for far and unknown places, that they would abandon their son, Abimael, at the Internado and never see him again. All they knew for now was that it was time to go. This place was now cursed for them.

In the dark of the evening, while the water from the heavens saturated the hills and the soil and the roots of every tree, the mountainside exploded. The gigantic rock which was the hillside above the cave opening came down in one piece, shattering

157

against the earth into boulders bigger than burros that rolled down to places where they wedged between mighty trees and larger stones left there from the mountain's previous madness. Water spewed out as if escaping from a cage. The groaning died down as if the mountain was finally relieved, but the water continued to gush steadily with less pressure but greater quantity.

This night, Ruben was sleeping peacefully, undisturbed by the wind and rain. Miguel lay at his side, restlessly. The rain in Mexico City had been heavy at times but rarely fell with the same fury. He was thinking of the Internado and the growing pools of mud. He'd made promises to the students and to the Directora. Now, with the return of Ruben, was he compromising his commitments? He was trudging through the school year faithfully, and he had a right to a personal life. Yet he imagined the children in their bunks, frightened in the storm. Then again, even if he were there, what could he do? He felt something within that told him to go back, as if he were called to duty.

He shook Ruben's shoulder. "Ruben."

Ruben half woke from his slumber. "Hmm? What's the matter?"

"I have to go back."

"Then go to the bathroom."

"No, Ruben, I have to go back to the Internado."

"What?" He rolled over to look at him with squinty eyes. "You're crazy. It's only Sunday. You don't have to go back till tomorrow. Go back to sleep."

Miguel lay quiet for a moment and stared at the ceiling, listening to the wicked weather. He could not go back to sleep. He lifted his legs into the air and with one movement brought them down to the floor as he stood up. "I know it sounds crazy, Ruben, but something is wrong." He flicked on the bedroom light.

"Yes…It's wrong for you to turn on the light right now. Are you nuts? Listen to the rain outside. You can't go anywhere. There are no taxis, no buses, nobody around."

"I know, Ruben. I am crazy." His eyes were wide with worry. "I'm sure this is stupid. But I have to go back to the school right now."

Ruben sat up in the bed, rolled his eyes for a second and then conceded: "Fine. If you're going, then I'm going. There is no way you'll make it to the school alone. What do you think might be the problem?"

"I don't know. I don't know. I just feel like I should be there right now, like something is going to happen. Maybe it's this weather that's just driving me crazy. You know, the way they say horses get before earthquakes or whatever."

"Well," said Ruben, "you better hope horses don't go too crazy because we're taking Micha up to the Internado."

"Really?"

"There is no other way. I'm telling you. Look at the water pouring down. We'll be lucky if we don't get ourselves killed." Ruben started scrambling for his clothes. "But like we said, someone has to be the strong one when the other one loses it, right?" They wrapped up in plastic parkas to keep out some of the rain and headed down to the stable in the treacherous night.

Micha was kept at the hacienda of the mayor's brother-in-law. It was a relatively large ranch on the outskirts of town. It was in the opposite direction of the Internado, but Ruben was right, there was no other way of getting there.

When they reached the hacienda, the barn door was banging in the wind but, once inside, they found it eerily quiet, the animals attentive but not hysterical. Half a dozen horses, a pony, and a couple of mules stuck their heads out of their stalls to see who was coming. Miguel and Ruben heard the snorting of pigs, and the awakened pair of llamas used as pack animals stared strangely at them. The men leaned up against Micha's stall and took a breather.

"Are you sure you need to do this, Miguel?"

"Yes, I'm sure. Trust me," Miguel replied. "You don't have to go if you don't want to."

"Yes, I do. We're in this together."

He crouched into the stall and started to mount the saddle on Micha. She was a brave mare, she would make it.

Once on the road, she didn't seem to mind a bit. She seemed to sense the urgency of the mission and made no complaints as they galloped to the end of town and up the curvy highway. Her feet were steady on the wet pavement though the running water had eroded potholes nearly everywhere. It was as if she treated the added weight and difficult weather as a challenge, as she put her head down and pushed on.

Miguel wrapped his arms as tightly around Ruben's waist as possible while still holding the flashlight in one hand in case a car actually drove down this way. He didn't want to be the emergency that they went there to prevent. Micha began slowly on the upgrades and water battered their three faces.

"We may have to turn back!" Ruben shouted into the night.

"No!" returned Miguel, who dismounted the horse. He grabbed the reins from the front and led them up the hill. His legs strained to gain footing, withstanding the water and the cold. Lightning added surges of adrenaline. He trudged on, though, knowing that the road would slope back downward right around the bend. He knew every stretch of it for the hundred times he'd been down it. The road would slope down and then there'd be a straightaway and then a final curve before they reached the bridge at the inlet to Comalticán.

By the time they reached the top of the hill, Micha was panting heavily. Ruben got down to let Micha rest. And though the downhill section would be easier on the legs, the wind on this side of the hill slapped them in their faces. Two fallen trees lay motionless across the road. There was no way that cars would get in or out of here right now.

Micha carried them down the straightaway, slowly but steadily. There was only one more curve before they made it. As they approached the curve, they heard the roaring of the river. With every step closer, the noise grew louder and louder. As they rounded the turn, Comalticán came into view. The ridge of homes that normally lit up the nighttime with the lights in their windows was eerily dark save a couple of houses with solitary kerosene lamps. Miguel couldn't even make out the Internado, whose two streetlamps were the brightest in all of Comalticán. The power was most certainly out.

The worst problem was at the bottom of the curve. The bridge was partly knocked out, the water rushing between the two sides where the center of the bridge used to be. The water was rising slightly above the level of the road. The concrete held up better on the downstream side where only a small part of the bridge had been washed away. In the middle, there was about a two-meter gap of raging river. When the water came up above the level of the bridge, it splashed hard against the leftover railing.

They approached the bridge cautiously. Miguel could see the cemetery across the way and made out the fallen power post. A few people were gathered around it in a circle. They were little people, students. Something had gone wrong.

"The longer we wait to cross, the higher the river's going to get!" shouted Ruben over the turbulence.

"Look over there." He pointed toward the post. "Something's happened over there."

Micha's hoofs pounded the ground anxiously. Ruben prodded her closer. He nudged at her ribs. "Come on, Micha!" She looked at the water as it kicked up from the bridge, calculating her footing, doubting the jump.

"Let me get off!" said Miguel. "You can make it better without me."

"And then what are you going to do? You can't cross that by yourself, Miguel. I'm not leaving you here."

The bridge was a frightening trap. One slip and they'd all be in the river. There would be no hope for them. Then one of the students noticed them from the power post. She came running toward the river where she was waving her hands and screaming. It was Angelica, a slender girl from Miguel's class, and then she was joined by a small group of others who beckoned for them to cross.

Ruben dug his heels into Micha's sides. "Come on, Micha! Heeah!"

Miguel was jolted by her start, and he was unready for the gallop straight toward the bridge. He clung tight to Ruben's abdomen and stuck his head into Ruben's back looking straight down where he saw their thighs and feet and the oncoming wa-

ter underneath as they flew over the broken bridge. Water
pelted their legs but Micha's hoofs caught solid landing. Then
Miguel realized he could breathe again.

They hadn't a second to celebrate their triumph, for the
children were frantic and desperate. They ran back to the post,
signaling for Ruben and Miguel to follow.

Miguel recognized the Directora right away, lying in the
slippery clay. She was grabbing her left leg which she had suspended in the air and the falling rain. It was crooked at the
lower end and her teeth, so prevalent in her smile, were now the
largest feature in her grimace. She endured the pain silently.
The children had unsuccessfully attempted to ascend the clay
slope and seek help from the closest neighbor. Even on all
fours, the children could not make it up.

Beside them lay the fallen power post whose thick black
cable lay in the same brown clay. It had fallen like a tree, its
cement base unearthed like vanquished roots. The Directora
must have come to see the post when the power had gone out.
The children must have followed her or searched for her when
she hadn't returned. Their curiosity often got the best of them; a
lucky thing for the Directora this time.

Miguel pulled the black umbrella from the saddle on
Micha, not as protection from the rain but as a makeshift splint.
He pulled his belt off and wrapped it around the umbrella and
the Directora's lower leg. He was afraid she'd go into shock.
Then they lifted her up, careful of her leg, and placed her
tummy-side down in front of Ruben on top of Micha. There
was no other way.

Though Miguel thought of bringing her back down to Arbolito, the chance of crossing the river had greatly diminished.
They'd have to look for help here in Comaltícan.

Micha seemed to concentrate as she took the clay hill one
step at a time. Where a person's long foot and flat sole slid
down the clay, her round hoofs made her sink in. It was a tough
climb up, as she pulled her hoofs over and over against the suc-
tion of the clay but she made it in twenty arduous steps. The top
of the slope was level mud and gravel, an easy ride to safety.

As Miguel helped the children struggle up the slope in

Micha's footsteps, Ruben brought the Directora to the first house with light. The people there welcomed her as if she were Celine Dion and, having few medical supplies, called for neighbors who brought more neighbors, all with their favorite remedies. Before long, the Directora was on a queen-size bed with clean sheets, a towel on her forehead, tequila shots at her side complete with salt and lemon, and a doctor of gynecology from the social security hospital who had retired more than twenty years ago. He set her fractured leg in the company of about twenty neighbors, a handful of children, Ruben and Miguel, and, of course, a pair of neighborhood dogs.

Twenty-six

AS IF MOTHER NATURE HERSELF had finally exhausted her anger, the gray clouds opened to let the baby blue sky prevail again, the sound of birds chirping could be heard, and tiny flowers sprang up everywhere in multitudes of refreshing colors. The river water began subsiding, little by little. The government was aware the blocked highway would halt the commerce in the entire area, so bridge repair was urgent. Road workers came to rebuild the bridge in exactly the same design as before. Reinforcing or expanding the bridge would have taken a much greater investment. It was almost cheaper to rebuild the bridge every five years (and under a different elected official each time). The potholes would wait till summer.

The Federal Commission of Electricity repaired the downed electric cables within a week's time. It left enough time for the villagers whose homes were illegally connected to the cable to disconnect them and then reconnect them when the work was complete. Frequent roadside billboards warned of federal fines and prison time for electricity theft, but few were inclined to change their ways. They had never seen anyone get caught or punished, so why pay?

When the mayor came to examine the bridge, he stopped by the Internado and recognized the "heroes" with a small school ceremony and a certificate: "Ruben Sepulveda and Miguel Hernández are hereby recognized by the Municipality of Arbolito for Model Citizenship and Bravery." He also recognized Viviana Muñoz, his own niece, for "Leadership and Professional Guidance," for Miguel was clearly influenced by her fine tutelage. Even Micha, who bucked at seeing that bridge again, received a flower wreath around her neck and, her favorite treat, carrots. The Directora sat in her wheelchair, having become amazingly dexterous in the short time that she had it, and not a smidge less respectable. She carried on her duties as normal, including the clandestine organization of the recognition ceremony which she had secretly requested.

The part most appreciated by all was the *carne asada*. The mayor had dug into his pockets to bring a posse of cooks and their barbecues. The children enjoyed the treat of fresh tortillas, hearty meat slices, green guacamole piled high in great bowls, and spicy salsa. Afterward, the boys played soccer in a nearly dry field while the girls jumped rope and played tag and gossiped in the courtyard.

Miguel's true achievement was not earning the certificate but earning a spot back on the Directora's good side (which she knew he never had lost). Paradoxically, this recognition gave him a place not inside the Internado but outside it. It gave him the confidence to move away from the Internado to Ruben's apartment without jeopardizing his position.

Teresita made her way to the Internado for the ceremony, too, along with her entire family, whom she introduced as part of Miguel's family. They savored the tacos and used the event as their own celebration for having made it through another winter season. The river water had come dangerously close to their house. Teresita had had the entire family prepared to evacuate to the home of a neighbor and family friend downstream, whose house was a few meters higher than theirs. They would have been unannounced, but she knew that true friends never closed the door. The water never rose that high, though, and Teresita laughed with joy, "Guess we made it another year, right?"

Even Doña Conchita made it to the Internado with a real reporter, who interviewed the heroes, the witnesses, and the rescued. She thought a story about a local heroine would fit nicely into the museum at Arbolito. "Mayor's Niece Oversees Rescue" read the headline. Miguel was called "the trainee" and Ruben and Micha were mentioned as accessories.

The pleasant weather was a reprieve to everyone as people greeted one another in the town streets again, business started moving again, and the roads and floors were finally clean. Business at the candy store picked up, too, which was a help to Ruben. He was able to pay a nurse from a local clinic to check on his mother twice a day, as well as to clean up Carmelo's dog shit that was piling up in her patio. This was a relief to all three of them—Dahlia, Ruben, and Carmelo.

Children playing happily out in the yard made Miguel think how different this was from the rusty bars that surrounded his primary school in the northern so-called suburbs of Mexico City. So-called because they were closer to slums than suburbs. Children were kept indoors or inside the confines of the school grounds for fear of eight lanes of ruthless traffic on the freeway, rabid street dogs that roamed in packs scavenging the garbage heaps and taco stands, or any one of the neighborhood gangs of former students, then dropouts, who looked for entertainment, mischief, and sustenance amongst the weaker of the species.

Miguel loathed the unsupervised outdoors back then, only risking trips on his own to see his grandmother. But the school itself was the least of many evils; there he sometimes found solace, despite grumpy teachers and dreary schoolwork, with an occasionally enthusiastic instructor and his many friends. Little did he imagine he'd someday be in the position himself of making choices that changed the lives of children. God only knew if the grumpy teachers had long before been those same enthusiastic instructors.

The popular game back then was called "can." The kid who was "it" had to shake a gravel can between his hands and throw it as far as he could over his back, as a bride throws her bouquet. The other children would sprint away, in any direction from the can. When it finally stopped rattling, they were frozen in place and "it" obliged them to call their steps. They'd guess steps to the next person and, unless the first guessed correctly, the person whose guess was closest to being right was the next one to be "it." A pointless childhood game that required nothing but garbage and gravel was, at the same time, such a fond memory in the files of his brain.

The children at the Internado had their own version of the

can game. It provoked the same giggles and laughter, though, that brought back some nostalgia as he watched and listened to them. His primary school friends' faces appeared, their smiles and four-step handshakes, their jokes and nicknames, especially his best friend, Pedro. And then the abrupt words that took him back, "I think he's gay. My father likes him," from a quiet yet resentful little girl. Brenda's words took him back like time travel to Camila Martinez, who yelled on the school lot, "I think he's gay. Pedro likes him!" Those same words made his blood freeze in sixth grade and now again as the teacher of the sixth grade.

He snapped awake from his trance and saw Brenda there, unaware he was listening, as she chatted away with her classroom buddies on the field. His muscles automatically kept from moving like those of a scared dog who hid the same fear. Once again he felt cast into the limelight, now a "school hero" with his *best friend* Ruben. What business did they have mixing his personal life with his job? Would there be no place in this entire province free of constant judgment? The words that wounded him some fifteen years ago seemed no less venomous today.

He walked away from where he had heard them, hoping to not return the judgment on the little girl, hoping that her words would dissipate into the wind and that the other children's esteem for him would prevail. She was right, after all, to be resentful of a father who so obviously put her needs behind his own addictions. Miguel was ashamed to have fallen so easily into the trap of Tomas. What had he gotten for it? A weekend of pathetic punishment disguised as pleasure and now, potentially, months of rumors, reminders, and regret.

During that month that he had officially moved in with Ruben, hers had hardly been an isolated comment. True, he was ecstatic with the relationship. He had never believed that he'd be in such a functional relationship where "home" was actually a pleasant place to return to. He paid for it, though. When he had stayed with Ruben in the past, he hadn't actually moved out of the Internado. This time his absence from the teachers' quarters was more noticed, and not just by the students. The envy of other teachers sprouted up along with the wildflowers; they wished for an occasional moment in the spotlight, though they did little to earn it. And in town, Doña Conchita couldn't help but propagate the latest and exciting adventures of others that had nothing to do with her life.

Ruben began to visit the Internado more often again. His arrival was met each time with happy hollers from the black-haired sea. It only took a single comment or laugh or doodle, though, to remind them that the world was not one of blind love. Of course, those who sometimes created those comments or jeers might not have meant anything bad by it. They might not have realized that everything makes a difference. People sometimes get so used to their way of doing things that they don't consider the effects on others, the fire it may start or the fear it may create.

Ruben spent an afternoon reading to a small group of students in the shade of a pine tree. They were so enthused in his company. Imagine his surprise, then, at the penciled picture he found beneath the tree, two men together beneath that same pine tree, a heart between them, the letters "R & M," and one's hand on the other's crotch. Which student drew it was not obvious; but someone leaving the crinkled white ball in their sitting place, mocking the same person who dedicated his time to them, Miguel and Ruben could not understand. They tried to rationalize it, to think of it as children and their ignorance, but the message was clear. Miguel knew what it was like to be in a place where he didn't always feel welcome.

Miguel kept his promise, nonetheless. He was faithful to the work. He continued to give his heart and soul to the children who were equally constant in challenging him, demanding of him, and growing because of him. He had to admit, though, that the thought of the school year ending a few months down the road would be another fork in the road for him. Whether to stay or leave was becoming unclear. Abimael, Johana, and their friends were sometimes concerned as they watched Miguel and Ruben talk through the windows of the classroom. They looked so somber at times. And those children knew that the relationship, the one between them and their beloved teacher, was a two-way street—they had to give as much as they received.

Then Ruben stopped coming for awhile. Some of the children had a group meeting. Perhaps they had scared him away. The teachers were getting sick of them, they hypothesized. They had no idea that Ruben's mother was sick, that he went to bring her money, take her dog to the veterinarian, check in with the doctor, and stock her kitchen. Children always thought it was all about them.

Miguel stayed home at the apartment alone. He found it curious this time how occupied his evenings and weekends were. He checked on the employees in the candy store downstairs, reviewed the sales, swung by to check on Micha, and worked all night on lesson plans and grading. How had he ever had time to lose with Tomas when Ruben was gone the last time? There were so many productive things to do. But more than anything, he noticed how secure he felt tending the nest and knowing that Ruben would soon return.

Jesse took a particular liking to the Directora in her wheelchair. She was like a reincarnation of his mother. He was drawn to her like a magnetic pole. There was some yearning in him that tugged at his heart, and so he pushed her gladly at every chance. But it was more than the wheelchair; she transmitted a hidden energy to him.

The Directora was child-sized in her rolling chair. She rolled along the concrete courtyard, her eyes still overseeing the children as they played. Their eyes met hers at an even level but there was something about her that made them experience her differently. She was no typical adult. Her head seemed to float among the crowd like a spirit. Her demeanor was confident and omniscient yet gentle. She made them feel as if she could see right through to their young souls and timid hearts. She was the voice of wisdom and truth, as if her dark face had been here in the mountains for centuries, since the days when half-naked peoples hunted and roamed. She was a niece to the Sun.

That made her mother the Sun's sister. She was a storyteller whose tales passed on a culmination of lessons from generations of her people from the coast of Veracruz. Her ancestors had been there through the great storms of Mother Nature and

the great invasion of the metal-clad men from the east. They
had been there through foreign diseases and domestic slavery.
They wrought life from the very jungle around them and sang
songs from days even longer ago. They cherished the gifts of
the earth—bloody meat, fine fruits, long colored feathers, curv-
ing conches, and crystal clear water. The gods of the stars
watched over them through the tribulations which they sent
them so they could judge their valor and endurance. Their respect for natural order became entwined like the mix of blood
of local peoples and foreign ones in the DNA of their flesh, like
the mesh of ancient beliefs and Catholic ones. She was a testa-
ment to history itself. And now she sat in her wheelchair, the
sacred chief of this modern yet indigenous tribe, with the inheritance bestowed upon her by the centuries.

"Directora," Abimael and Johana asked her, after having
discussed the issue at length in their favorite leaning place in
the courtyard, "what is it about Maestro Miguel and Ruben?
Why have other kids talked behind their backs at times?"

She saw innocence when she looked into their eyes, and
openness. She gazed up into the blue sky where the stars were
obscured in the daylight. She answered in as few words as possible, "All people are of equal worth but that does not mean that
all people are the same. Many people, young and old, do not
understand that."

"Why do they spend so much time together and live together, Directora?" they clarified.

She paused again before she spoke. She had the type of answers that even children would wait for. "They make choices,
just as everyone does, about following their own paths and
about who they love."

They were still not satisfied. "But is it true, Directora?"
they urged her. "Is it true what those silly children say, that they
are not normal? That they are like perverts?"

"What do you think, children? Are they not normal? Are
they perverts?"

The two looked at each other. "No, Directora, they are not
normal. They have treated us far better than *normal* people.
They have taught us so much more."

"Then why are you asking me?"

"Well, it just doesn't seem fair," they explained, "that they treat us so well yet people do not treat them the same in return. People seem jealous. They act weird sometimes. As if it mattered to them. Even the other teachers talk behind their backs."

"You are wise people," she said to them.

"Why doesn't everyone just love them and let them be?"

"I don't know," she said.

"They are kind of like a nice couple, like Johana's parents, who try so hard for us."

"Yes, Abimael. Yes, Johana. You are right."

"Why don't they get married, then?" Johana asked her.

"My dear, they cannot get married in our churches nor in our state offices. They are not recognized like that here. That is only between a man and a woman, because that is what some people believe is right." Her patience did not diminish.

"Is that why they are not treated with the same respect, Directora, because they are not married? Because God did not make them a man and a woman? Maybe this is what is right for them."

"Maybe that is the answer, my dear. You will know the answer when it sits well with you. It will make you feel calm instead of apprehensive." She put her hand on the girl's shoulder. "Do you treat them with respect?"

Johana just nodded her head. She looked over at Abimael who was in agreement.

"Then you have done your part, children, and that is all that you can do."

"But we don't want them to get sick of these people and leave. We want to do more, Directora."

"Well, child, perhaps one day you will."

Twenty-seven

THE WHEELS OF HER WALKER clumsily ascended the steps of the municipal palace and they shuffled along the floor and down the hallways with such a clamor that the registrar, the safety inspector, the on-duty deputies, and the mayor's secretary were all warned of her arrival long before she actually got there. She had closed the museum for "official business" and was willing to wait until day's end to have the mayor's ear. But he attended to her rapidly and with earnest attention, for he was aware of her propensity to linger indefinitely and sermonize adamantly. It was more expeditious to let her have her way than to discuss the contrary.

"Children should learn the importance of history and culture, Mr. Mayor," she began, quite the same as the year before and the year before that.

"Yes, Doña, of course they should." He did believe in respecting his elders, after all.

"When I was a young girl, we felt it a privilege to visit the local museums and historical sites and hear about the important steps that our forefathers took to build the beautiful places that we enjoy nowadays. Children these days do not appreciate things. We must teach them."

"Yes, Doña. I agree entirely," he responded as emphatically as she spoke.

"You know, Mr. Mayor, that every March children come from the schools and the Internado to experience my museum and hear of the secrets that it holds."

"Of course, Doña."

"The city has always hired a bus to bring them, Mr. Mayor," she informed him.

172

"And we shall again this year. Just tell my secretary the date and I will see to it."

"I will check the calendar," she said, "and I trust you will see to it."

He nodded and smiled politely. "Of course, Doña," he said as he opened the door for her. She laboriously exited, mumbling random thoughts on the subject as she made her way back down the hallways and back to the museum, which she re-opened. She double-checked the empty calendar and then crouched down into a vinyl chair that squeaked as it accepted her weight. She sat there in the artifact-filled room, a stored artifact herself, and mumbled herself to sleep.

The Directora handed out the museum field-trip schedule the following week. Grades kindergarten through two on Monday, three through five on Tuesday, and six on up on Wednesday. Miguel's group would go on the last day, then, which gave him enough time to remind students of proper behavior and gratitude. They had no interest in the museum after having heard different versions of the same story every year they had been there, but they were excited at the simple hope of shooting baskets in the lone basketball court outside the municipal palace and running free in the town center park like the pigeons that had usurped it. With any luck, they'd have a basketball that bounced this year.

The February cold did not ease. It seemed to freeze the very marrow in Miguel's bones. And the weight of Miguel's duties at school did not let up, either. What was once such a joyful position was now a non-stop challenge. Nothing had changed but time and he wondered how he had had so much energy earlier in the year. He wasn't the only one. In truth, all of the teachers were feeling the weariness of the positions that they had chosen; it was simply part of the reality of teaching at that time of year.

For Miguel, though, living in town made transportation more difficult, and his day even longer. Then, coming to help Ruben in the candy store made even weekends feel a drag. The two were so focused on stocking the shelves and cleaning the floors and keeping the books that they had little time for each other. Again, it was reality. The field trip to the museum would be a fine change of pace. There would be one day he wouldn't have to worry about planning every second of activities for nearly fifty people.

The snickering he'd heard one day from a group of boys didn't help his attitude, either. Perhaps it wasn't even about him, but he felt a definite paranoia that people were constantly talking about him and Ruben. At times he ascribed it to their ages. Children would be children. Besides, no matter how he looked at it, it was still rewarding to guide them down their pothole-filled roads one step at a time. Perhaps it was their lack of awareness of his guidance that sometimes disappointed him. They walked in his steps but oftentimes hadn't the faintest notion of it. He still promised himself to never be an indifferent instructor. He knew it was worth it. If he expected students to maintain their motivation, he would have to be their model. The reality of the job, he began to understand, was that it was a long-term commitment. In the Normal school, they practiced hour-long lessons or week-long units, but a full year was a different story. And not only did he get to know the students profoundly, in the best and worst of ways, but that relationship was a two-way street.

The yellow bus had three children on every bench and a few kids surfing in the aisle, their legs wedged between other legs, stuck as if in quicksand. The children cheered in unison down the curves of the one-lane highway, held their arms up as if on a roller coaster, and leaned toward the far side on turns as if to tip the bus over. It was better that they get their giggles out now, Miguel figured, than to embarrass the school down at the municipal palace. The Directora rode in the front like the leader of a guerrilla pack, her sunglasses black like a movie-star's. She laughed with the children so long as their laughter did not suggest mischief.

When the children shuffled off the bus, the first group was herded through the arched palace entry, a remnant of the Spanish colonists, and directed into the first small room of the museum.

"In 1910, Pancho Villa himself, actually named Doroteo Arango, rode through these hills recruiting for his cause," began Doña Conchita, addressing the first round of students from where she sat in her chair behind her walker. Children crowded around the display case in the center of the room and overflowed through an open doorway into the second room that was separated only by a section of wall perhaps two meters long. Pictures hung crookedly all about the rooms, black and white portraits of dead people whose feet once stomped on these hills and whose seed still flourished in these parts, at least some of them. The children, pre-warned, maintained silence as they respectfully looked at a rusty pistol used to kill someone some time ago and dusty earthenware found somewhere in the hills in some cave or other. Doña Conchita's voice droned along steadily as the children stomped each other's feet and pulled at one another from below the line of sight. The line of students rotated throughout the room and chanted, "Thank you, Doña Conchita!" before they were excused to the free outdoors and the next group of kids was crammed in.

She started again, "In 1904, Pancho Villa himself, actually named Doroteo Arango, rode through these hills, recruiting for his cause... ."

Abimael and Johana ran outside in the town center. It was filled with trees and plants in a geometrical pattern, the typical gazebo the center point, and tall metal lampposts at every twenty paces. Those that were still intact held up five white globes, one in the middle and the four others like moons around a planet. Rose bushes occupied the majority of the fenced-in triangles. Pigeons paced the square in hopes of finding some leftover popcorn or a benevolent seed donor. Teresita stood near a dry fountain, her ponytail enveloped by a pink beaded net that she had found on a park bench, and it looked like the wagging tail of a short-haired dog. She was selling tamarindo suckers, brownish-red, spicy-sweet paste on wooden sticks wrapped in plastic.

The kids raced around the square, keeping Maestro Miguel

within earshot. His group was to be the last group for the tour, a perfect arrangement for those who wanted to take maximum advantage of the nearly clear sky for their outdoor enjoyment. Too soon the sky would darken and force them back inside.

Before long, they were herded not to the museum but to the cafeteria down the street, where they were treated to bean and cheese tacos and atole, a cornstarch thickened milk drink of chocolate and cinnamon. They packed the long straight tables of the restaurant in rows like Pancho Villa's army. Underage waitresses served the lukewarm tacos from beneath the folds of dishtowels in large baskets while the children drank their hot atole from warm cups between cold fingers.

Abi and Johana huddled together and discussed the apathetic face of Maestro Miguel. "He's not the way he used to be," they agreed.

"He probably thinks that we don't like him any more," said Abi.

"But we never did anything against him, Abi," Johana said.

"Of course we didn't, *guey*. We haven't done anything *for* him, either," he said to her.

"What are we supposed to do? What do you think we can do?" she said.

"I don't know, Johana. Show him that he belongs, just like he showed us," he said with an emphatic, wart-free face.

"Last group!" shouted the Directora. "Maestro Miguel's group to your feet! It's your turn to go to the museum! Be respectful, children!" And without any other word or instruction, they made their way to the door, arms at their sides, and marched to the museum.

"In 1908, Pancho Villa himself roamed these hills," started Doña Conchita who, by this time, was visibly tired. Her eyes blinked for long moments between sentences. The children watched her as they smiled and held in the noise of their giggles.

"Was he here for the Revolution?" asked Miguel loudly, helping to get her back on course.

She perked up in her chair, the big locks of her white hair jiggling like gelatin. "Who?" she asked.

"Pancho Villa," he clarified. "Was he here in 1908 for the Revolution?"

The children now could not control their laughter but she carried on in unawares.

"Pancho Villa was from the north, Maestro," she explained. "It was Emiliano Zapata that was here in the south."

She saw the children giggling but assumed it to be a response to his obvious ignorance.

"I thought you said it was Pancho Villa."

"No, no, young man," she chuckled with the children. "Emiliano Zapata was the one who came through here early on in 1906. That's when my parents came to see him right across the street in the town square."

Nobody even noticed Abi and Johana who were debating in whispered voices in the second room. Their eyes shifted in the darkening room's late afternoon light and their little hearts raced. They had finally discovered a way to give their teacher his rightful recognition.

As they exited the museum, Abi looked strangely chubby again, his waistline inflated, as they passed Doña Conchita in her fading consciousness. It had been a long day for her, with the telling of many stories, the recalling of many facts, and the sizing up of over a hundred future gossip-makers. As soon as they said their thank yous and passed the threshold, the children shot out of the museum door and fanned out in chaos about the town center. Miguel shouted at them to return but his calls disintegrated in the large outdoors. He tracked them down one by one and sent each directly to the waiting bus.

The ride back to the Internado was much more subdued, the students having filled their bellies and exhausted their energy. But for Abi and Johana, it was a crucial time of planning. They huddled near the back with a few confidants from the classroom, including little Rebeca, the now-conversational Xochitl and Misol-Ha, David the rodeo roper and guitar player, and several others of definite trustworthiness. Not included were Jesse, Orfil, Juan, Brenda, or any others of questionable reliability.

The children skipped dinner and began to put their plan into action. They loved the excitement that pushed adrenaline through their veins, but they each understood the seriousness of the situation and believed in the plan with utter sincerity. It could not be foiled or compromised in any way.

Though Miguel did not eat, he did have cafeteria duties. The little ones had gone to the museum earlier in the week so they had to be fed. He stirred and mashed the cauldron of brown beans and then served the bread from the Captain's encrusted trays. The Captain had kept a low profile for months, secluded in his bakery across the field, the smoking chimney and daily bread the only signs of his continued existence. The thought of the Captain and his episodes with him, which now seemed like ages and ages ago, made Miguel smirk. How naïve he had been just six months before.

The excursion into town had been exciting for the kids, but for Miguel, on constant vigil, it had been rather tiring. He felt like this job had had more and more days like that. He wished, at times, to feel the same enthusiasm that he felt a few months back. He knew that all teachers had a similar psychological cycle throughout the year, but more than that, right now, he wished to be in private with Ruben, snuggled against his partner and cocooned from the rest of the world.

Abi intercepted him outside the kitchen's back door with those same frantic eyes as when Don Coco came with the ice cream cart. *Now what is it?* Miguel thought, but then he immediately recognized something different in Abi's demeanor. He pulled at Miguel's hand and coerced him into the darkness without a single sound.

"Maestro," he whispered to Miguel behind the cafeteria.

"What is it, Abimael? What is wrong?"

Abi still held his hand and looked up into his eyes. "You know that we love you, right?"

"Um, yes." His response was delayed as he tried to figure out where this conversation was going.

"We do, Maestro. We love you," he said. Then he whispered, "Do you trust me?"

"Abi, what is going on? Did you do something?"

"Maestro, do you trust me?"

"Yes, I suppose I do trust you, Abi."

"Then follow me quietly. We can't let anyone see." And he tugged at his hand as he led him passed the dormitories, staying close to the buildings, and he headed for the storage room on the far side of the perimeter. He pulled the great door open and persuaded Miguel inside. Almost nobody saw them.

Miguel had entered this room on various occasions. The building was a single room that had four rows of heavy wooden shelves stacked to the ceiling with boxes. Some were marked "Christmas decorations" while others said "gardening" or "Señor Pacheco," probably some teacher's things from long ago and long forgotten, but most were stuffed to the top without any indication of their contents. The shelves stopped far short of the wall toward the back of the room, leaving an open space perhaps twelve feet wide and twenty feet long. Larger articles had been stored there in the open space but were now pushed between the aisles created by the shelves. A single light bulb illuminated the area from the end of an electric cord that hung from the ceiling.

Miguel searched the room for answers to the questions that were in his mind but Abi pushed him swiftly toward the open space with both hands on his back. "We haven't got much time, Maestro."

Ten children were lined up in the room, shoulder to shoulder, in their cleanest uniforms. Xochitl and Misol-Ha came in their colorful indigenous dress. There were roses in their hair the same red and yellow colors as the petals that were strewn all about the floor.

"Hello, children," he said. "What is going on? What is this?" he asked.

They stood at attention and smiled but did not answer him. It was Abi who spoke for them: "We want you to know that we care for you, Maestro."

"Thank you, Abi. I do know that. I am sorry if things aren't quite what they used to be."

"No, Maestro. It was our fault. You have always done your part. You have accepted us and helped us to learn. We owe you more."

Miguel was moved and responded slowly, though still conscious of his role as the adult here, the leader. He laughed lightly, nervously. "No, you don't owe me anything. I owe you."

"Maestro, we brought you something."

Miguel looked to the far side of the room. He recognized the patent leather knee-high boots of Teresa, and her broad and happy face appeared from behind the dark shelf. She smiled without saying a word and pulled at someone from where he was hidden. Ruben stepped out into the light. He was more handsome than ever, freshly shaved and standing tall in a black suit of antique design. He grinned proudly as he looked at Miguel, whose bafflement was replaced by amazement at Ruben's beauty.

Miguel's face lit up brighter than the bare light bulb, and he looked around the room at the children, whose eyes were glistening and whose faces could barely contain the smiles they had on their faces. "Well, thank you, children," he said as he began to embrace the children about him. "He looks fabulous. You didn't have to bother... ."

"That's not what we brought you, Maestro," interrupted Abi. "Ruben is just helping us."

Miguel let go of the children and returned to the place he was standing before them.

Xochitl and Misol-Ha had been given the next duty. In unison, they took a single step away from each other and revealed the item that they had brought for their teacher, their beloved friend. Their brown hands suspended the fluffy white wedding dress of Doña Conchita, slightly faded with time but still as beautiful as the day that she had been married in it several decades before. In fact, it was even more beautiful in this context away from the morbid display case of the museum, where it had been buried with Doña Conchita's soul the day it was placed there.

His math skills seemed to take a momentary dive for he still hadn't summed up two and two. "It's...it's...very pretty," he said.

The children and Teresita gazed at him, still smiling in anticipation. Everybody loved a wedding.

Then it clicked in Miguel's brain. Two and two were four. His eyes opened wide in surprise. His head swiveled slowly toward Ruben who awaited him in the faded black suit of Doña Conchita's betrothed. *Are you crazy?* he asked them in his mind. Ruben read his thoughts but only responded with a single shrug of his shoulders.

Misol-Ha and Xochitl placed the dress against Miguel's chest to size it up. It looked like a perfect fit, they agreed. They led him behind the shelves from where Ruben had appeared, a veritable changing room. *There must be some misunderstanding*, he thought, as he suddenly found himself in the darkness with a fifty year-old wedding dress and a dozen of his favorite people in the whole world waiting.

Did they think he was a woman? Did they think he was a drag queen? A transvestite? They seemed so determined, enthusiastic, and sincere. How could he let them down? The place was quiet despite their presence. He hadn't much time to think. How could he get out of this? What if someone else walked in? And marriage...did they expect him to get married? Not that he didn't want to, of course. Didn't he? This was just a game, really, a gesture. No big deal, right? He shook his head in the darkness and laughed to himself as he thought of home in Mexico City. In a million years he would have never imagined *this*.

Miguel remembered a guy back home in Mexico City who had begged on a street corner for years. He was a young man, really, whose name was Lalo but people could barely tell this by asking him. Only people who knew his family knew his name was Lalo, because they said it was. He had a nervous system disorder that prohibited him from speaking clearly. He could barely enunciate a single word intelligibly, not even his own name. The same disorder kept him begging on the street corner. He couldn't really walk; his form of movement was more of a crazy kind of strut, rather like a drunken, ludicrous hip hop dancer. It wasn't out of meanness that people would laugh; his walk was just so out of the ordinary to people who had never seen him before. But when they looked at his face and the exertion that his walk required of him and the snot that was encrusted on his unshaven face because he couldn't lift his hand to clean himself, they were often inspired to deposit a coin in the bag that hung from his neck. A sign that read "God Bless You" had been woven into the cloth bag by his siblings. With every donation to the bag, he grunted neither "thank you" nor "may God be with you" but "Give it your all!" He even said it to people who didn't donate. He must have said it five hundred times a day—"Give it your all! Give it your all!"

Lalo did not feel sorry for himself. He was simply different. When people laughed at him or looked at him, he believed it to be a natural reaction, like the way people might respond to someone particularly tall or fat, or maybe someone whose legs had been chopped off. They didn't mean anything by it. In fact, he was aware that it motivated them to give up their money. It sparked an idea in his mind.

After a long discussion, or whatever his interaction with his sisters could be called, he recruited their help. They did not understand him at first, and they didn't want him to humiliate himself, but he was a stubborn Taurus just like his grandfather. He went out the next day in drag, complete with his older sister's dress, his younger sister's cheap makeup, and someone's wig. Perhaps it was his way of spiting the gods or an expression of his cynical sense of humor, but it made him feel liberated from the confines of his crippled life. It didn't earn him much more money, though, so he didn't continue with this costume, figuring it wasn't worth the effort. But he did show the people of the world, or his neighborhood anyway, that he wasn't afraid, nor should they be. Lalo was not a beggar and he wasn't a drag queen, either; he was a motivator. If Lalo could do it, then Miguel could do it, too.

With a certain doubt, he untied his shoes and placed them side by side against the shelf. He pulled off his socks and the soles of his feet felt the cold and earthy floor. There were no appropriate shoes for him, so he'd go barefoot. As he took his shirt and pants off, he heard the animated whispers of his waiting audience. He sucked in his breath down to his nervous stomach, wondering if he'd regret this day. He was in the final moment before doing something that he might later wish he hadn't. It was his final chance to turn back.

"Give it your all," he thought one more time. He looked into the darkness at the end of the aisle of shelves, where the single bulb cast distorted shadows. Give it your all...to this job, to these children, to this relationship, to this life. What more did he have to lose, anyway? He imagined how he might regret *not* having done it.

The dress slipped on easily enough. It had a smell of dampness and age, though the dress, stained brown with time, was surprisingly soft and comfortable. Miguel tightened up the laces at both sides of his ribcage. His hands cupped the small pouches at his chest and it occurred to him to stuff his socks in the emptiness. But this was not a fashion show; he thought the better of it. He ran his hands through his hair as if to prime it for the veil that clipped on with a comb-like plastic brooch. He arranged the veil in front of his face as if to hide not his innocence but his embarrassment. His heart beat wildly. Finally, he took one last breath of stale storage room air before stepping out into potential humiliation.

The children had formed two lines on either side of the small space. When he stepped out, he looked down at the rose petals on the floor and the white cloth that enshrouded his body. When he raised his head, he looked through the thin veil first down the aisle to where Ruben stood up straight beside Teresita. He then glanced around to see the beaming faces of the children to whom laughter had not occurred. It was probably one of the proudest and most beautiful moments in all their lives. It was neither a silly game nor a whimsical gesture but a true confirmation. Their collective speechlessness made tears well up in Miguel's eyes. Far from feeling ridiculous, he felt enveloped by their gift as by the veil about his head.

Then he focused on Ruben, who stood there grinning joyfully. In such a short time this man had become such an important part of Miguel's life, indeed, the most important part. He hadn't expected to ever feel this way again after his incarceration with Salvador. There Miguel stood in what might have seemed a mock rite of passage, an appeasement of the children, a skit. His heart was now filled with the weight and splendor of this moment's reality. It had required no proposal, no invitations, no bouquet, no reception, and very little planning. It required only the belief of these twelve jury members. Because they believed in it, it was real.

He took a single step forward. Two of the children raised their hands to their faces while Xochitl and Misol-Ha grabbed each others' hands behind their backs. Abi, at the end of one row, stood tall and proud, as if admiring his own work of art. Johana's face was bright. It was like her fantasy in a forest, a glorious princess in a white wedding dress with a long train floating behind her, and a nobleman at the altar. Teresita attempted to recall the words of the priests that she had heard in her lifetime, on television and with relatives, but not her own wedding, since she had never actually had one. Ruben, on the other hand, took in the incredible moment and trusted that the words would come to his mouth when the time was right.

The Directora was observant, patient, and prudent. From her office, she had heard the click-clocking of Teresita's boots in the entrance hallway. She sensed the absence of some of her favorite people. She heard something in their silence, smelled something in the air. She saw the slightest glimmer of light from between the wood panels that formed the storage room wall halfway across the campus. Her approach had been nonchalant, investigative. There was more to learn by allowing whatever was going to happen than by interceding and aborting it. Whatever it was, she knew it was better that she discover it than anybody else. She certainly did not want to attract the attention of others, for there might be delicate human feelings involved.

Her hands had been gentle on the metal doorknob of the storage room door. Her feet, free of the wheelchair, limped quietly. She intended to react to the situation, whatever it might be, and not let the situation react to her. She positioned herself stealthily in the darkness of the row of shelves closest to the door, her shortness removing any need to crouch. She could make out the back of Ruben and the straggly hair of Teresita from her location. She suddenly felt protective. She waited in the distance like a mother bird might watch her chicks' first flight. Sometimes the best teaching occurred in the absence of the teacher.

Miguel made slow steps past the children, who viewed his face through the white veil. He felt ambivalent, both secure and vulnerable, both excited and afraid. He stepped fifteen paces or so in what seemed like half an hour, until he stood face to face with Ruben and in front of Teresita, who had taken her place, as the only other adult in the room, as the mistress of ceremonies. She adjusted the Irish cap on her head to an appropriate tilt, pulled up the sleeves on her jade green polyester blouse, and cleared her throat dramatically.

"Our Father, who art in heaven," she began in a bold voice that made Abi cringe for fear of discovery. She lowered her voice to a near whisper, "I haven't taken confession for a few years, now. That doesn't matter, does it?" Those who heard her answered with shrugs of their shoulders. "Okay....Our Father, who art in heaven, hollow be Thy name.

"Beloved friends, we are here in this storage room, right? In secret, right? Because you asked me to bring Ruben here, since there was not any other place to do this. I mean, where else would we have gone, right?" She chuckled to herself. "But that doesn't matter, right?

"I mean, we should have been in a church, right? I guess. But not everyone can do this sort of thing, you know. Imagine if there were like a brother and a sister, right? I mean, they couldn't, either. Anyways, that doesn't really matter right now, either." She maintained the smile on her face but inside her heart started to race. She had obviously never done such a thing before and she meant not to mess it up but the memories of weddings weren't exactly coming to mind. It might have helped if she had paid attention to them.

"Dearly beloved friends, we have come here to celebrate the friendship, or, you know, of Señor Ruben here to my right," she took his hands and raised it like a boxer's, "and, um, Señor, or Señora, um, Señorita, well, Maestro Miguel here to my left." She then raised his hand in a similar fashion. Johana smiled out of politeness but was not convinced that this was going the way that they had hoped.

Then, from the darkness, the outstretched hand of the Directora deliberately tapped Teresa's shoulder. Teresa looked at her as her brain registered a new piece of information. As if someone had turned up the switch on a dimmer, the twenty-four eyebrows in the room rose in unison. The Directora motioned Teresita to the side as she took her place where Teresita had been speaking. Miguel opened his mouth to say something, though he did not know what it would be, for his heart had fallen from a cliff and had surely taken his voice box down with it.

The Directora's warm hands grabbed and lowered the hands that Teresita had raised like those of boxers in a ring and simply held them for a moment, as if to transfer her good intentions and sooth their thoughts. When she let go, Miguel raised his hands to pull back the veil and see her better.

Her voice was quiet and her words slow, as if written and rehearsed especially for this occasion: "Children and Teresa," she paused to look at the audience, "we have united here with two beautiful people who have a true affection for one another. This is not the beauty on the outside that I refer to, but the beauty that people can have inside, regardless of what they look like or what they are wearing or whether man or woman. So we unite not to judge but to celebrate a decision these two have made to be together and work together toward happiness."

All listened thoughtfully and attentively, soaking in the words as if Plato had been addressing them.

"Let it be clear," she continued, "that we are to never think of them as a man,"—she held her hand toward Ruben,—" and a woman,"—she indicated Miguel. "Neither of these men is a woman. Rather, they stand here today representing the balance of personalities, talents, and beliefs that make a relationship greater than the sum of its parts. They represent the black and the white, the strength and the delicacy, the masculine and the feminine, and the left and the right that we people can find between us and also within each of us. It is this balance that makes a relationship healthy.

"We are all both teaching and learning here in a moment that we must never forget, that we must cherish, and that we must also protect from ridicule, for there are ignorance and fear that we have all witnessed outside these wooden walls. Your presence here and the creation of this rite show your own wisdom, sincerity, and love. Let this be considered sacred for all of us. If any of you do not agree, then promise silence and take your leave now."

All the children stood there decisively, heads up proudly. Though they did not all capture or understand every single word, each of their young minds comprehended the seriousness and power of the proceedings.

"Very well," she said. She turned her face to address the man at her right. "Ruben, you have been an honorable assistant to this school and a worthy partner to Maestro Miguel. You have become a part of our family through your positive deeds and your generosity. You have willingly given of your time, resources, energy, and soul. We give you the same respect that you have shown us time and time again. Now, I invite you to express yourself and your part in this ceremony."

He licked his lips as he looked at her and then looked at beautiful Miguel in front of him. He knew the words would come.

"You have opened your doors to me and opened your arms to me," he started. "Though I did relatively well in school, I never felt the closeness with the others like I feel with you." He turned his head alternately to the Directora and to the children. "I want to thank you for embracing me so dearly. Though I first came here for Miguel, I now feel a separate attachment to you too. Count on me to give the same affection that you are showing me.

"I never imagined that I would be in this situation. My relationships have always been very personal and private. But, let me say this," he now turned his gaze directly to Miguel, "Miguel, I had always dreamt that I would find a person with whose life my life could meld. I enjoy our intimacy together and I also value the way that we have expanded our relationship to include people like those who are here, my family, and even Micha. I cherish what we have and the promise of ever greater times. Though I had never thought of marriage exactly, I freely

commit who and what I am to you. I proudly promise to give all
that I have in my being to this relationship and to the prospect
of an ever-better future." By this time, his two hands had found
Miguel's and their eyes were fixed upon each other.

The room was quiet for a moment. Then, without a cue,
Miguel began his discourse: "I came here on a windy road that
passed through the foggy heights and the river-bed bottoms of
these green, faraway mountains. I came to find myself and,
therefore, fill the hole that I never could in Mexico City. I had
no idea that the crazy bus ride of shifts and turns was the start
of the same kind of life here. I imagined everything would be
docile and simple. I guess the human experience is just not so.

"I have been on a high road with Ruben though I do feel
that I've fallen into a rut here at the Internado. It is a heavy responsibility that I feel, and I have let that weight drag me down.
I am sorry if I have betrayed you," his face now turned toward
the children. "I am sorry if I have not given you what you deserve. You have reminded me how real our work together is for
everyone and what powerful people surround me. I forget, at
times, that you give as much or more than you take. Thank you
for the gift of your presence and acceptance. The least I could
do was put on a stolen dress for you."

The group laughed momentarily in much-needed comic relief.

He turned back again to his partner. "Ruben, something in
my soul still cannot believe that our relationship hasn't become
a failure like my pessimism caused me to expect. When I wake
up, you are still there and still as good to me as you have always been. You are amazingly confident and strong, even when
the thunder comes and the rain falls down." This brought a big
smile to the Directora's face where it stayed, as she quietly ob-
served from barely a meter away. "You have taught me to see
that life can be different...and better.

"I do not know what destiny has in store for me, or for us.
But I do believe in it, whatever it is. It's as if the energy of the
world moved all the pieces into place for us and we needed
only to act upon our good fortune and accept it. Now, it is our
own energy that will determine the outcome. For my part, I

promise to give you my energy each and every day. Though there may be no signed papers here, it is our decision to be together that gives it legitimacy. And though we may not be in a cathedral, I believe that God is present with us today and has been from the start. May He bless us and be with us for all of our days."

Then the room was quiet again until Teresita, from behind the Directora, pronounced loudly, "Amen."

The Directora smiled again from where she presided and then once more took their two hands. Abi and Johana looked at each other. "The rings," they said, "the rings!" They looked over at Misol-Ha and Xochitl, who had no idea about the appropriate sequencing of things. Abi and Johana pulled at their elbows and led them down the short aisle to where Ruben and Miguel stood.

"We have rings?" the Directora inquired. Abi and Johana nodded their heads. "Okay, we may now exchange the rings."

The two black-haired girls pulled from beneath their colorfully adorned white dresses a pair of identical woven bracelets. They were about half a centimeter wide and depicted the change from day to night with a bright orange Sun against a yellow sky. The sky then changed to dark orange and red and then the blue sky of the night accented by white and yellow stars. They offered the bracelets to the young men with outstretched hands. "For your many days and nights," iterated quiet Misol-Ha.

"Okay," corrected the Directora, "you may now exchange the bracelets." And the couple took turns fastening these new symbols, depictions of time, balance, and the cycle of life upon their wrists, Ruben's bracelet beside the silver one already given to him by his mother.

Twenty-eight

SPRINGTIME FLOWERS were the freshest thing the museum had seen for a long time. The Directora waited inside, the door was wide open but there was nobody there. Then she heard the scrapings of Doña Conchita's walker from down the hall, a slow and menacing sound.

"It must have been the school children," she explained in a disturbed voice to the police chief who walked at her side. "They were the last ones to visit," she said as the two entered the room. Their eyes opened in surprise to see the Directora sitting there so early in the morning. Doña Conchita ignored the flowers in her hands. "It's a good thing you're here, Directora. We have a very serious matter to discuss."

"Oh?" said the Directora with utmost sincerity.

Doña Conchita remained standing, her hands gripping the handles of her walker with fury. "Yes! It seems we've had a robbery! And it was one of your students."

"What?" said the Directora. "How dare they!"

Doña Conchita signaled her over to the other room.

"I'm sure we'll get to the bottom of this, Doña. What ever was stolen?"

"Of course they'd take what was most valuable..." The mouth of her wrinkly face stayed open and her droopy eyes stared blankly. "It was my dress," she completed her sentence slowly as she looked at the display case where her dress used to be, and found that her dress and the suit lay there just as they always had.

The police chief stood behind the two women with this thumbs wedged in his black leather belt beneath his round stomach. He looked at the Directora and their eyes met and rolled upward together as if agreeing on Doña Conchita's senility.

190

"Perhaps you couldn't see them for the glare of the light," proposed the Directora as charitably as a cat.

"I guess I won't be needed, then, ladies," said the officer as he stepped out.

Shocked, Doña Conchita hadn't moved from where she stood. But her eyes slanted suspiciously as she took in the condescending smile of the Directora. The Doña suddenly felt like the helpless prey of this feline. She had seen so many better days when her blood ran fast and her heart pumped strong. She barely had the energy to complain anymore, let alone stand in the ring for a cat fight.

"Don't feel bad, Doña," said the Directora, "It could happen to anybody." She put her hand on the old woman's shoulder and pushed the colorful bunch of flowers to her bosom. "The children sent you these flowers in gratitude for their enlightening and liberating experience."

Somehow this marriage reminded Miguel of his time back in Mexico City. The rain in the summertime is as predictable as government corruption, yet still people get caught in the deluges. A few years before he had left for the Internado, Miguel had been visiting a friend down in Coyoacán, a quiet, upscale, artsy neighborhood some ways south of his house. On his way home, the rain turned on like a fire hose, and he found himself walking blocks and blocks in a downpour that changed the sidewalk curbs into riverbanks. His clothes were like steeped sponges, both from the falling water and the splashing of cars. His shoes squeaked at every step, and his wet socks, stained black from his fake leather shoes, would be pried off and wrung out at home hours later.

A week afterward, the skin from the bottom of his feet began peeling off like the shells of hard-boiled eggs. He thought of a guy whom he knew named Antulio. He had met him at a party that was thrown by a gay friend and his three gay roommates. Antulio was being treated for AIDS at the free clinic that was funded (or under-funded) by foreign charities and supplied with leftover drugs by American pharmaceutical companies in search of tax write-offs and good public relations. Though he had many visible sores and was emaciated, the first thing they asked to see each time he went to the clinic were his feet. Miguel presumed that they could tell something about his condition just by looking at his feet. Fucked-up feet meant fucked-up health.

So the first thing he thought of when the skin was falling off his feet was Antulio and HIV. He didn't say anything to anyone, least of whom his mother, of course, not wanting to hear the bickering sermons and endless I-told-you-so's. But he did head for the clinic, where he was immediately asked to take off his shoes.

By that time, there were large patches of skinless meat on his heels and on the balls of his feet. The raw tips of his toes were red and nearly bleeding. He could hardly walk without wincing. He was sure he was infected, and it must have been late stage, too. They drew his blood, and he then agonized for two weeks .

He had not only suffered the pain of every step he took and the shame of secrecy and anxiety, but he contemplated the early end of his life, the slow death made even more tortuous by his family, as well as the humiliating disintegration of his physical being. He imagined the longed-for dreams that would never come true and the exotic places that he would never witness. He pictured his gravestone, untended and forgotten in some corner of a cheap cemetery. When they told him he was HIV-negative and prescribed him anti-fungal cream for a severe case of athlete's foot, it was like the reincarnation of hope itself.

He suddenly saw his entire life from a different perspective. He laughed at the little things. He dreamt anew. Of course, since nobody close to him knew of his struggle, it was an entirely internal experience. To everyone else, everything was the same; but to him, the world was a new place.

Now, in Comalticán and Arbolito, far from that trying time in Mexico City, he fingered his new bracelet and felt like hope had arisen again. In town, the streets seemed quaint and clean. The candy tasted sweet and rich. People were friendly and cheerful. Ruben and he worked the same routines but did them while whistling. The Internado was like a place that he recognized, but his eyes opened up to its newness and splendor. There was green grass he had never noticed before and birds singing in the blue air. There were smiling children, playful dogs, skillful teachers, even good-tasting beans and bread.

Miguel also refocused on the children. He knew that the work with them would sometimes taste bitter. But he also reminded himself that these were children—young people without all of the faculties of adults. They were the sons and daughters of faraway construction workers, road builders, rock movers, harvesters, folks who sold sugar cane to infrequent cars that they stopped on the highway, folks who were unemployed or uneducated, who hunted, gathered, borrowed and bartered. He remembered again that he was their only hope. He could not count on them to fulfill his needs, but he must fulfill theirs; he must show them the way.

His eyes frequently fixed on his bracelet, this inconspicuous trinket that represented a life-changing experience. The threads reminded him of pixels on a computer screen, the squares of solid colors comprising each image. His days seemed just like that bracelet, with the Sun in a clear sky. They were peaceful again, pleasant and productive. The children were like the sunshine itself that made the daytime warm. But the bracelet revealed the truth. The nighttime was coming.

Public schools, including the Internado, did not celebrate Easter, unlike Christmas, or carry out any Easter-related festivities. This, of course, was because schools were secular. However, schools were closed all of Easter week, which was the first week of April this year. Families came from the hills to pick up their children without the fanfare of the Christmas festival and, before Miguel knew it, the children had said their goodbyes and the Internado was vacant. He hadn't thought about it much until now, but a certain fact was becoming more and more obvious—the school year was nearly over.

Seven months ago it had seemed like he'd be here forever and that the year would never end, yet now the time was fleeting. What had been more like an insignificant fact someplace in his brain now seemed like an inevitable approach to the edge of a cliff. He would have to make a decision. He was a student teacher, and there was no job promised to him here. There were no teachers planning to leave, after all, and all of the class-rooms were occupied. The understanding at the Normal school was that student teachers do their year of service and return to the city. But he was married now, right? And what of his students, with whom he had renewed his relationship? Then again, even if he were to stay somehow, he would have a whole new set of faces to work with. Another big decision to make... would life never let up?

He found solace on Micha's back, soothed by the rhythmic sound of her hoofs on the ground, Ruben's strong torso to which he clung, and his back on which he rested his head, en-joying the moment and postponing thoughts about anything bigger. It was their first ride up the river since it had subsided to its normal levels. Birds were dancing in the air and chirping in the trees, insects buzzed and flew about, and the clear water rippled and flowed. Miguel breathed in with eyes closed and then exhaled slowly to breathe in once more.

Signs of winter's fury were all about. There were mangled branches stuck high up in the trees and miscellaneous things like tree trunks and fence posts, even a child's bike, wedged in cracks between boulders and bases of trees, wherever the forces of nature might have left them. Huge uprooted trees lay about waiting for the termites to get them or the next storm to move them along.

Miguel and Ruben expected their beach to be different or maybe not even there at all. They didn't expect it to be four times bigger and more inviting than ever. Fine sand formed a half-moon where it met the river. It came up steeply from the rivers edge to form a solid beach bank high above the water. Not a single rock or branch or piece of trash was upon it. It was as if the god of the river or of the mountain invited them home.

They took the invitation. They sat directly on the sand to feel the grains between their fingers. They took off their shoes to feel the same between their toes. Then they lay together in the nature, moment by moment feeling closer and closer. Their hands traveled their bodies while their lips met. Before long, shirts became untucked, pants become unbuttoned, then clothes came off piece by piece, until finally they made love on the sand, on their beach, beneath the trees and before the gods that presently presided.

———————————

Their next trip was out to Molino, where Dahlia lived. Ruben hadn't spoken with his mother for a while but had been faithfully depositing the money in her account every week as he had promised. When they entered the house, it looked quite the same, but it smelled like dog piss.

Carmelo, the Chihuahua, was the first to greet them with yappy barks and less than ferocious snarls. He was Dahlia's new son, but far from a perfect child. He had chewed a sizeable hole in the seat cushion of the living room set and marked his territory in every room of the house. Though a tiny dog, his little hairs were all over the place; they had proven impossible to keep off the furniture and floor for any reasonable amount of time. He had nothing to worry about, however, for his big eyes, floppy ears, and underbite smile had won Dahlia's heart over in the first week that she had him. When it came to children, she had learned to take the good with the bad.

At least she was more mobile. The wound in her leg had finally closed up and her strength had returned enough for her to walk about the house. She could make it well enough to the bathroom and front door, and had learned to cook while sitting down. She was thrilled to see them both and gave them the most genuine of hugs, the kind that last longer than normal with not a single moment of awkwardness, as she said to them, "It's good to be close to family." Her prognosis was positive for the time being, although she'd be checked semi-annually for recurrence or metastasis of the tumor. Her faith in God was as strong as ever, and there were numerous members of her church willing to lend a hand when she needed anything.

Mosquitoes in Molino were a problem. The small dam that had been built on the river for the mill created numerous standing pockets of water, the perfect breeding ground for the biting bugs. Dahlia was quick to remind anyone who was careless enough when entering, Miguel in this case: "Close the screen door! Close the screen door!"

It reminded him of the cockroach infestations they had at times back home. His mother had always said it was because of the dirty dishes piled up in the kitchen, the food bits on the floor, the lack of attention that they all had for the house and their chores. Miguel knew it wasn't true, though. Cockroaches were in everyone's house, all the time, but more in the hot weather. They would climb up the walls, walk right over your back in the middle of the night, scurry in the cracks, and duck between spices and breadcrumbs and the oil bottle in the kitchen cabinets. It was not as if they were spying, waiting for the alleged pile of dirty dishes. They lived there.

One day she ran from the kitchen into the living room where the entire family was sitting. She had the most horrified expression on her face. "Raid—Home and Garden!" she screamed, "Raid—Home and Garden!" She expected them to all get up and dash for the insecticide, but instead the whole family burst out in laughter. Even she couldn't resist the moment and her look of horror changed to laughter, too.

She had found a black leg floating in the top of her coffee as she poured in the powdered creamer. It looked quite strange to her at first, the jagged edges, the knee joint, the tiny claw at the tip. Then it clicked in her head. She looked through the tiny hole in the nearly empty plastic bottle of coffee creamer. Sure enough, there was a four centimeter carcass of brown cockroach at the bottom. Their laughter had become stunted a bit because everyone had used cream from that bottle. But the moment was never forgotten.

From that time forward, anytime anyone in the family saw an insect in the house, they screamed, "Raid—Home and Garden! Raid—Home and Garden!" Sometimes they sang out in unison as they jumped about frantically but it always ended in laughter. Ironically, he thought, such an insignificant snippet of life represented one of the few joyous times with his family that he could remember. He wondered how his mother might be now, what the current cockroach count was, how sealed the coffee creamer might be, how close she kept the Raid—Home and Garden, and how often she thought of him.

Twenty-nine

"WE'RE GOING TO START A PROJECT TODAY, class," were the first words that he said to the children upon their return from break. "I know that many of you had a chance to spend time with your families over the break, and with your mothers. I know that some of you no longer have your mother, or maybe haven't seen her for a long time. I understand that, for I have not seen mine, either. So, in honor of the upcoming Mother's Day in May, we will be writing an essay!"

"Ughh," they all moaned, as their shoulders dropped.

"No, no. This is an important essay. It is a chance for you to tell about your mother. In addition, we will be creating an homage in the form of an altar to all of our mothers for, even though we all have different relationships with our mothers, it is one of the few things that we all have in common—we all have mothers. We will all discuss an artifact, an item that represents our mothers, that we will place on the altar. We will write a letter or an essay to explain why we chose that particular artifact, and what the symbolism is of the item."

"Do you mean like the shrine at Day of the Dead?" they asked.

"Something like that," he answered, "but most of your mothers are not dead."

The children's facial expressions changed. Most were enthusiastic and pensive, wondering which item might represent their relationship with their mother the best. But others felt a silent pain. Jesse's pain was dull, one of longing and sadness. Others felt homesick when they thought of their mothers. Abi's sensation was more like that of a dagger being stuck in him in the darkness where he was abandoned and left to fend for him-

197

self. Miguel knew the task would not be as easy as it sounded for many, including himself.

The daylight hours increased and so did the temperature. With each day Miguel seemed to appreciate more and more the pleasantries of his work, the spirit of the children, the quiet times at home with Ruben, the frolicking water of the river, their beach, the bustle of the town, and the frequent meeting with familiar faces in the street. Each day seemed to pass faster and faster like grains in an hourglass that seemed to fall faster when there were fewer and fewer of them. June was known for graduation, supposedly an advancement to bigger and better things. To where would he advance? The thought spurred the fluttering of butterflies in his stomach, like the ones he felt when he got here, only bigger and stronger ones.

Mother's Day came faster than the gas guys who block your line when you haven't paid the bill. The class made a shrine of an old table that was crammed into the corner of the classroom. As the children came up to the table, their faces showed the reverence for the one topic that no one had the audacity to disrespect. They read their essays one by one and left the artifacts on the shrine. There was a pineapple, a multi-colored scarf, a tea cup, a hand-held broom, a plastic red heart, a tortilla holder, a miniature carved cane, a shot glass, a string of plastic beads, and a chocolate bar. Jesse spoke with a cracking voice and watery eyes. He left a candle in a vase with a portrait of the Virgin of Guadalupe that he lit at the end of his reading.

Then it was Abimael's turn. He stood up confidently but did not make eye contact with anyone on his way to the front. He unrolled a crinkled piece of paper filled with erasures and crossed out words. He held it firmly between his hands and began to read:

Dear Mama,

Thank you for walking with me down the slippery trails. Thank you for taking me with you when you knew I would have otherwise been left. Thank you for tucking me in the warm bed and leaving the night-light on. And for running your fingers through my hair and humming some songs to me. Thanks for showing me how to eat right with a fork and a knife and also for reading the books to me like *The Three Bears* and *Aladdin*. Thanks for showing me that you still loved me even when I was ugly and short and fat. I know that you didn't give birth to me, but I don't really care. Since you took me into your pretty home next to your coffee roaster with your daughter and husband and workers, it must be because you truly thought I was important. You didn't care that you didn't give birth to me, so why should I? I don't think I would have made it without you.

That other lady, Moo-Moo I used to call her. She must have thought that this place was like some old garbage dump and that she finally took out the trash. I'll bet Moo-Moo doesn't know that favor that she did for me. She took me outside the darkness and brought me to the light. A guy can dream out here in the hands of people who care about him.

Moo-Moo, you stay in your cold cave and may you never come out. Just be careful it doesn't fall in on you. The gods have a way of getting back, don't they? Isn't that what you told me? Oh, and say hi to the bats for me, those flying rats, since you speak their language, too. Don't worry about me, Moo-Moo, I have a new mother that is better than you.

His hands wiped tears from both sides of his face that had dripped down his cheek and hung like stalactites from the bottom of his jawbone. He snorted in the mucus that had accumulated in his nose and then his eyes took a quick survey of the class before he looked down toward the floor again. Then, he chanced a look at Maestro Miguel, whose quiet smile was like a harness around his heart.

Johana sat near the front, and she knew that he knew that she was there for him. She was happy to share her mother with him, though she had never known he felt like this.

Finally, Abimael pulled out from a jacket pocket a terra-cotta coffee cup, with the hand-painted image of two children walking beside a woman in a large dress. He placed it on the altar. The woman's hair seemed to blow far in the breeze and the sunshine seemed to kiss their faces.

Miguel stayed in the classroom after class. His chin sat in the palm of his hand and he stared at the red brick wall across the room from him. He hadn't realized that teaching would be such an emotional job. They were not always happy emotions, but they were always deep ones. Happiness was not always a necessary feeling, he thought; it was the depth of emotion that gave richness to life.

He stood up at his desk and gathered his coat and backpack. He did not have kitchen duties that afternoon. Then he took a last glance at the shrine to motherhood and all the assorted things upon it. Not a single person had failed to complete this project, not even himself. He recognized the spray can in a corner of the table, the one behind the pineapple, the only item left unexplained to the class: Raid—Home and Garden.

He closed the classroom door behind him and hurried out the gate. It was Mother's Day and he had a phone call to make.

The trip home was unusually fast. The bus showed up by the cemetery almost immediately and the driver was crazier than a taxi driver in Mexico City. *Maybe the driver has to get home and call his mother, too*, Miguel thought. When he climbed up the stairs to the apartment and opened the door, the telephone seemed to be the largest feature of the entire place. It seemed to be goading him. His feet started to get cold. He didn't need to call her, it wouldn't be the first year that he hadn't. He had been here almost a full school year and she had never called him. Perhaps she didn't have the number but, if she had tried hard enough, she could have gotten it.

He thought of Abimael and his bravery, his willingness to stand up and say what he felt. If a twelve-year old boy could do it, he could too. At any rate, probably nobody would pick up at home. He could just leave a message, get credit for having called, and not even talk to her. He picked up the phone and dialed quickly before he changed his mind.

It rang once, twice, three times. He was in luck. Then he heard the phone pick up on the other side. *What do you want?* he expected, or *Miguel, I knew you'd never call!* or *What do you need this time?*

"Hello." It was her voice. Of course, she didn't know who it was yet.

"Happy Mother's Day, Mom," he said, alert as a metal detector in a mine field.

"Miguel," she answered. Then a short pause ensued. "How are you?"

How are you? he wondered. *How are you?* What happened to *I was sure you had forgotten about us! How are you?* How on Earth was he supposed to answer that? His mind raced and his heart paced. Just three short words. He was waiting for the other shoe to drop. But it didn't. It was as if she were actually waiting for his response.

"I'm good, Mom. How are you?" The metal detector was still on high.

"Miguel, I've been thinking about you. I'm so glad that you called."

"Well, how is everyone?" he asked. Surely this would bring things back to normal. Certainly there would be disaster to discuss and messes to clean up. Someone must have fucked up by now.

"Pretty good, Miguel." Her voice was strangely peaceful. "Actually, we're pretty good. But what about you...how are things working out there? I've thought so many times about calling you. I just...well, you know."

"Things are great here, Mom. I'm living in a little town called Arbolito. I'm working with a great group of students. I've learned a lot. Changed a lot. It seems like they like me and the Directora says the nicest things about me."

"Wow. And here I thought that you'd have such a hard time and it sounds like you're doing amazing things. I know I wasn't always that supportive, Miguel. You probably have thought the worst of me."

He could not believe the words he was hearing. "Things

were hard for all of us for a long time, Mom. I understand."

"You don't have to excuse me, Miguel. I know I wasn't the best. I am sorry for that."

He was speechless and sat motionless in the chair, stupefied.

"I was thinking, Miguel. Your school year is over soon, right?"

He still didn't answer.

"You know," she said, "I've heard about some job opportunities out here in the private schools. Not the public ones, but the private ones where the pay is better and the kids are better. Miguel, we only live once. I know things were tough for a long time but we only have this one chance to get it right. When you get back, we'll find you a good job and we'll work things out better. No?"

"I…I don't know, Mom. I haven't decided yet."

"It's time for you to come home," she told him. "I would like you back. We deserve to have another chance."

"Umm…I will think about it," he answered still in shock.

"Miguel," she said, "you can start a new life here. You can find a partner, too, I'm sure. You know, a woman…or a man, it doesn't really matter."

His heart stopped. A *man*? How dare she say it right out in the open. It was against everything she ever taught him! A *man*! Was she trying to say that she accepted that he was gay? Was she trying to say it was okay? Had the metal detector hit a mine? He was baffled.

"Are you still there?" she asked.

"Yes, Mom, I'm still here."

"Well, you think about it, okay? Will you promise to call me soon? And I will keep looking for you…for a job, I mean."

"Okay, Mom. I will call you. Happy Mother's Day." He let the phone fall to the table. His head stayed perfectly still, almost as if he were catatonic, as gravity pulled a bit of saliva from his open mouth. His lips came together to form a final word that he mouthed in the solitude. "Maybe."

Thirty

MIGUEL REMEMBERED that, at first, his mother had told him one hurried morning, "You're not getting out of school. So get up and get dressed. What, you didn't finish your homework for today?" That's what he had expected from her. He tried to pull the covers off but was freezing cold. His fever was going up, his throat ached.

When she actually looked at him and registered what she was seeing, her demeanor changed. His face was swollen and pale, his eyes were sincere. Why did she always have to respond like that? She sat on the bed next to him and then tucked the blankets back around him as they were. "No, my son," she said. "You are sick. We're staying home today." Her purse dropped to the floor and her compassion came out.

She spent the entire two weeks of his chickenpox bout at home with him. She cooked for him whatever she thought might stay down. And when the red blisters were all over his body, she comforted him and talked to him in those quiet moments when they were alone. She brought in paper for tic-tac-toe and made him a special seat on the couch with blankets and pillows and a drink nearby for times they sat together and watched early morning shows or tried-and-true children's programs. He didn't even recognize her.

He hardly remembered ever having seen that side of her. She never rubbed in his face the income she lost during those two weeks. She never once complained when he couldn't finish the food; she didn't call him ungrateful for it, or wasteful. She did not pressure him to get up or get better, but let him return to life when he was ready. She attended to his every need, and showed the maternal instinct, alive and well, that so often

203

eluded her. And then, on the day that the rash cleared up, his appetite returned, and his energy came back to him, her old attitude returned.

"You're better now. Time to get up and get to school. You'll have a lot of work to catch up and I've got bills to pay so let's get moving."

It was time to get back to life, he knew, and he found it easier to forgive her for her insensitive tone now that he had witnessed another side of her. He had seen that she loved him. Chicken pox, it turned out, was one of his favorite childhood memories.

"I can't leave the candy store," Ruben said to him.

"You can open a candy store in Mexico City," Miguel replied.

"Besides, my mother needs me. I am close to her here. And what about Micha? Would you expect me to give her to the stable boy? I'm not leaving her either."

"I know that there would be sacrifices. But what gives you the right to be close to your mother while I can't be close to mine?"

Ruben frowned. "Come on, Miguel, I'm not talking geography here. You know that I have a closer relationship with my mother than you have with yours. I'm sorry but that's the way it is."

"Exactly. That's exactly true. Your relationship is more stable and solid than mine. Mine needs repair. So shouldn't I go and repair it?"

"My mother is sick," he retorted.

"My mother has been sick for thirty years," Miguel said blankly.

The two looked at each other as they sat on opposite sides of the coffee table.

"Besides," Miguel added, "let's face it. I won't even have a job here."

"We can work together in the candy store if everything else fails."

"No. I don't want you to support me. Anyway, people get

sick of each other if they spend too much time together."

"Oh, now you're getting sick of me?" Ruben asked.

"That's not what I meant. You'd probably get sick of me. Don't you think we need balance to keep us healthy?"

"Well, some job is bound to open up. There is always something to do."

"You mean like maybe the Captain will finally drink himself to death? Then I could be the baker! This is a small town. It changes slowly. I don't see anything opening up for me here," Miguel explained. "But in Mexico City, there are hundreds of schools. Thousands. The Department of Education is huge. There are always jobs there. And there are always people who want candy."

Ruben shook his head. "Not gonna happen, Miguel."

Miguel was sitting up straight in the chair. His hands grabbed the armrests firmly and his knuckles turned white. "You left for a month when your mother called."

"That was different."

"Not really."

"Is that what you want? To leave?" asked Ruben. He looked down at the bracelet on his wrist. *Sentimental trinket.* The thought made him look away from Miguel to the window.

Miguel's bracelet was hidden beneath his sleeve. His mother could get sick like Dahlia, too. *One never knows. This could be my last chance.* He looked at Ruben, whose face was still turned toward the window. He did love him. But sometimes relationships ended for pragmatic reasons.

Ruben ran the brush through Micha's cappuccino-colored hair. While he tended her, she stayed still and calm, and occasionally made a grunt or flapped her lips. She had been a faithful friend to him for so long. She had known him through his move to Arbolito, the opening of the store, countless trips up and down the river and into the mountains, long conversations, and even longer silent times. She watched over him at the beach with Miguel, and she had been the true hero in the storm.

They knew each other so well. She could feel his energy, read his face, respond to his tones. And he could interpret the simple stomp of a hoof, the swishing of her tail, the tosses of her head from left to right or up and down. He moved the brush over her high back, over the spots that he recognized well, and then combed out her black mane while she batted her long eyelashes. Then he stood in front of her as they looked at one another face to face. Her eyes were brilliant like black opals, and her gaze was tranquil.

"No," he summed up their conversation. "We're not going anywhere, are we?"

She agreed in silence.

"I mean, I love him but this is not the sacrifice that we should be making. I won't give up everything and bet on hope. He will have to make a decision."

She bowed her head into his stomach, asking to be scratched behind the ears.

"He can't expect to come here, meet a person, and believe the person will leave everything and go to…Mexico City, of all horrific places. He has what he needs here, don't you think? There are other ways for him to make peace with his mother."

She kept her head down.

"It is time for us to trust that he will do the right thing."

She looked up at him and exhaled strongly through her nostrils. She said so much without saying anything at all.

That same day brought hysteria back to the Internado. This time, however, Miguel was part of it. When the buzz hit the school and all the children scrambled for cups, Miguel understood the urgency—Don Coco was back with his ice cream for the first time this Spring. One never knew the next time he might arrive.

The ice cream was delicious, there was no denying it. There was nothing else like it—creamy and smooth, perfectly sweet, textured with tiny pieces of coconut, flavored with a hint of pineapple, every bite packed with refreshing flavor for a sunny afternoon. More than that, it was a time of bonding for the whole school. Classes stopped, people dropped what they were doing, and the entire population gathered around, found a spot on the baked concrete or patchy grass, and enjoyed a break from routine life. It was a mass exercise in appreciating the small things in life.

The Directora oversaw the event, as always, from a couple of steps back. If Don Coco had come to Comaltícán every day, her reaction would have been different. But she, the constant observer of people, saw the benefits of the controlled frenzy in their glowing faces, the connection between the children and their teachers, and, of course, the laughter. It was like a two-day team-building retreat bundled into fifteen minutes—a bargain!

She noted Miguel, too, and the carefree way that he commandeered his students. Compared to the other classes, she noticed, his students were gathered near to him, though they had not been instructed to do so. They interacted more frequently with him than other students did with their teachers, and they frequently called for his presence among them. They liked him and trusted him. She knew that even the smallest situation was a reflection, a microcosm, of the big picture. She also knew that children told the truth, but not always with words. He was a good person, trustworthy, generous with himself, and a truly gifted teacher.

Thirty-one

"**I** FOUND A JOB FOR YOU," she said. The phone call was historic, he realized. It was the first one she had made to him, not just this year, but in his life. He felt again he was in uncharted waters.

"This is a great opportunity," she continued. "It's a job at the Lázaro Cárdenas Academy just outside the Cuitláhuac metro station. It takes fifteen minutes to get there from here! Not only that, it's a full-time, pension-track position."

"Really?" he responded, his eyes shifting back and forth with his thoughts.

"Yes. Do you remember Señora Chavarín, an old friend of your grandmother?"

"Yeah, I guess."

"Well, she's finally leaving her position…and she wants you to have it."

"Really? Why?" he asked.

"Well, I told your grandmother how well you're doing and she still talks to Señora Chavarin because they live so close. I'm sure your grandmother put in a good word for you, maybe asked her as a favor, and now she's promised you the position."

"Grandmother?" he said. Mentioning his grandmother was like pulling puppet strings on his heart.

"Of course," she said. "Did you think she forgot you?"

"No, Mother, I know she didn't."

"Well, she may be an old and simple woman but she has a few friends in decent places. She was giddy about it. She probably thought of it like the only inheritance she can ever give you."

Tears filled up his eyes and then fell to the floor at his first blink. His grandmother had taken such a backseat in his life out here.

208

"What should I tell them, Miguel?" she asked. "You can't refuse this. These jobs don't come up very often."

"I know," he answered. "I, I'm not sure just yet."

"What? Not sure? Miguel, what else will you do? You've got to take this."

"I know," he said.

"You're not going to waste it, are you?" she asked.

He recognized this line of questioning. Was she going to tell him how ungrateful he was next? Or how stupid he was for not jumping on it? Was she going to demean him?

"Miguel," she said. He braced for her next words. "Remember where you are from. You are from Mexico City, D.F., *el Distrito Federal*, pure *chilango*, one hundred percent *DFeño*. You have done good things and we are proud of you. Don't you think it's time to come home?"

Her words were not what he expected. They made it through his defenses and into his brain. She was right, strangely. Maybe it was time. And his grandmother's image tugged at his heart. Somehow his thoughts had meandered away from her. How had he let that happen? Why was life such a painful game to play? He could only imagine her wrinkly face and her strong hands that would caress his cheeks. How he would love to see her in that moment, to be in her home again on those couches, decades old even then, from his childhood memories. How he would love to buy her a new living room set and see the delight in her face. How he would love to get her the hell out of that neighborhood where she lived. Why had he let himself become so distant from her?

All these years he complained to himself. He had been dealt such a bad hand, he had so little to work with, it was everyone else's fault, the world was an ugly place. Hadn't he become the same thing that he was complaining about? Now he knew that he could be different, and powerful, and decide his own fate. He had responsibilities and he had influence in this life. Maybe it was time to go home and sort it all out. Maybe it was time to make up for all those years and put things the way they ought to be.

The heavy wooden door of the storage room at the Internado creaked loudly as he opened it. He had come for the school's graduation garb and decorations, and began to look among the many boxes that contained the decorations and costumes for the entire year's events. In a sense, what motivated everyone in the school was the "next big thing." If it wasn't Mexican Independence Day, then it was Christmas. If it wasn't Christmas, then it was Valentine's Day. The events broke the otherwise monotonous trip of life up into more meaningful and manageable pieces.

This event seemed to be the last big deal—the closing ceremony. But this event was different, and of more personal significance for the students because it represented a big step, no matter which grade level they were completing, and a good-bye to their teachers. There was also the unspoken understanding that this could be it, this could be the last promotion at school for any one of them, because nobody knew what the future had in store, where their families might end up next, what call of duty might pull them from their studies, or when their parents might inexplicably extract them from their current settings. Many of them would not finish secondary school or go on to preparatory school, much less the university. Many of them would complete their educations here. Thus, this ceremony was meaningful for them all.

Miguel's thoughts perused the entire year. He had seen so many changes in the children. Physically, they seemed to grow like banana trees. Emotionally, many had developed and become more self-confident, more conscious of others, more understanding of the world in general. And academically, many had made strides in their abilities. Of course, they were not the only ones who had changed this year.

He looked down at the floor where the back of the storage room was still cleared from his wedding day. The children, the dress, Teresita and her speech attempt. It was just a memory now, and it caused him to smile. One hand felt the bracelet on the other wrist. His mind echoed his own words from that ceremony: "…this hasn't become the failure that I was wired to expect… Now, it is our own energy that will determine the outcome. For my part, I promise to give you mine each and every day." He had said those words with such sincerity, but they had faded to the back of his mind, found their way into a long-term memory file like a dusty photo in an album on a bookcase.

The rose petals were still on the floor, darkened now, nearly black, shriveled where they lay. The Sun had shone so brightly that day and the future looked certain; now there was darkness and obscurity. He had not imagined the choices he would have to make between his own mother and Ruben, between work and unemployment. It was so unfair. The petals were motionless, they seemed to him like mere remnants of a bygone day as he focused on a new one. "It is our decision to be together," he heard his own voice in his head. Was there no other choice? Could he not have the best of both worlds?

Enough of that. His window for decision-making was closing. His time for preparation for the ceremony was also winding down. He located the box he was looking for and pulled it down from the dirty shelf and closed the padlock on the heavy door.

He had been anxious the entire day, hoping for resolution yet fearful of the uncertainty. It seemed to him like so much was at stake. And he had learned that there was little turning back in life. The conversation with Ruben was serious from the beginning, their faces like those of businessmen in negotiations.

"Maybe I'll just go for a while. You know, just the summer, to see what happens," said Miguel.

"The whole summer? Exactly what do you think is going to happen?"

Miguel hadn't thought it all through. "I don't know."

"I mean," explained Ruben, "what's the best thing that can happen? You make up with your mother, get a great job, get used to the city again? What happens to us, then? You'd never be back."

Miguel hated these talks. He hated confronting reality when it meant making choices between things that could not be reconciled.

Ruben continued: "Or you fight with her, nothing changes,

and you come back angry and depressed to me, the second-best option, to pick up the frayed ends of what you left? Either way, it's not a good look for us."

"You don't know what would happen."

"It happens with Micha and me all the time. We pass some side path and hope to go back and explore it some day. But that day never comes. Life has a way of taking us in directions we would never have imagined but rarely gives us the chance to redo anything. You can't go back in time and change your mind on everything."

"Sure," said Miguel. "It's easy for you to judge. You get along well with your mother. You are an hour away. You talk to her all the time. What do you care? You don't know what it feels like."

"Do you think it was always this way between my mother and me? I've had my bad times. It wasn't perfect…it still isn't."

"Well, what did you do? Obviously you fixed it. Obviously you had your time to make amends."

"It took a long time, Miguel. It took years."

"But how? What did you do?"

"I left the door open and waited for her to walk through it."

"But how long were you going to wait?"

"As long as it took."

"Exactly! See? Mine is walking through it right now," said Miguel emphatically.

Ruben shook his head. "Who is walking through whose door?" he asked.

"What do you expect?" Miguel's voice rose. "She's my mother!"

"You're an adult now. This is your life. I am your *husband*, remember? Your life is more stable than hers. You have more to lose by leaving here than she does by coming here. Leave the door open. Let her come here."

Miguel ended with a big sigh and a headache.

There was something the old man must have recognized in Ruben. Perhaps it was his gaze or his walk, or maybe the way his pants were slightly tight around his waist and buttocks, unlike the over-sized and baggy trousers on most men his age. He hadn't been in the candy store before, only passed it, but he had been on the hunt all morning throughout the town for truffles or bonbons or liquor-filled candies, something classy for his Sunday social. He wasn't going to find those kinds of candies here nor in all of Arbolito. That was something he'd have to bring back from his next trip to Monterrey. But he did find something else that he found familiar and intriguing.

"You're not from around here, are you?" Ruben asked, noting his curious glances. The old man was clearly energetic and clear-minded. He wore an argyle sweater and corduroys with pressed seams, definitely not a local, and his silver-rimmed glasses and gray hair made him look rather intellectual for these parts.

He pushed his glasses up his nose before addressing Ruben. "I beg your pardon. I've lived here for thirty-eight years! I suspect you are the pilgrim, the imported help."

"Actually, I own this store."

"Well you might try a course on aesthetics," replied the old man, as he looked about at the cramped aisles and clear plastic bags filled with candies stacked up to the ceiling. Then he grinned and looked at Ruben from above the rims of his spectacles. "It's nice to meet you, umm…"

"Ruben," came the response and the outstretched hand.

"Gerardo Ivan," said the man.

"Funny we've never met before," said Ruben. "You must live downriver a bit."

"No, we live three and a half blocks from here," he said, pointing behind him with his left hand.

"Three and a half blocks?"

"We keep to ourselves a bit. You know the tall wall a few doors down from the laundromat?"

Ruben nodded his head.

"That's the place."

"Okay. You live there with your…"

"Maestro Julio Jimenez. Perhaps you've heard of him? He's retired now but worked in the preparatory school as a music and art teacher for over twenty years."

"I'm afraid not. Sorry."

"Don't apologize. Maybe you don't get out of this dank place."

"Not that much. But I'd figure that at least Doña Conchita would have mentioned you."

"Doña who?" he asked.

"Doña Conchita…don't you know her?"

"No. She must have a different social circle."

"I guess so," said Ruben, perplexed.

"In all honesty, we don't spend all that much time here. We also have homes in Mexico City and Monterrey. We come here to get away from it all."

"Get away from what?"

"The racket," said Gerardo Ivan.

"What racket? What do you do?"

"I'm an antiques dealer. And so ready to retire. And yet I just can't seem to get entirely out of the pool, you know? Julio retired years ago."

"That's funny," said Ruben. "My friend Miguel is just starting as a teacher. He works up here at the Internado."

"Well, I hope we can have him down to meet him. I am sure that Julio and he would have plenty to talk about," replied Gerardo Ivan. "Teachers always get overly enthralled with their work. They need to commiserate. I suppose antiques dealers do, too."

"He's down every night. He lives here upstairs with me." He pointed up with his left hand.

"That's perfect. We'll expect you both for dinner, then. Tomorrow, all right?"

"I'll check with him. If you leave me your number, I'll let you know."

"It's settled then. Tomorrow at seven. Perfect way to pepper the week. We'll be waiting for you."

With that, he held out his hand one more time and walked away in the direction from whence he came.

Thirty-two

MIGUEL FELT MORE LIKE A MARINE BIOLOGIST than an oceanographer. What he had oftentimes seen as a sea of black heads had transformed. He had seen the depths, as if he had donned mask and snorkel, and had dived beneath the surface. To his amazement, he found each person to be like a different species of fish. Each had his or her ways of moving and surviving, habits of eating and socializing, and each grew in his or her own way. A vast world had opened up to him, little by little, over the nine months during which he was submerged. It had taken a long time to learn about each child, but now even thinking of any two of them as alike would be ludicrous.

He watched them in these waning days, his last couple of weeks with them. They exerted themselves in their final tests, they chatted gleefully with their friends, they passed the days joyfully in what had become a new home to them: this school and this classroom. They marched up the mountain again like troopers and dove from the boulders down at the swimming hole in their final outing. They had become a cohesive bunch. Trust had been a foundation into which they sank their roots, and from which they grew in spurts.

What will become of them? he wondered. What would become of *him?* Might he and they just say goodbye in mid-June and never see one another again? That was the norm in a school, wasn't it? He had no contact with his former teachers. And even while he was still attending school, he had barely spoken to the teachers of whom he was fondest—a quick "Hi, Maestro," and a rare word at first, but gradually his interest had faded as he stepped ahead in life and left the past behind. Was that what was in store for him with these students?

Miguel had never expected such sentiment. He had had no idea how human these people were. He had expected toothless, lice-ridden mountain folks, but found in their place untainted humanity. He had also found Ruben. He had thought he left Mexico City last summer for obvious reasons, but it turned out that the true reasons were the discovery itself. He knew that life was sweet-and-sour. He lamented having lived so sweetly this year for he feared that sour was at the door.

The wall was high, white, and simple, and succeeded in blocking out everything behind it from the world. It left little for people to talk about; it left them only with their speculations, but it was actually so blank as to cause disinterest. It had no adornments whatsoever and encompassed the entire property. Ruben pushed the doorbell button, the only punctuation on the otherwise blank page.

The interior was as astonishing as the exterior was bland. It had a manicured lawn that stretched some ten meters from the interior of the wall to the doorway of the house. A pair of concrete lions licked their paws at either side of the entrance to the house, and small palm trees stood at attention behind them. The house was two stories in height; the soft light from its many paned windows was inviting to any who penetrated the fortress. Gerardo Ivan greeted them at the door and introduced them to Maestro Julio, who waited behind him.

Julio's cheeks were red and his round face glowed. The lines on his face revealed a life of experience, but his brown eyes were well-rested and peaceful. He had a tender smile like that of a person they'd known for years, and his smooth warm hands were like accepting friends. He gave them a hug after the handshake. "Come in and see the house," he said.

The first striking features were the large plants that were carefully arranged about the house in elegant vases. Paintings lined the walls and books abounded on the shelves, on the tables, and any other place that they might find space. The light that had shone through the windows was from candles that were lit in every room. Miguel passed a copper-like statue in a niche in the wall. It was a nearly naked man with a masquerade style of mask that came down below his chin and formed a point like a bird's beak. He was in a pose that revealed his defined muscles to perfection, standing upright on his hands like a gymnast on the torso of another male gymnast of equal muscularity. The statue was perched on a base that stood perhaps half a meter off the floor and it reached up to Miguel's eye level. He couldn't help but touch it and his hand withdrew quickly at the cold feel of real copper.

"We built this house thirty-eight years ago when a decent person could still construct a place for less than the cost of a new brain," said Julio. "As soon as we met, we started it and we've added to it and knocked it down and repaired it what seems like a thousand times. The job of tending a nest is never finished." He laughed out loud. "And that's just one house." He looked over at Gerardo Ivan. "But it is our favorite, isn't it?"

"I still don't know why we have so many houses, Maestro Julio. You say it's because we travel around all the time, but I think it's time to sell them."

"I wish we had that problem, Gerardo," said Ruben. "We can barely seem to keep it all together as it is."

"It's *Gerardo Ivan*," he answered. "And, you know, time changes everything."

"We have noticed," said Miguel, "how everything changes in ways that you least expect."

"That is true," said Gerardo Ivan. "But then again, life isn't random, either. We have greater control than we think. It depends on what you are really after. An alcoholic can stop drinking if he really wants to. But sometimes we just don't know exactly what we want. We get torn, we get scared, and we let time decide."

"The old sage," interrupted Julio. "You don't have to deliver your sermon to these boys, Gerardo."

"It's *Gerardo Ivan*! And it's not a sermon. I mean, don't you wish we had had someone our age to talk to when we were their age?"

Julio raised his eyebrows and looked away. "You can't teach an old dog new tricks. Unless, of course, he has an interest in learning them! You are a stubborn old fool."

The dinner, cooked for hours during the long afternoon, was as superb as the house and as the company. After the dinner and the wine, Gerardo Ivan centered a small plate of hazelnut-filled dark chocolates on the table.

"Gerardo Ivan! I thought you couldn't find them!"

Gerardo Ivan looked at the three of them with a big smile. "I still have my secrets, my dears. I still have my secrets."

The children at the Internado were anxious and excited. Their parents, extended families, guardians, and friends would soon begin to trickle in. The children would leave for the summer, some never to see this place again. Others would move on to the next grade; saying goodbye to their school friends and teachers, they would cross the stage before hundreds of people. Everyone would be watching them—their families, the Directora, the mayor, their schoolmates, and all of the teachers. Emotions ran high.

The school was adorned, once again, with those items that Miguel had brought from the storage room. There were colorful ribbons and long signs that read "Congratulations!" Long streamers ran between buildings and trees. Men from town, once again, brought hundreds of folding chairs for the masses. The Sun beat overhead, making Miguel's armpits sweaty and his shirt sticky.

Considering the perfect consistency of time, every second on the clock ticking exactly alike, it sure had a way of dragging in some moments, whizzing by in others, and then by the end seeming like it never even happened at all. He couldn't believe that this day had arrived. He couldn't believe that he might find himself once more in the pitiful place in Mexico City that he called home. He imagined his mother's eyes and the lack of ceremony when he arrived. He imagined the anticlimax. But even that was up in the air now. Like the children, he wished for time to stay frozen in happy moments like this, but he also wished to move on. *We do have control, as Gerardo Ivan said, but still not so much as to control time.*

The Directora walked from place to place about the campus. She showed no signs of nervousness. Rather, she seemed to enjoy the process, the moment, the people's enthusiasm and nervousness. Her joys were, in a way, vicarious. In her life, she had lived moments like this what seemed like a hundred times. This rite of passage was a story repeated in a different place and different time upon the same Earth and beneath the same Sun for millennia. Life was a beautiful thing to see if you knew how to simply watch it the way you saw the Milky Way spangle across the black night, the way you caught a falling star every once in awhile.

By noontime, the school was filled again with folks who came from their distant homes for their children and with the many spectators who came from Comalticán and Arbolito to support the school, or to support their families and friends. Some came for the pure nostalgia and some came simply for the sake of not missing anything. The school that would be empty in a few hours was packed; every chair and place to stand seemed to be occupied.

The mayor spoke first, bellowing into the microphone about the greatness of the school, of the state, of the country, of himself. His words were loud but faded into the sky as if they had been soaked up and carried by the passing clouds like benevolent sponges. Of course his constituency would elect him again, so why did they have to hear his words? But they kept their thoughts to themselves and behaved appropriately.

When the Directora took the stage, the audience focused. They actually did desire to hear her message, her comments about the students and teachers, and the words *see you in August*. She lowered the microphone to her height but she smiled like a giant. She was a slow, purposeful speaker who scanned her audience from left to right and focused on individuals with her eyes, as if talking to them specifically. She had a gift with her ways and with her words.

"Students," she began, looking at the many faces of the young people sitting in their whitest uniform shirts and cleanest pants and skirts. Some had tears in their clothes, or tiny holes. Others had scars and defects. But she had learned years before the sacred lesson that Miguel had begun to experience. In reality, she never stopped marveling at the experience of teaching the Earth's magnificent children.

She continued, "You are the divine inspiration that paints
this school with brilliance. You young people make the mountains green in the springtime and you make the river flow. They
want you to be part of them. They know that you will be their
keepers, that you will one day conserve them and protect them.
We know that one day, you will have the responsibility of lead-
ing us forward. You may find yourself in the coffee plantations
on the highest peaks of this beautiful state or harvesting mangos
or guavas or bananas in the lowlands. You may be in a court-
room or police department or hospital tending to the needs of a
modern society. You may become an artist or a dancer or a mu-
sician, filling the world with splendor and opening the eyes and
ears and minds of those who have forgotten how to see and hear
and think. You may someday find yourself in the busy streets of
Mexico City or beneath the grand arches of Rome. You can be
whatever you choose, wherever you choose. We hope to have
served you well and that you will pass our service on. We are
counting on you."

Her pause cued the applause of the people. She waited patiently and then turned her direction to the row of teachers and
the row of student teachers behind them. "Maestros, we thank
you for your gifts. You brought a gift to your classroom every
single day. You wrapped it with care and tied it with a bow. At
times, though, your students did not want the gift. They refused
it or might have even thrown it on the floor and stomped on it
or tossed it back in your face. You did not get offended, you did
not give up. Perhaps you got discouraged at times, but you reminded yourself to find your inspiration in them, to bring a bigger gift the next day wrapped even more beautifully and even
more temptingly. You knew what they needed even when they
did not. Maestros, we thank you for your gifts." The crowd
once again erupted in applause.

After a few more words began the process of introducing
the teachers and their classes one by one. The people buckled
down for the lengthy ceremony but remained attentive to the
names and faces they knew that would walk across the stage
and, of course, for any mishaps or antics that might occur. Ap-

plause was strong and loud at first, but inevitably died down after the first three or four classes.

The sunlight was fierce in the early afternoon, and the eyes of the spectators that were not protected by hats or sunglasses were squinting and tearing. The show proceeded. Kindergarten, then first grade appeared, then second and third, fourth and fifth. Miguel's class grew restless and anxious though he turned around from his seat in front and smiled at them. They were next.

"Our next class is the sixth grade," said the Directora. The students rose in place as they had rehearsed. The Directora then gave Miguel the most sincere and motherly smile, one probably not noticed by anyone else but him. "It gives me great pleasure to introduce... ." Miguel braced for his name. "Maestra Viviana." She stood next to Miguel and raised her arm up, people clapped from their seats. "She has been working on many projects this year for the Internado and has left her classroom largely in the very capable hands of Maestro Miguel Hernández." He raised his arm as his students began screaming and applauding to high heaven, which set off a wave of recognition from the entire school and crowd. It filled him like a cold beer on a hot day.

"I would also like to recognize," the Directora continued, "his partner, Ruben, if he is in the stands."

Miguel flushed. He couldn't believe his ears. It was like a tequila shooter. *Partner*!

Ruben stood not far from the stage and stepped forward, waving, as the crowd continued to applaud wildly. Miguel took a deep breath and then noted the smiles and support among the people.

"He has been Maestro Miguel's partner in the classroom and has volunteered countless hours and countless bags of candies to the betterment of the class." They continued applauding notably louder than with any other class, bringing back those who had drifted away.

"I'd like to say that Maestro Miguel has been a wonderful addition to our school campus this year, as have many student teachers. He is a gifted teacher who truly embraced the children, the Internado, Comalticán, and the entire state as his own. He came here from Mexico City but now seems to be just like one of us from Puebla. Indeed, he should be called not Miguel Hernández but Miguel Poblano." The crowd once again gave a round of applause for him. "We hope to have you one day as a permanent teacher here. You are home," she concluded, as she continued to look at him.

He felt his breath quicken; his eyes watered, and the year passed through his mind in quick flashes. Those same children who stood before him and whose faces formed a mental album in his brain were a real part of him, as real as any important people could ever be. Their families who encircled them with grateful recognition of a job well done, of a challenge success-fully met, and who showed the same respect for his *partner*, suddenly made life for Miguel, and its next step, strikingly clear.

The children passed before him on the stage. They were taking their next steps, as they hugged him perhaps for the last time ever. He realized that he was now among his family, albeit one that he had fallen into yet helped to form, one that was ex-tended and fluid, one that was leagues away from the one he left in Mexico City. The Directora was right—he was home.

Epilogue

IT WAS YEARS after Miguel had forgotten about the stabbed Santa Claus dolls, left there by Juanito's father as a simple prank suggested by the Captain. Miguel and Ruben donned cold weather garments and walked down to the cathedral at the town square. The traditional Christmas decorations adorned the streets and homes; the busy townspeople scurried from shop to shop despite the cold.

Miguel and Ruben passed adolescents playing soccer on the concrete basketball court next door to the church. Well-dressed families and godparents were waiting outside its great wooden doors where Teresita sold marshmallow reindeer. The couple nodded at Johana's parents, who had braved the slick roads for the occasion, and then they proceeded to a pew inside the cavernous building. The last time they had set foot in a church was for the funeral of Ruben's mother, who had endured several years of treatment and pain before finally succumbing to the persistent cancer. They hoped this would be a more joyful event.

They sat beside Gerardo Ivan and Maestro Julio, who were flamboyantly decked in fashionable garb. Two rows ahead the Directora sat alone, her graying hair and bifocals betraying her age. She was absorbing this step in the lives of her adopted offspring as a warrior might receive another bear tooth to add to his collection. She turned and waved at Miguel and Ruben, but then turned forward, as the ceremony was about to begin. She would see them soon enough on their volunteer nights. Near Miguel and Ruben sat a number of Johana's family as well as dozens of friends. The other side of the aisle was filled with people unfamiliar to Miguel who were celebrating the simulta-

223

neous baptisms of other children.

Johana's mother stared lovingly at her little granddaughter, who was quiet in Johana's arms. She had intended to protect Johana from her older daughter's fate of falling for a menial worker by sending her to the Internado. Her dream of having a wealthy son-in-law had been destroyed, but the shock seemed to have worn off by now. At least her wish for her daughter's happiness was fulfilled. Now she really was Abimael's mother—his mother-in-law. And he stood proudly, as shiny as the day he walked into the classroom with no more warts on his face.

As the priest carried out the ritual of lighting the candles, wetting the children with holy water and blessing them, Miguel watched the families and thought of his own mother. She would visit again soon to break away from the stresses of the city and her never-ending struggle to make ends meet. He was grateful that she finally had come through his door.

The church bells tolled at the end of the proceedings and the people emptied out of the building, tightening their scarves and bracing for the weather. They would head to receptions with stewed goat and warm tortillas and then return to the routine activities of their lives. Likewise, Miguel and Ruben would return to the candy store and prepare for another busy day. They bore the same expressions of exhaustion as they always did this time of year. But they lived happily nonetheless, through their many ups and downs, fights and fits, summer heat waves and winter floods, strides and setbacks, and all of the other things that constitute love.

About the Author

Born in San Francisco in 1970, **Erik Orrantia** lived in the San Francisco Bay Area until 1997. By that time, he had earned a Bachelor's Degree in Psychology and a Master's Degree in Counseling at California State University in Hayward. His original intention was to build a practice in psychotherapy.

He then felt a calling to explore the world and entered an International Study Program in Mexico City where he earned a teaching credential. He currently works as a middle school teacher in San Ysidro, California, along the Mexican-American border. He was voted Teacher of the Year in 2008 for his school district.

He has traveled extensively throughout Mexico. He now spends most of his time in Tijuana with his partner and dedicates his free time to writing.